Chapter 1 *UNRESTRAINED*

By Tom Mohr

Garth Williams was the lone night watchman at a remote
construction site northwest of Calgary, Alberta. He had finished
his walk-around and opened the door to his pickup truck to
retrieve his thermos of coffee. He didn't hear a sound as a dark
figure crept up behind him and deftly cut his throat. Three other
men appeared out of the darkness and went to work on the steel
doors of the locked container van that stored the dynamite and
primers. There was no need to be quiet so they used chisels and
sledge hammers to remove the pins from the hinges. The two
doors that were held together with a hardened chain and padlock
crashed to the ground as one solid piece. The men quickly
removed several cases of dynamite and a carton of electric primers
from the van and loaded them in Garth's pickup. They left Garth's
body where it fell beside the truck. The man who had cut Garth's
throat climbed into the truck with one other man and drove off
with the other two men following in their Jeep. They drove on
through the night toward Creston, British Columbia "We will meet
Omar a little south of Creston, BC on a logging road he has
marked on this map. He has arranged to get these explosives into
the USA." Ahmed told his companion. "Are we to drive this truck
across the border?" The other man asked. "No Abdul, he and his
men have purchased some off road vehicles that will allow us to

sneakthrough the woods, away from the normal border crossing
points." Ahmed replied.

"How will we get to Las Vegas? We can't drive all terrain vehicles
down the highway that far." Abdul asked. "We have a truck
coming to meet us once we get into Idaho. We will ditch the
ATV's and load all of us and the explosives in it. We will get
another vehicle in Montana once we are clear of the woods." It
was nearly daylight when they arrived at the rendezvous point
outside of Creston. They had to wait a while for Omar to arrive so
they went over the road map to plan the route from Libby Montana

to Las Vegas. They were parked at a camp ground near a trail head leading into the woods.

Since it was a week day there were no other cars at the camp ground. A short time later Omar arrived on a Polaris ATV. He told the others to follow him with the pickup and car.

He led them about three miles up into the woods on a very rough abandoned logging road. There they met the rest of their group at an old log loading deck. They loaded the dynamite onto two of the ATV's and then drove the truck and jeep up into the brush on a skidder trail until they were stuck, but out of sight from below. Omar had stashed the pickup and trailer he used to haul the ATV's up an adjacent skid trail. There were eight men in all and four machines. They had to ride double but the big Polaris machines were each equipped to hold a passenger and had a rack behind for carrying supplies. Omar had purchased rifle scabbards, common accessories for these machines, to hold the four assault rifles they had with them. He had a US Forest Service topographic map showing the area of north Idaho and western Montana that their contacts in the USA had provided them. The trails they were to use were marked in red highlighter as well as the meeting place on the Yaak River in western Montana The Iranian, Naheed, who had made this same trip before, smuggling other terrorists into the country Led the way. They crossed

the border in deep woods on a game trail where there was no fence of any kind or any real evidence that it was the border between two countries.

CHAPTER TWO

That same day in a small office in Greenwich Village, a secret counterterrorism task force met to discuss some new leads that had come in from the CIA, FBI and the NSA.

Jake Powell was the senior agent, in charge of this group of men whose job it was to protect the country from terrorist acts. This task force was formed by Doug Small, the deputy chief of

Homeland Security. Doug was a close friend of the president and made certain that the president was fully insulated from any direct knowledge of their existence or operations. From his position at Homeland Security Doug coordinated all the intelligence from the various agencies and funneled it to Powell via a secure internet account or an encrypted phone line. His former work in military intelligence and the NSA, gave Doug the skills he needed to recruit and secretly run this kind of undercover operation. He and Jake Powell had worked together on many covert activities and trusted each other completely. Doug and Jake had recruited the four other operatives all of whom had served with one or the other. All were military trained and each had special talents well suited to the task force. The men were drinking coffee and comparing notes when Jake entered the room. They could tell from his expression that something was happening. "Listen up!" Jake said as he stepped to the front of the room. "I just got word that some terrorists are crossing the Canadian border near Mel's home territory in north Idaho." Everyone came to rapt attention as Jake lit up a satellite map on the near wall.

"Right about here, between the Moyie River in Idaho and the Yaak River drainage in western Montana, the border patrol has picked up the trail of some Muslim extremist

group that left the Calgary area after robbing a remote construction site of several cases of dynamite. They have apparently crossed the border using some four wheel drive ATV's and are moving through the wilderness on logging roads and game trails. We need to go immediately into the area and intercept them before they get out of the backwoods.

It's suspected that they have people in place to receive them and their cargo somewhere near Bonners Ferry, Idaho or over in the Yaak River area north of highway two. Grab your gear, we leave in ten minutes." A private jet was waiting at the executive air terminal when they arrived at JFK. They loaded their gear and got on board quickly with practiced precision.

Jake said "We'll land at Fairchild AFB in Spokane and meet up with some Delta Force guys that happen to be training at the Survival School there.. We'll get on a transport with them and parachute into the area north of Moyie Springs. They'll drop in dirt bikes and ATV's loaded with automatic weapons and night vision equipment. This will be a night jump into wooded terrain so watch out for trees. The LZ will be in a clear cut area but the winds can be unpredictable in those mountains. They have a thirty hour head start from the border so we should intercept them before daylight tomorrow. Any questions?" "Just one Jake, do we take them out or try to arrest and interrogate them?" Tyler asked.

"Stopping them is our first objective. If we can keep one or two alive for interrogation, so much the better. But don't hesitate to kill, we can't afford for any of them to get out with those explosives and whatever else they may be carrying." Jake said. After one more check of their equipment they all settled in for some sleep. Although it was early in the day they all had the soldier's ability to sleep whenever and wherever it was possible, and they knew they might be in action for many hours or days without rest.

The flight went smoothly and they arrived at Fairchild AFB in Spokane, Washington just before dark. Their unmarked jet taxied into a large hangar before the men got out. When Jake stepped out onto the floor he was met by a large man in camouflage fatigues.

"Lieutenant Powell, as I live and breathe, I thought they would have played taps for you by now old timer." He said as he grabbed Jake in a huge bear hug. "Not yet Rusty, there's still a little life left in these old bones." Jake said as he pried himself loose. Jake Powell stands six feet three and weighs two hundred and fifty pounds. Rusty Edwards towered over him and had no problem lifting him off the ground. It was all Jake could do to extricate himself. By now all the men had gotten the gear out of the jet and were standing in a half circle with Jake and his giant friend. "We really don't have time for old home week Rusty, we need to get loaded up for a night jump into Indian country" Jake said

"The transport you're standing by is loaded and ready to go as soon as you get your guys on board. I loaded everything you asked for before you landed. Are you sure you don't want a couple of my men to go in with you?" Rusty asked. "You know the drill, we were never here and no one but you and the pilot know about this "training flight" we're taking." Jake reminded him. "Just leave what's left of the equipment in the woods when you leave, we'll retrieve it as part of the survival school training program when you're gone. Good hunting!" Rusty said over his shoulder as he headed for the door at the other end of the hangar. Jake went into the cockpit to go over the drop zone coordinates with the pilot as the rest of the men checked out the vehicles and parachutes in the rear of the transport. The flight from Fairchild to the drop zone area only took about twenty five minutes after they had reached their designated altitude of 20,000 feet. They would descend to 9,000 feet for the jump after getting well past civilization to avoid detection.

"Night vision in place? Aye sir, static lines attached? Aye sir," was asked and answered just as the rear door opened. "On my count, release the vehicles" Jake commanded.

"Three, two, one, go" he said as Mel and Ron released the bikes and ATV's into the night. Two by two the men jumped out the door followed last by Jake Powell. Night vision goggles made the landing possible if not easy. The men all landed safely with no one ending up in the trees and all the vehicles landed intact. The bigger Honda ATV had a silenced .30 caliber belt fed machine gun mounted on a swivel above the driver's head, operated by the gunner standing on a rack behind the driver. The second smaller ATV

carried the communications equipment and an infrared thermal imaging scope. Ty rode the smaller ATV and operated the electronic gadgets while Nate drove the larger one with Ron manning the machine gun. Jake and Mel rode the silenced dirt bikes ahead. Both machines had gps units mounted on the handlebars. Their night vision equipment allowed them to ride with the lights off. About an hour into the ride Jake got a nice surprise, his satcom buzzed in his ear and Rusty's voice came over the earpiece. "Dirt digger this is eye in the sky, over" Jake motioned to the others to stop while he returned Rusty's call.

"What are you up to, eye in the sky?" He asked. "I thought you could use a little help so I have a Cheyenne with IR and thermal imaging checking your position against any warm bodies in the brush. I'm sight and sound proof so the bogey's won't know I'm here. Same drill, I was never here" he said. "Hold on digger, I just got a contact about two clicks northwest of your position. They're moving slowly but in your general direction. They must be on a game trail; they're too erratic to be on a logging road. Have one of your guys scout ahead on these coordinates and see if there is a good ambush point in their path." Jake entered the coordinates into his gps unit and told the others to spread out and

wait while he rode ahead to scout the terrain. Mel grabbed his arm and said "we're within about half a click from an old mining claim that I remember from hunting in this area, let me go ahead and take a look. I'll go about half way on the bike and then on foot until I find the spot." Jake agreed and Mel took off. About twenty minutes later Rusty came on the satcom again and told Jake "Your man is heading right for the bad guys and getting pretty close. Hold it, he must have turned around, he's heading back your way. Now he's stopped. They must have heard him or me, they had been running with their lights on and now they've stopped and turned them off. They don't know I can see them with thermal imaging." Just then Mel came over the satcom "I found the old mine dump, it's perfect for an ambush if they are on the only decent sized trail north of it. Move up quietly until you come to my bike and then come on foot straight up the trail to me, over." "Roger that, we'll be on your tail in 15, out" Jake replied. They moved out in single file with Jake in the lead followed by Nate and Ron and then Ty on the small ATV. Just as they came up to Mel's bike Rusty came over the satcom again "Your bogeys are moving again with their lights on so they must have decided they didn't hear anything after all." Mel appeared out of nowhere and motioned to Jake to be quiet and follow him. They moved ahead and to the east a little and came upon an old mine dump. It was about 100 feet higher than the terrain around it and gave a perfect view of the trail. The trail crossed a narrow but deep creek just above the dump with steep banks on both sides. Beyond the dump the old mine's spur road lead off to the east. Jake stationed Nate and Ron with the 30 caliber, in the brush alongside of the road just east of the dump. Ty left the small machine down the other trail and came up to Mel and Jake's position on foot. Since the enemy was running with their lights on there was no need for the electronic gear. Jake

and Ty dug in behind the lip of the dump near the top and laid out extra ammo and grenades. Mel disappeared into the night somewhere west of the trail. Moving silently through the trees and brush Mel inhaled the sweet smell of willows and damp leaves. It calmed him and reminded him of his days growing up. His night vision goggles allowed him to maneuver quickly through the dense forest. The eerie green glow they cast on the surroundings was as familiar to Mel as the smells and sounds of the forest. He expertly worked his way past the group of ATV's and positioned himself a few yards north of the last vehicle. One man, carrying his weapon over his shoulder, had walked ahead to join the others. One man was standing near the rear four wheeler taking a leak when Mel approached him from behind. His hand went to his zipper just as Mel snuffed out his life with a perfect knife strike. Mel pushed the man down into the brush and then ripped the spark plug wire from the machine. Then he quickly made his way back toward the mine dump.

Jake got that prickly feeling on the back of his neck just as the flickering of the lead machine's lights came into sight through the trees. He could faintly hear the ATV's running over the sound of the night wind and the rushing creek. Rusty came back on the satcom "They have four machines total and eight warm bodies and they are about two hundred yards uphill from your position. I gotta scram outta here for now; I'm low on fuel, good luck digger." A few moments later the first ATV appeared at the top of the bank above the creek. He stopped and a second machine pulled along side. They left their lights on and the machines running. One man appeared from behind the machines and started down the bank toward the creek. He was carrying an AK47 over his shoulder and had a long stick in his right hand. He was about to probe the creek for depth when

someone shouted to the leader "Naheed, where is Omar? His machine is dead and he is missing!" Muzzle flashes flickered through the heavy brush accompanied by the sound of men running. Jake and Tyler opened up with their silenced machine guns and dropped the first man in the creek and then shot out the lights of the two visible machines. Mel appeared out of the woods to the west and joined Jake and Ty at the mine dump. The terrorists were now down to five men and three machines. Mel had disabled the one ATV. The other terrorists gathered behind the front ATV and began firing at the men on the mine dump. Suddenly the front machine leapt forward followed by the other two.

They careened down the bank into the creek in single file. The first machine flipped over as it hit the opposing bank throwing the driver and passenger over the handlebars. Ty took them out with a burst from his gun as the second and third machines crossed the creek and roared past the base of the dump with their passengers firing wildly. The lead machine exploded in a huge ball of flame as Ron hosed them down with his .30 caliber machine gun. The last machine and passenger met the same fate as Nate moved the ATV

into position on the spur road so Ron could blast them with the 30. These two machines had apparently been carrying the dynamite. Then all was quiet except the sound of the rushing creek and the crackle of the dying flames from the burnt ATV's. Mel made a sweep of the area above the creek and gathered the bodies of the dead terrorists. Jake and Ty removed all the identification they could find on the bodies by the mine dump while Ron and Nate did the same with what was left of the men from the other ATV's. "What should we do with the bodies and the wrecked machines?" Ty asked. "We can lose the bodies down the shaft of the old mine, no one will ever go in there to find them" Mel said

"I think we can put what's left of the ATV's in there also if we move a couple of timbers

from the opening" Jake added. They worked quickly to open the portal wide enough for the ATV wreckage to fit through and then shoved the machinery and bodies into the opening. Each piece clattered against the sides of the shaft before finally splashing into the water, the same was true for the bodies. "Some of these old mines are hundreds of feet deep and this must be one of the deeper ones" Mel said. Nate set C-4 charges expertly around the portal and closed the entrance forever with a muffled blast. "Mount up, lets go home" Jake said as he led off on his dirt bike. They rode quickly back down the trail and headed for the small airport near Bonners Ferry. A quick call on the satcom had their plane waiting for them when they arrived at the airport just before dawn. The sight of military camouflage painted dirt bikes and ATV's at the airfield was only a minor curiosity for the locals as they drove by heading for another day working in the woods. The survival school guys had done things like this before and no one paid much attention. Over the state line in Montana, on the Yaak River side, a rented Ryder box van was parked on a side road above a ratty old bar called "The Dirty Shame". The two men inside waited until past noon and tried to raise the terrorists on their mobile phone a few times. When they eventually decided the plan had failed they drove out of the woods and east toward Libby, Montana.

On the return flight Jake went over the ID's and other items they found on the dead terrorists. There was no mention of who was supposed to meet them, only a number for a disposable cell phone. There were instructions on how to build a fire bomb from dynamite and drums of gasoline. The terrorists had planned to leave the bomb in a truck on the top floor in one of the parking garages at a Las Vegas casino. The effect would have been to cause a huge explosion near the elevators and spread the fire to all the floors

of the hotel and casino. It wouldn't have been the first casino they had bombed; they had done it before in Malaysia. But if they had

succeeded it would have been the first time for such an attack in
America.

CHAPTER THREE

Back at the office, Jake sent an encrypted report to Doug Small.
Return mail said "Nice work, two of those you identified were on
our terrorist watch list, definitely Al Qaeda.

The others were Canadian citizens from a mosque in Maple,
Ontario; a suburb of Toronto. The RCMP is checking into
activities around that area. This could be a new source of extremist
sympathizers." "Take a couple of days off, you guys earned it. Get
some R&R and get back here on Monday" Jake said as he packed
up his briefcase and headed out the door.

Monday morning when Jake came into the room he told the men
he had just gotten a copy of a new CIA report from Doug Small.
The CIA had been tracking three suspected Al Qaeda terrorists
who were supposed to be carrying stinger missiles. The CIA had
lost their trail when the suspects entered Mexico. DEA agents
working on an investigation along with Mexican authorities near
Guaymas were tipped off that three men had stolen a pickup truck
in that area. Mexican police had discovered the stolen truck a few
kilometers north of Hermosillo. "I think the only thing we can do
is meet the DEA guys in Hermosillo and see if we can help them
figure out how the suspects are traveling and which way they're
going. I have us booked on a flight to Tucson out of JFK in two
hours.

When we get there we will be met by a DEA plane that'll take us
into Mexico with the arms and supplies we need. Let's move out."
Jake instructed. It was after dark when they left Tucson and flew
to a small airfield north of Hermosillo. The airstrip was abandoned

and had no lights. A few flares were burning on either side of the
narrow gravel strip, the only indication that there was a place to
land the plane. Evidently the DEA pilot had plenty of experience
making night landings. He sat it down with hardly a bump. Two

Chevy suburbans that appeared to be civilian pulled up near the plane with their lights off. A man wearing a baseball cap, fishing vest and khaki pants greeted them and told them to load their gear into the back of the two trucks. The other driver was similarly dressed and only nodded at the men as they climbed into his truck. The plane turned around and taxied to the opposite end of the gravel strip and then roared off into the night. The two trucks headed north toward Santa Ana. Jake rode in the lead vehicle with Sam Corona the DEA agent in charge of the search. He told Jake that the Mexican Police had found a man and woman murdered in a ditch just out side Santa Ana. The police had identified them from a wallet found near the bodies. A check with the California DMV

had shown that the couple was from Fresno and owned a Winnebago motor home. The two trucks arrived at the crime scene a little south of Santa Ana just before dawn. The bodies had been removed and technicians were just wrapping up their investigation.

Agent Corona got out and walked over to a uniformed man he seemed to know. The others remained in the trucks. After a brief conversation punctuated by hand gestures and pointing he returned to the truck. "They have the description and license plate for the Winnebago. Unfortunately there are many ways out of Santa Ana and it won't be easy to find them once they get off the main roads." He told Jake. Then he got on a cell phone and called the border patrol offices in Nogales and Yuma. He explained the situation and gave them the description of the motor home. "They probably will ditch the Winnebago and try some other means to get over the border, but you never know. Maybe the Border

patrol will get lucky." Jake said when Sam got off the phone. "What we really need is airborne reconnaissance, if they get off the main roads the Mexican police will never spot them from their cars" Sam said. "Pull over so I can get out and use my satellite phone, I'll see what I can do about some overhead assistance." Jake instructed. They were approaching a Pemex gas station and Sam pulled in beside the pumps. Mel got out of the second suburban and came over to Jake while Corona and agent Newton, the other DEA man, filled their tanks. Jake brought Mel up to speed on the situation and told him he was calling Doug Small to see if he could get some air power and maybe some satellite assistance finding the Winnebago. Since it was too early for Doug to be in his office Jake called his home. When Doug answered Jake filled him in on the situation and asked for his help. Doug said he would make it a top priority and get everything he could into the air as soon as possible. Jake and Mel were joined by Ty, Nate and Ron beside the rear vehicle. They were trying to decide whether to split up and take the two most likely routes toward the border or wait in the Santa Ana area until someone spotted the motor home. Before any decision was reached Corona came over and said the Mexican police had spotted the Winnebago on route 2 headed north toward Sonoyta and had given chase.

A gunman in the Winnebago had shot at the police car and caused the driver to swerve off the road. The right front wheel had hit a boulder and was torn off, disabling the car.

Neither officer was injured but they lost sight of the Winnebago. Jake's crew jumped back into the DEA vehicles and took off toward Sonoyta. Corona alerted the Border patrol that the suspects were headed for the Sonoyta area and then drove flat-out up highway 2. It took about an hour to reach the disabled Mexican patrol car and there were two more on the scene when they arrived. They drove on past and kept going toward the

border, monitoring the Mexican police band as they went. No one had seen the suspects.

US Border patrol units were spread out covering the likely crossing areas between Lukeville and the Organ Pipe Cactus National Monument area. Tribal police were alerted and would watch the border where they could on the Papago Indian reservation. Other Mexican patrol cars were heading southeast on route 2, from Sonoyta. Sam decided to pull off the main highway onto a side road that appeared to be well traveled. They parked the two Chevy's in a wide spot just north of route 2 about 50 miles southeast of Sonoyta.

Everyone got out and stretched their legs. "I doubt they will try to cross at Lukeville or any regular border crossing with the Winnebago." Sam said. Jake agreed and contacted Doug Small to see if they were getting any closer to having satellite surveillance. Doug told him that the Defense Department had ordered a satellite to change course and pass over the suspected area, but it would be about 3 hours before it would make the first run over their area. Sam spread a large map out on the hood of his truck and showed them where they were and the most likely roads that would be good enough for the Winnebago to navigate toward the border. He and agent Newton talked it over and decided they should split up and have a look at a couple of the more traveled roads in the immediate area while they waited for word from elsewhere. It was agreed that they would split up and keep in contact by satcom. Mel said he thought they would probably try to hide the motor home somewhere until after dark and suggested they look for any barns or buildings that could hide a Winnebago. The afternoon passed without any more sightings.

It was getting toward dark when the two DEA vehicles met at a crossroads a few miles from where they had originally separated. They decided to go back to the main highway and head toward Sonoyta. Sam wanted to check out some other dirt roads closer to town.

"Maybe we should look south of the highway. They may have gone a little south to wait until dark, figuring anyone looking for them would probably concentrate on the north side, toward the border." Ron suggested. Agent Newton agreed and said he knew of some abandoned mining sites with some good sized buildings still standing a few miles south of route 2. There were two of these sites not far apart on the same road. He said they had uncovered a pot growing operation in one of them about a year ago. The terrain south of the highway was rough desert with rocky hills covered in sage brush, manzanita and cactus. It was dark when they came to the hill above the nearer of the two old mines. Jake and Mel took over driving when they left the main road. They used night vision goggles so they could leave the headlights off and they removed the tail light bulbs so the brake lights wouldn't give them away.

There was only one building that could have hidden the motor home. The doors had been removed and all the glass was broken from the windows. Ron and Nate slipped down the bank and crept up to look in the side windows.

Finding nothing they walked back up the road to the others. They drove a few more minutes and came upon the second old mine. It was in slightly better condition than the first with two buildings still standing that were large enough for the motor home. A faint glow was visible coming from a broken window on the side of the building nearest the hillside. It went away, glowed again and then disappeared, most likely a cigarette. The men spread out and approached the building silently from all sides. At the front of the building the large corrugated metal doors had been pulled closed, leaving triangular shaped flat spots where the sand and gravel had been disturbed. Mel arrived first and crawled along the building below the windows. He was about to raise up and sneak a look inside when they heard the engine start. Seconds later the doors were knocked off

the building as the Winnebago burst out and roared down the draw. Taken by surprise the men fired at the rear of the vehicle shattering the back window and the tail lights as it careened wildly and disappeared around a bend. Ty was closest to the front suburban so he ran to it then drove down and picked up Mel and Ron then tore off down the draw throwing a spray of rocks and dust behind him. The others ran back up the hill and got in the other unit. Jake spun it around and headed back the way they had come. "Where does that other road go?" Jake yelled at Newton in the rear seat. "It connects to the highway about five miles east of this one." He replied. Then he added. "It was washed out about a mile below the highway when we were here before." The men were jammed into the seats and holding on to keep from beating each other up with their weapons as the Chevy slid and bounced down the rough road. Jake had it floored and never let up; when they got on the paved road he was hitting 90 miles an hour. "Is that the road?" Jake yelled as they approached a side road with a single strand of barbed wire strung between two wooden posts. "Yes!" Corona and Newton yelled back in unison. Jake slid the truck sideways and gunned it down the road straight through the barbed wire. About a mile from the highway they came to a dry river bed and stopped. It was really more of a sand wash but it looked passable. "Are you certain there is no other way for them to get out?"

Jake asked. Newton replied that he was sure there was no other way they could get that motor home out of the area. Jake parked the truck cross ways of the road just out of sight below the brow of the hill leading up to the wash. There was no way the Winnebago could get by it if they got that far. Mel's voice came over the satcom. "Where are you?"

He asked. Jake told him they were waiting at a dry wash on the same road and gave him the gps coordinates. Mel said they had slid off the road and got stuck and were just

getting the suburban back on the road. "Keep your lights off and go easy. We have them trapped between us. I don't want you eating a stinger if they see you." "Roger that. This road is so twisty I don't see how they can make any time and they could ambush us pretty easily." Mel replied. Up ahead the Winnebago was stopped. One of the men took a shoulder fired launch tube and loaded a stinger missile into it. He positioned himself beside a large boulder where he could watch for any vehicles coming up the hill. The other two watched and listened from near the motor home. The night sky was full of stars but there was no moonlight and they had no night vision equipment. There was a slight breeze that made soft sounds in the brush and there were a few bird sounds but otherwise it was very quiet. After a short while one of the men said "Maybe they ran off the road or their car quit. They should have caught up to us by now. We would hear them if they were getting close." Ron and Mel had come up through the desert on foot and were almost even with the man holding the stinger. Ron was about fifty yards to his east and Mel about twenty yards on the west. Ron was watching Mel sneak up on the man when someone started the motor home. The other man was signaling to the stinger man with a flashlight presumably to have him return. He had gone about three steps when Mel took him from behind and broke his neck.

Both other men were already in the motor home and didn't hear or see a thing. Ron made his way quickly down his side of the road while Mel picked up the stinger and jogged toward the motor home. He slowed up and walked quietly for a few moments to let Ron get into position near the door. Mel bumped the back of the vehicle with the end of the tube and made a grunting sound. One of the other men leapt out of the door to see what happened. He had a pistol in his hand. It didn't matter. Ron shot him twice in the heart with his silenced M-4 automatic. Mel had

dropped the launch tube and snuck around the front of the vehicle, below the driver's line of sight. Ron said "Come quickly" in muffled Arabic. The driver stuck his head out the door with a Mac 10 in his hand. Mel pulled him out of the door and knocked him out cold with a vicious punch to the side of his head. Ron bound the man's hands and feet with tie wraps and wrapped a strip of duct tape across his mouth. Ron called Ty and had him bring up the suburban while Mel called Jake and told him what they had done. Jake said for them to wait there for him. "We'd better get the Mexicans involved in this now." Sam Corona advised "Give me time to get a handle on things first." Jake said. They got in the truck and drove across the wash and down to where Mel and the others were. There were two more tubes and four additional missiles found in the Winnebago along with a handwritten plan on how to shoot down an airliner. Jake and his crew loaded all but one launcher and missile in the suburban behind the Winnebago. They took the live prisoner and put him under a tarp in the back of the suburban. "We'll take your truck back to where we landed. You can call the Mexican authorities after we are well clear of here.

When they get here tell them you and agent Newton shot it out with these guys. You only found these two assholes with the Winnebago. Thanks for your help. We were never here." Jake told him and patted him on the back. Mel put one round in the other dead terrorist to make it look like he was killed in the gun battle. Jake drove them back to the mine road and out to the highway. He arranged for the DEA pilot to meet them at the dirt strip near

Hermosillo. They loaded everything into the plane and took off for a secret airstrip near Alamogordo, New Mexico.

CHAPTER FOUR

When they landed they taxied down a ramp into an underground hangar where they were met by a tall balding man in civilian clothes. Jake addressed him as Commander Mulligan. Ty and Nate had the prisoner by his arms and carried him between them with his feet off the floor. They stood him up in front of Commander Mulligan and cut the tie wraps from his feet so he could walk on his own. They didn't remove the tape from his mouth and the tie wrap from his hands until they sat him in a chair in an interrogation room. He was still groggy from the sedative they gave him in Mexico. Ron told him in Arabic "You are our prisoner. You have no rights. What happens to you will depend on how well you cooperate. If you answer our questions truthfully we may allow you to live." He glared at the men around him and said in accented English. "You are wasting your time. You will get nothing from me. I will go happily to Allah if that is my fate."

"He's all yours commander. Let us know if you get anything useful from him." Jake said

"You can count on it Jake. If he doesn't give us what we want I'll cut him up and feed him to the pigs like the last one you brought me" Mulligan said with a wink that the prisoner couldn't see. With that Jake and his crew left to make arrangements for the trip home. The next day the network news had the story of how a joint effort between US and Mexican authorities had thwarted a plan to shoot down a civilian airliner with a shoulder fired missile. It went on to describe a heroic gun battle waged by Mexican police against Al Qaeda terrorists who had murdered a California couple and stole their motor home.

"Nice work agent Corona." Jake thought to himself when he saw it on the news. The next couple of weeks passed quietly. Nothing new seemed to be happening.

CHAPTER FIVE

"How will we deliver the explosives, Mustafa?" Muhammad asked. "It is simple my friend. "With the help of Allah we will drive two trucks into the tunnel, and abandon them near enough to the entrance to escape on foot to the getaway cars." Mustafa replied.

"We will have to practice several times to get the timing correct and arrange for safe escape routes." He continued.

"Will not the repeated runs with the same vehicles create suspicion?" Muhammad asked.

"Not if we don't actually abandon them during the practice runs. Fifty thousand cars go through that tunnel every day. We will just record the times necessary to be in the right area during rush hour and observe the possible escape routes."

The six terrorists sat in lawn chairs inside the barn of Yousef Ibrahim in rural New Jersey, drinking strong coffee and planning the destruction of the Holland tunnel. Ibrahim was not the master mind of the group but owned the small farm which was being used as a base for the terror cell. All of the men were Muslim students in the country on student visas except for Mustafa and Yousef. Mustafa was an experienced terrorist leader supposedly raised in Morocco who had several terrorist acts to his credit, but none in the USA. He never gave anyone his real name and went only by Mustafa. Yousef Ibrahim was a chemical engineer and businessman whose New York based company owned the small farm. The farm allowed not only a safe hiding place but also a legitimate reason to purchase nitrate fertilizer for explosives. None of the group stayed at the farm on a regular basis and they had only met here for the first time. Two of the students had older panel vans and used them for regular transportation. They would become the deadly bomb carriers. Yousef said. "I will begin construction of the explosives as soon as I have enough material, which will be very soon. No one should come near this farm again until we are ready to load the explosives." Mustafa told the others. "I will work out the plan and the practice schedule. We will meet at various locations for the practice runs. You will each call me on my cell phone on Wednesdays for instructions.

One by one the men went out to their cars and the two vans, ever watchful for surveillance in the dark shadows of the farm.

Youssef and Mustafa remained behind. "Why don't we just have the boys drive the vans into the tunnel and become glorious martyrs? It would be a simpler and safer plan." Youssef asked. "Because I have greater plans for them at a later time.

Besides, if we keep letting the volunteers die in these operations, sooner or later we will run out of true believers. It is getting harder to get people into this country unnoticed; we must protect the ones we have for as long as we can." Mustafa replied.

With that, Mustafa slipped out the side door and disappeared into the woods. He never let anyone see what he was driving. Youssef busied himself with plans for the chemicals and detonators before leaving in his Mercedes.

CHAPTER SIX

Finishing his coffee Jake opened the meeting saying "Gentlemen, we have had reports of possible sightings of the terrorist known only as Mustafa, in the New York City area in the last month. I believe the name Mustafa means "chosen one" in Arabic. He is believed to have come into the country from Canada under an assumed name using a diplomatic passport. The British had spotted him in Turkey then he disappeared about two months ago. The name on the passport belonged to a Moroccan diplomat who was found murdered in Istanbul last week. He had been missing for about three weeks when his body was discovered.

"We think Mustafa made it into Canada and then to the US using the stolen passport.

Here we have two fairly grainy photos of him taken last year in Spain. He is expert at hiding and changing his appearance which makes him dangerous and likely to turn up anywhere. We want to know if he is here and what he is up to. An FBI informer says he thinks he saw him at a mosque in Brooklyn last week but was not able to verify his identity and the man he saw has not been seen since." Jake explained. "I want Nate to check out the mosque and see who goes there. Don't go inside and don't be seen too long near the place, just sniff around for any known faces or suspicious groups. Ron, I want you to go to Miami and check out the lead we got on that Muslim professor and his wife.

There may be nothing to it but have a look around and get back here if nothing is happening. Doug says the FBI is watching them so don't get caught snooping around; I don't want to have to explain what we're doing there. Mel, you and Ty see what you can find on that report of several small purchases of ammonium nitrate in New Jersey going to the same farm. Transportation has been tracking new fertilizer shipments since Oklahoma City and they think this may be something. This appears to be a new customer buying small quantities at fairly close intervals. It started about the time we heard that Mustafa may have entered the country. I don't believe in coincidences, so check it out."

As the men left Jake pored over the morning terror reports looking for anything that might lead to the discovery of any new activity by any of the suspected terror groups and Al Qaeda sympathizers under the watchful eyes of the various government agencies. He couldn't lose the feeling that Mustafa was indeed here and planning something. But what? And where?

Nate found the mosque in a quiet Brooklyn neighborhood at the end of a strip of small businesses. He drove back up town and found a parking lot where he could leave his car out of sight. He was dressed like a teacher or college professor and he carried a well worn briefcase containing a hidden video camera when he boarded the metro bus. When he got off the bus he walked to a bookstore/coffee shop near the south end of the strip of businesses.

He bought a newspaper and ordered a cup of coffee and sat at a table outside.

From here he could clearly see the entrance to the mosque. He arranged the briefcase next to his chair so its hidden camera could record the scene at the mosque. It was near the time for midday prayers and people were entering the building alone, in pairs and in small groups. He was sipping his drink when he noticed a black Ford sedan pull up and park up the block from where he was sitting. Two men got out and walked across the street where they separated. One went directly into the mosque while the other walked past the mosque and disappeared around the building. The one heading into the mosque was obviously a Muslim while the other appeared to be a middle aged black man in sweats with a walkman plugged into his ear. Nate guessed they were FBI and he got pictures of both. He decided not to risk being seen and walked up the street to the bus stop where he caught the next bus back to his car. He called Jake and told him what he had just seen. Jake told him to come back to the office so they could look at what he had captured with the digital video camera. Natvar "Nate" Patel had served with Doug Small in Vietnam as an ordinance expert. He had been one of the best at defusing mines and booby traps and had gone to work on the bomb squad in Philadelphia after the war. The only son of Indian immigrants he had gone into the marines after his parents were killed in an automobile accident. His dark hair and complexion made it possible for him to pass

for someone of Arabic descent, perfect for undercover surveillance of possible terror groups. He spoke fluent Arabic and understood several regional dialects. Everyone called him Nate. He had readily accepted the job offer from Jake Powell and took early retirement from the Philadelphia bomb squad.

CHAPTER SEVEN

It was hot and humid in Miami when Ron Pierce stepped off the plane, even though it was after ten pm. He picked up a rental car and booked himself into the Hilton airport hotel for the night. The following morning he headed off toward the University of Miami district. The FBI report indicated that a U of M professor and his wife had been observed in the company of some Arabic students who were suspected of connections to Al Qaeda. There appeared to be increased recent activity among the suspect students, two of whom had taken trips to New York on several occasions. Ron decided to go to the campus and look around before doing any specific inquiries on the professor and the suspect students. Ron Pierce was the intellectual in Jake's group. He had been a language specialist with the CIA after Vietnam. Like the others he was in fine physical condition and deceptively strong despite his slim appearance. He spoke several languages including Vietnamese, Japanese, and Spanish and lately had become accomplished with two Arabic languages while operating in Afghanistan. His blond hair which was graying at the temples and his deep blue eyes ruled him out for undercover work with Arabic groups.

He was highly skilled at hand to hand combat and preferred edged weapons for close encounters of the deadly kind. He wandered leisurely around the campus checking out the student union, the library and the student bookstore. He noticed several Arabic students going into the student union lounge around three o'clock. They had just left the Language

Arts building where professor Abashir held his Islamic Studies classes. He sat on a bench, holding books he had brought along as props and watched the door to the student union for a while. About ten minutes later the professor walked out of the Language Arts building and across to the student union building. Ron got up and went in after him and watched from the refreshment counter while the professor sat at a table next to the four students. He was too far away to hear their conversation clearly but thought he picked up the words New York and Mustafa from one of the students. He got a large Coke to go and headed outside. He sat back on the bench and watched the door for a while. None of the students came out of the front entrance, only the professor. When the professor headed back into the Language Arts building, Ron decided to go to the lot where he left his car. As he approached the lot he saw an older Toyota leaving with two of the students visible in the front seat. The other two were in the back but he could not see them clearly through the darkly tinted windows. He decided not to follow them and then called Jake.

He related what he had seen to Jake who asked if he got the license plate on the Toyota.

He said yes and gave the Florida plate numbers to him. Jake said "sit tight in Miami for another day while I run this plate and maybe take a look at the professor's residence tonight after dark". "I'm on it" Ron said. Later that evening he cruised through the neighborhood where the professor lived and made note of the vehicles in the driveway.

There was a Volvo wagon and the Toyota Corolla he had seen the students in earlier. He wrote down the license tags and moved on out of the area. Later the Corolla turned out to be registered to one of the students; the Volvo was the professor's. Ron parked the rental car two blocks over and took a slow walk back toward the professor's house. He killed some more time walking around the neighborhood and back to his car. He was about to

drive away when the Corolla came past him going the other way. Inside were the four students he had seen earlier. He decided to give them a few minutes head start and then follow them. He stayed behind far enough to keep other cars between them and finally they pulled into an apartment complex near the campus. They pulled in next to an old Ford van, got out and went into a ground floor apartment.

Ron called Jake again and told him what he had seen. Jake said he knew the FBI was watching these guys and told Ron to come on home. They would watch the FBI reports on them for a while unless something new happened.

CHAPTER EIGHT

Mel Denison and Tyler Cheney looked over the Department of Transportation report on the suspect fertilizer purchases and decided to split up. Ty would go to northern New Jersey where

most of the fertilizer was purchased and Mel would go to the
address where the product had been shipped.

Melvin, "Mel" Denison had been in the same platoon in Vietnam
as Doug and Nate and like the other two was an expert marksman.
He had a physical presence that was difficult to define, just over
six feet tall about one hundred eighty pounds, not exactly muscular
looking but somehow you knew he was a man you did not want to
mess with. He had light brown hair and deep dark eyes that could
give you chills when he focused his intense gaze on you. He had
grown up working with his father and older brother in the woods
of north Idaho. He worked summers and weekends starting at age
fourteen doing the same work as the older men. The work was
hard and the days were long but it gave him extraordinary physical
strength and mental determination. When he joined the marines
after high school he was in better physical shape than any of the
recruits or

officers at boot camp. Bow hunting with his older brother had fine
tuned his natural skills for moving through a forest without making
a sound. His exploits in Vietnam were legendary among the
troops; he could sneak into an enemy camp at night and kill or
capture a man without disturbing any others. It was said he could
"move through the woods like a puff of smoke". He had been
working as a hunting guide on the St. Joe River near St. Maries,
Idaho when he was recruited by Jake Powell for the task force.

Mel drove past several similar small farms outside Little Falls and
finally found the farm whose address was on the shipping invoice,
at the end of a dirt road. The name on the mail box was Esco
farms. No one seemed to be around, there were no cars in the
driveway and no one appeared to be working in the fields. There
was a tractor behind the large barn and several attachments for
plowing and harrowing. The fields did not appear to have been
worked recently and there were no crops growing anywhere that
he could see. Mel drove up to the house and knocked on the door,
there was no answer. He walked over to the barn and checked the
big doors. They were locked with a chain and large padlock. He
tried the side door and found it was also locked as were the small

and large rear doors. There were windows on the side nearest the house but they were smeared and he couldn't see inside. Not wanting to risk being seen breaking in he decided to leave for now and come back after dark. He called Jake "I found the farm listed as Esco Farms on the invoices from the fertilizer company. No one is around and it doesn't look like anyone has been working the farm or living in the house for a while. Everything is locked up but no problem to get in. Do you want me to have a look inside tonight?" Jake said

"Yeah, take a good look. Why would anyone need fertilizer on a non-working farm? Ty is running down the ownership. The bills were paid by a corporation whose address is in

Manhattan. Lay low until after dark and then go ahead and look inside the house and barn. I don't have to tell you not to leave any evidence you were there." "No problem boss, remember, I'm just a puff of smoke" Mel said referring to his old Vietnam legend.

Ty had talked to the bulk fertilizer dealer and got copies of the invoices for Esco Farms.

He had posed as an inspector from the Department of Transportation using false papers prepared by Jake Powell's connections at NSA. He traced the ownership of Esco Farms to an international trading company based in New York City known as PTC, Inc.

Tyler "Ty" Cheney was the youngest of the task force group. He was working in military intelligence in Iraq when a roadside bomb blew off his left foot and most of his left leg below the knee. He was recuperating at Bethesda Naval Hospital when he was approached by Jake Powell. He had worked hard to improve the prosthesis on his foot and lower leg as well as his general physical condition until he could walk, run or climb better than most normal people. He had a young face and an easy smile that belied the fierce warrior that resided deep in his soul. For a computer whiz like Ty, checking into international corporations was a breeze and he came up with the information quickly. He contacted Jake by phone "Esco Farms is owned by PTC, Inc. PTC stands for Phoenix Trading Company. It was formed by two brothers, Terrence and Joseph Abraham in 1996. The business address is in Manhattan. I found more than one Joseph Abraham listed in Manhattan but no Terrence. That's all I have for now. I'll keep checking and get back to you."

Mel killed time at a local bar until after dark and then drove back toward the farm. On the way he was passed by a man in a black Mercedes. He pulled off at another farm entrance and waited for the Mercedes to disappear down the road. He then went on down the road

until he was about a mile from the farm and parked the car in the trees away from the road. He walked right up the road until he was a few hundred yards from the driveway where he went into the woods and made his way silently toward the house.

The Mercedes was in the driveway and the lights were on in the kitchen area of the house. He could see a man sitting at the table with a laptop computer and a large paper bag. Mel crept up to the house where he could see through a window and watched the man typing on the computer. After a short while the man got up and removed some things from the bag. He placed a framed 8 x 10 picture on a side board and placed a candle on either side of it. He lit the candles and appeared to be praying on his knees.

After a while he blew out the candles and hand wrote a note on a sheet of notebook paper. He turned off the lights and walked out onto the front porch. He then stuck the note to the door on a nail that was already there and walked out to his car. Mel moved along the side of the house to the rear so he wouldn't be visible when the car lights came on. The car backed out and drove off into the night. Mel then went to the door and read the note. It was written in large elegant script. It said "Mr. Klepner, please prepare the tractor for operation and begin cultivating for a corn crop. Call me when you have finished or if you need anything. Joseph Abraham". He then picked the lock and went into the kitchen. He closed the door behind him and used a small maglight to inspect the house. It had not been used for sometime and what furniture there was, was old. He looked at the picture the man had placed on the sideboard and was surprised to see a young woman holding a newborn baby. He left the house as he found it and went to the barn, he had the padlock opened in ten seconds and slipped the chain off the doors. Inside he found some old farm equipment and a large workbench with a few tools on it. At the

rear of the room near the back doors there were two pallets stacked with bags of ammonium nitrate fertilizer. No other chemicals were found but there was a drum marked

"seed corn" off to one side. A side room appeared to be for tool storage, there was an old cement mixer, a fuel oil tank and some empty drums The barn smelled of old dust, hay and animal leftovers from an earlier period. He quickly left as he had come and relocked the chain on the doors. He was careful not to leave any footprints and headed back down the road to retrieve his car. He checked into a nearby motel and went to bed. The next morning he went back to the farm around ten a.m. and was surprised to find an older man in bib overalls and two Spanish boys working on the tractor behind the barn. They had just gotten it started and were hooking up the plow when Mel arrived. He walked over to the man and introduced himself as Mel Denison, crop insurance salesman. Bart Klepner looked him over and offered his hand. He told Mel "I'm just hired to do some plowing and planting for the owner, you would have to talk to him about crop insurance or anything else to do with the farm." "Have you worked on this farm for him before?" Mel asked. "This farm hasn't been worked for several years. When the new owner bought it I had harvested a good corn crop for the old family just before they sold it. The new guy met me here when I was finishing the job and asked if he could hire me next season. I gave him my phone number and told him to call when he was ready, but he never did until now." Bart said as he scuffed around in the dirt with his right boot. "When did he buy the farm" Mel asked. "August 2001, he said it was a surprise for his wife and new son. Look, I gotta get these boys to workin', if you want to contact the owner, here's his number." He handed Mel a scrap of paper torn from a feed store invoice with a scribbled phone number on it then climbed up on the tractor and took off to the field with the boys

following behind. "Thanks," Mel said into the distance and headed back to his car. He called Jake on the way back to the office and filled him in. "I met an old farmer who has just been hired to plow and plant the farm this morning. The note I found on the door last night had the name Joseph Abraham and this phone number." He repeated the number to Jake. Jake noted that it matched one of the numbers Ty found listed. "He told me an interesting story about the new owner. It seems he bought the farm just before 9-11 as a surprise for his wife and their new son. For whatever reason, they never hired him to come back and work the farm until just now. I checked out the barn last night. There are two pallets of bagged ammonium nitrate fertilizer out there and a barrel of seed corn.

Nothing in the house or barn indicates any intent or ability to make a bomb." "Ty found some information on the owner yesterday. He and his brother started a trading company in New York, with offices in the World Trade Center. After nine eleven they moved uptown in Manhattan. For now I don't see any need to bother this Joseph Abraham unless we see something that ties him to any of the terror suspects. What's your gut feeling?"

Jake asked. "It all seems pretty innocent on the surface, I saw the guy praying in front of a picture of woman and child in the farm house last night. But it would be a perfect place to hide out while building a bomb. The contract farmer, Bart Klepner, seems genuine enough." Mel added. "Well, come on back, we have other fish to fry" Jake said.

CHAPTER NINE

In a run down apartment complex in Lackawanna, New York, a woman prepared a simple dinner for two. The shades were drawn in the small apartment and the man was barely visible sitting on the couch watching the TV news. "How long can you stay?" the woman asked in Arabic. "Only tonight" he replied. The smell of garlic and curry filled

the apartment as she prepared lamb and vegetables for their dinner.
They ate in silence, she watching him and him watching the news.
When they finished, she cleared the table and placed the dishes in
the sink. He came up slowly behind her and held her around the
waist and pressed himself into her. She turned in his grip and
pressed her hips into him as they shared a deep kiss. Without a
word they moved to the other room where the couch also served as
her bed. They tore at each other's clothes and were soon naked on
the couch, kissing each other hungrily. He probed her mound with
his fingers, feeling the smoothly shaved area, a custom of
Moroccan women. Moroccan men abhor pubic hair as unclean.

When he entered her she squirmed with desire and her hips rose up
to meet his thrust until they collapsed in mutual orgasm. "Karim, it
has been too long." She whispered. She knew him only as ABD-
Al-Karim, also an alias; she did not know him as Mustafa.

"Asrar, soon we will leave this place of the infidels, I will come
for you." He lied. She was sleeping in the early hours before dawn
when he slipped out of her apartment. No one saw him retrieve the
BMW motorcycle he had hidden behind the dumpster. Clad in
grey raingear and a full helmet with a dark face shield he
disappeared toward Buffalo.

Asrar, whose name means "secrets", woke to find him gone. She
wept silently, knowing she might never see him again. They had
been lovers years before when they met in London. She had
moved to the USA with her brother, Fayez, who was a friend of
Karim's. Her brother had gone to teach at a University in Buffalo
and lived with his wife near his work. She was alone. She never
knew how Mustafa had found her.

CHAPTER NINE

Muhammad and Malik had returned to Miami when professor
Abashir called them on their cell phone. "Have you heard from
Mustafa?" he asked. "Not a word, and don't use his name on the
phone. You never know who is listening. I have felt like someone
has been following us since we returned. I have not seen them, but

I feel like the eyes of the infidel are always upon us. We are to call the Chosen One on Wednesday for instructions, do not call again." Muhammad snapped. On the next street over from the professor's house two men in a Direct TV panel van were listening in on a newly authorized tap on the professor's phone. "Jerry, did you get the number he called?" "Yes, I'm running it now" Jerry replied. "It's a throw away cell, no way to know who has it" he continued.

Jerry Johnson and Shane Martin were newly minted FBI agents with only three years experience between them but both were sharp and had the energy of the young. Neither one had any training in Arabic languages so they had to record the call for analysis by FBI interpreters. They continued to monitor the professor's line for two more hours but no more calls came. "Should we forward this one call or wait until we have more to show for our efforts?" Jerry pondered aloud. "I say we keep on this guy for a few more days before we do a formal report" Shane added. "Agent Jackson will want more than this for allowing us to plant that bug" Jerry concluded.

CHAPTER TEN

"I think I'll go up to Esco Farms for a little follow up this morning, just to see if the old farmer really did plow that field" Mel said. "All right, follow your gut, but don't make a career out of it. We may have something more pressing. It's only Monday" Jake said.

Mel drove up to the farm and pulled into the driveway. No one was around but the tractor was back behind the barn and the dirt appeared to have been plowed. Mel got out and

walked up to the edge of the freshly turned dirt. The sun was hot on the back of his neck and the smell of the plowed soil filled his consciousness. He knelt down and scratched around until he found corn seeds in the furrows. "I guess he really does want to raise corn" he said to himself as he returned to his car. He still felt he was missing something but couldn't put his finger on it as he drove back to the city. Jake and the boys were going over the weekend intelligence reports, looking for anything unusual or unusually familiar when Mel returned. "Anything interesting" he asked." "The Feebs have put a bug in that Muslim professor's house in Miami but haven't reported anything so far. No word on Mustafa anywhere. What did you see at the farm?" Jake asked. "The land has been plowed and planted, I found corn seeds in the ground, but I still think there is something fishy about the whole setup, but I don't know what it is." Mel said.

CHAPTER ELEVEN

Wednesday morning when the phone vibrated in the pocket of his rain suit Mustafa removed his helmet and stepped into the phone booth at a convenience store in Trenton.

He removed the payphone from its cradle and appeared to be talking into it. It was Muhammad calling from Miami. "Get your group together and bring both vans to New Jersey on Sunday. We will meet at the same place as last time at 8 pm. Go to the mailbox store on Broadway and pick up your mail. Check your men into two different motels near the truck stop. When you get your mail, there will be a new number for me. Don't call. I will meet you on time." He stepped out of the booth with his helmet on and rode away.

He turned into the large truck stop and rode slowly between two big rigs. As one began to pull away he slipped the cell phone under the trailer wheels and rode off. The phone was

smashed beyond recognition and the truck driver was totally unaware that the motorcycle or its rider had been there.

CHAPTER TWELVE

The Direct TV van pulled up to the curb, half a block from the professor's house just before 7 am. Agent Johnson opened the stainless thermos and poured two cups of black coffee. He handed one to Shane in the back of the van, set his own on the console and stepped out. He placed orange cones at the front and rear of the van and climbed back into the driver's seat. "Are we receiving the signal yet" "Yeah, it's coming in five by five, but no calls yet. He leaves for classes by 9:30 on Wednesdays, so we won't be here too long today" Shane replied. "What were those new keywords Jackson told us to listen for?" Jerry asked. "Mustafa and New York" Shane said. "Wait a minute, lets replay that last call from the other day, I think I may have heard those words or something like it"

Jerry said, suddenly alert. Shane shoved the USB connection from the digital recorder into the monitor and replayed the Arabic conversation. "There, run that back again, see, the professor said *Mustafa* and then the other guy got agitated." "Shit, we'd better get this to Jackson right away" Shane added. Just then, he heard a dial tone, someone was making a call on the professor's phone. "Did you hear from Mustafa?" the professor's voice. "I told you not to use that name on the phone" the other voice replied, angrily. "Do you have the cash we need?" The voice asked. "Muhammad, I sent it to the mailbox in New Jersey as instructed by Mus..I mean the Chosen One." Professor Abashir replied. "We need gas and expense money to drive to New York, how are we supposed to get there?"

Muhammad asked in frustration." "Meet me at the Library after my last class. I will give you what I can" the professor said with a resigned sigh. The call ended and the two

agents stared at each other for a moment. "We'd better get this to Jackson right now"

Shane said as he dialed Walter "Stonewall" Jackson at the FBI office in Miami. "Play it for me now, I have Marla from the language section here with me" Agent Jackson instructed. Marla gave him the English translation as the words came over the phone from both calls. "Why the hell am I just hearing this now? When did that first call happen?" Jackson demanded. "It was last week, sir. We didn't have any key words to look for at the time" Shane explained. "Forget the excuses and get your butts back here now! Get rid of the van and get two cars from the pool. I want you two to see if you can manage to follow these guys after they leave the professor, without being seen." Jackson said, calmer now.

Agents Johnson and Martin grabbed a pair of Fords from the motor pool, Shane in a white station wagon and Jerry in a blue sedan. They headed for the campus library and staked out the two possible routes leaving the parking area. Shane could see an older Corolla parked near the entrance and watched as two young men in U of M tee shirts got in. The professor came out and got in his Volvo wagon and barely nodded at the two in the Corolla as he pulled away. "I've got 'em, they're in the old blue Corolla heading your way" Shane said to Jerry on the two- way. "I see them, Shane, I'll let them pass me and then you follow them. I'll turn around in the lot and follow a ways behind you. If they turn off this street, you keep going and I'll stay with them. We'll just tag team these jokers. They'll never suspect a thing." Jerry said. The plan worked to perfection, they followed the old Corolla to an apartment complex not far from the campus. Jerry drove on past and parked the sedan on the next block. Shane drove by and picked him up after watching the men go into a ground floor apartment. They circled the block and parked the

wagon where they could watch the apartment without being obvious. They continued the stake out until 10 pm when the lights in the apartment went out. They waited a while and then called agent Jackson. "Change cars and split up, take turns going for dinner, I want one of you on that Corolla at all times. If nothing happens by daylight I'll get someone to relieve you. Call me if they go on the move." He instructed.

CHAPTER THIRTEEN

Jake Powell was in a cranky mood Thursday morning. Things were too quiet and he had a bad feeling that he couldn't shake. "Let's have another look at that video that Nate took at the Brooklyn mosque, maybe we missed something" He said. Nate set up the large monitor and played the video again. Part way through, just after the mosque started to fill up for prayers Mel walked in from the restroom. "Hold it, Nate, back that up a little." he said

"What is it?" Jake asked "That guy getting out of the Mercedes looks like our farm owner" Mel replied. Nate froze the picture and zoomed in on the man getting out of the Mercedes across the street. "That's him; I got a good look at him at the farm house the first night." Mel said. The man was about six feet, a little tall for an Arab, with black hair and a neatly trimmed mustache and goatee. He was wearing an expensively tailored suit.

"That mosque is not the closest one to his office or apartment, so he must have had a specific reason to go there." Ty added. "Maybe we should have a closer look at who else went into the mosque before and after our alleged farmer" Jake said. Nate ran the video back to the beginning and they all watched it with renewed interest. What they couldn't see was that after Nate had left, a man came out of the mosque and left on a motorcycle.

CHAPTER FOURTEEN

Wednesday evening Joseph let himself into a small warehouse he had rented down in the five points district. Inside he gathered some boxes containing chemicals, electronics, mixing and measuring equipment and placed them in the trunk of the Mercedes. He then drove to rural New Jersey to his farm. He opened the big front doors and then drove his car inside. He closed the doors and turned on the overhead lights. He began placing items from the boxes on the workbench. He worked diligently making up detonators and wiring them to cell phones he planned to use as receivers for his signal to detonate the explosives. He went into the side room of the barn where the tools were kept and retrieved an old cement mixer. Then he opened a sack of fertilizer from one of the pallets and added it to the running mixer. Then he added fuel oil from a drum he had brought out of the tool room on a hand truck. Using a hand pump he added the liquid until the mixture was the proper texture. He ran the mixer a while longer to get a thorough mix of ingredients. Afterward he pumped the mixture out into an empty drum. He repeated this process until he had eight drums of the explosive mixture known as "anfo" (for ammonium nitrate & fuel oil) irreverently known to miners the world over as "goat shit".

Inside each drum, in a zip lock bag, he placed the cell phone receiver, the detonator and one stick of Dupont 70 dynamite. One call from him could set off all eight drums at once.

The plan was to have four drums in each of the vans, enough for a massive explosion that would collapse the Holland tunnel, drowning hundreds and disrupting traffic into and out of New York City. Not to mention the fear and panic it would create. Satisfied with his work, he decided to visit the farm house and say a prayer for his late wife and son before driving back to the city. He took a quick look at the sprouting corn before leaving, surprised at how good it looked without the benefit of fertilizer.

CHAPTER FIFTEEN

Daylight came and with it the usual Miami heat and humidity. Shane awoke with a start.

He had dozed off while he was supposed to be watching the Corolla at the apartments across the street. He stared at the car for moment and realized it was still there. He heaved a sigh of relief and called Jackson. "The Corolla is still here and there is no activity in the apartment so far" he said. "Johnson will be there to relieve you in a few minutes Shane, go home and get some sleep when he gets there." Jackson instructed. At that time two blocks away, two men got into two old Ford vans. One white with rust spots on the quarter panels the other faded blue with similar rusty areas. Both had Florida license plates. The blue one headed for highway 27, the white one for highway 95 North.

Later at a rest stop on 95 near Fort Pierce, Muhammad parked away from the restrooms and changed the Florida plate to a New Jersey one. A little while later on highway 27

near Clewiston, Malik stopped the other van at a gas station and parked behind the building after filling up. He changed the Florida plate for a New York one, stolen on the last trip.

Around ten o'clock agent Johnson tired of watching the Corolla and decided to walk over to the apartment and knock on the door.

He planned to ask for the apartment number of a Susan Johnson if anyone answered the door. It wasn't necessary, no one was there. He ran back to his car and called agent Jackson. "They have flown the coop" he said breathlessly when Jackson answered. "How the hell did that happen? Is the Corolla still there? He asked angrily. "Yeah, its here but no one is home. I knocked on the door and then peeked in the window when no one answered. They had to have left some other way." Johnson added. "All right get back here, we need to check all of them out and see

if they own any other vehicles." Jackson ordered. They had the names of all four suspects and ran them through motor vehicles to see if there were any other cars in their names.

Only the old Corolla registered to Muhammad Harun-Al Rashid showed up. "Let's try the professor and his wife" Jerry suggested. "Bingo! The professor and the wife each purchased Ford vans last month. Both are E-300 panel vans, one is a 1990 the other a 1992. The older one is the professor's, its white and the other is registered to the wife and its blue." Shane exclaimed. "Get FHP on it now! Give them the description and the plates. Have them pulled over for some bogus traffic or equipment violation and get a look inside. Maybe they can detain them until we can get a good tail on them. I want to know what they are up to." Jackson said. He sent an urgent e-mail to the New York and New Jersey field offices. He also decided to give Doug Small a heads up, just in case Homeland Security had something happening in the same area. The new era of info sharing was finally starting to take hold at the FBI.

CHAPTER SIXTEEN

"Nate, why don't you get into Arab drag and go back to that mosque for evening prayers"

Jake said. "I'll have Mel back you up across the street, just in case. Mel can take some more video on the outside while you check out the faithful." Jake added. Just then Jake's computer beeped signaling an instant message on the encrypted account. "It's from Doug.

Those students Ron checked out in Miami are on the move. The phone tap paid off when Doug sent the keywords Ron suggested. The FBI thinks they are driving north in a couple of old vans. Apparently they slipped out of the surveillance in Miami and got out of town in vans owned by the suspect professor and his wife. He sent the description and plate numbers to us but says the Florida highway patrol has not spotted either van so far."

"Maybe we should have another look at Joseph Abraham, I could tail him for a few days and see what he's up to" Ty said "I agree, I want to keep an eye on him now that we've seen him at the mosque" Jake said. With that said, Ty headed off to Manhattan to start watching Joseph Abraham. Mel and Nate left for Nate's apartment to get his authentic Arabic Muslim costume and wire him up for the hidden camera and recorder. They decided to leave Mel's car a ways up town and both ride the bus to the mosque area. Nate got off directly across from the mosque and Mel continued to the next stop and got off.

He walked slowly down to the café where Nate had been before and repeated Nate's earlier moves by buying a paper and a coffee and sitting at an outdoor table where he could point the briefcase camera at the entrance to the mosque. Nate had walked to the entrance of the mosque by the time Mel was situated and he blended into the crowd entering for evening prayers. Mel noticed a man dressed in something that resembled coveralls walking up toward the mosque. He couldn't tell where the man came from or how he arrived. He entered the mosque in the midst of a small group. No one seemed to notice him. Just then Mel felt a vibration from his cell phone in his breast pocket. He pulled it out and placed it up to his ear. It was Ty, he said "You won't believe this, but I am following Abraham and it appears that he is headed for the mosque. You should see him on your left any moment" Mel glanced around as he replaced the phone in his pocket and caught sight of Abraham's black Mercedes pulling into a parking spot near the mosque. Inside, Nate took a place near the outer aisle and put his prayer rug down in front of him.

The call to prayer ended and all present began bowing to the floor placing their heads on their rugs. When the praying was complete he rolled up his rug like all the other people

and strolled slowly among them toward the front entrance. He photographed as many as he could, but the size of the crowd limited his viewing capabilities. Many small groups stood around and visited, some went up to speak to the Imam. He didn't recognize Abraham standing next to a man in grey coveralls of some kind. They appeared to be in deep conversation with each other. The man in coveralls looked vaguely familiar but he kept his face turned so that Nate couldn't get a decent look at him. Nate had not seen Joseph Abraham at this point except in the original video and didn't make the connection.

He decided to go on outside and hang around the doors for a while before leaving for the bus stop. He got another look at the man in the coveralls as he came out of the entrance and walked up the street and was sure he got a frontal face shot with his hidden camera.

He was looking back at the entrance when he heard a motorcycle start up just past where he had last seen the man in what he thought were coveralls. He then realized the man was wearing a motorcycle rain suit and full helmet. Nate only saw the back of the man and the bike and couldn't see a license plate. Too many people were crossing the street and he lost sight of the bike right away. He walked casually across the street and up to the bus stop. Mel watched him go and then waited to see Abraham come out of the mosque alone and return to his car. Mel pulled out his cell phone and called Ty. "Your Mercedes is just pulling out, heading in your direction" Mel said softly into the cell phone. He watched the bus pick up Nate and then slowly walked up the street to the bus stop to wait for the next bus. He used the fifteen minute wait to video as many of the remaining "faithful" as he could as they passed by. Later he and Nate were in the car heading for the office when Nate suddenly remembered why the motorcycle guy looked familiar. "Did you notice a guy in grey coveralls at the mosque?" Nate asked. "Yeah, it seemed like an unusual outfit for a Muslim going to prayers" Mel answered "Do you have any of those photos of the guy we called Mustafa, with you?" Nate asked. "Not in the car, we have copies at the office; do you think it's the same guy?" Mel asked. "I didn't get a good look directly at his face but I think I got some pretty good video we can look at when we get back. He was in a pretty serious looking conversation with a taller guy in an expensive suit." Nate said. "The guy in the expensive suit was our alleged "farmer" Joseph Abraham. Ty tailed him to here and is following him as we speak" Mel went on.

CHAPTER SEVENTEEN

When Mustafa approached Yousef in the mosque he motioned him to join him at the back of the room. There they placed their prayer rugs next to each other and did not speak until prayers were concluded. "When will the instruments be ready my friend?" he whispered to Yousef. "They are ready now" He replied. "Good, I will finish with the choir practice by Monday; we can load the instruments on Tuesday night and perform the music on Wednesday morning." Mustafa said cryptically" "It is set then, God willing"

Yousef said. As they separated he slipped the barn key into Mustafa's pocket. Mustafa left first and Yousef stayed behind a short while as earlier instructed.

Ty followed Abraham's car until he pulled into the parking garage at his condo complex in Manhattan. He had made no other stops on the way back from the mosque. Ty called Mel and was told to come back to the office. When he arrived the others were going over the new videos Mel and Nate had taken at the mosque. They had determined that the motorcycle rider was indeed Mustafa and Nate's video showed him talking with Abraham inside the mosque. Now that they had connected Abraham to the terrorist Jake laid out a plan to investigate him. He instructed Ty to bug the man's home, office and car

so they could listen to his activities. They would also rotate following him whenever he traveled anywhere in the car. He also got word to the highway patrol in both New York and New Jersey, through Doug, to look for the motorcycle. They had only a vague description and no plate but at least they could watch for a lone rider matching the description. Ty waited then followed the Mercedes to Abraham's office and watched him go inside before placing a powerful transmitter under the driver's seat. He had no problem with the keyless entry system. He left and headed back to the man's condo. The condo had an underground garage with an automated gate at the entrance. He waited until a car came out and slipped inside, unnoticed. He had a good look around the condo but didn't find anything incriminating. He placed bugs in the kitchen and desk phones as well as the one in the bedroom. The rooms were tidy and well decorated with fine art and expensive furniture, all of a Middle Eastern motif. There were several pictures Ty assumed were of family members and a baby. It was a newer building with views of the skyline from the living room. None of the rooms were very large, typical for Manhattan.

He checked the bugs for live signals before leaving. He slipped out of the garage and walked back to his car. He drove back toward the man's office and parked on a street a block away. He could hear a radio or TV playing in the background of the office and the sound of typing. Abraham had no secretary or other employees in the small office. He apparently did all of his business by himself using the computer and telephone.

Mel drove up to the farm on Saturday and found no one there, as usual. He decided to have a look in the barn, so he slipped in the side door this time in broad daylight. He found only a couple of bags of fertilizer still on the pallets. He thought either the rest had been applied to the corn field or had been removed for some other purpose. There was a

strong odor of fuel oil and there was a stain on the floor where some had been spilled. He checked in the tool room and found that the cement mixer smelled of fuel oil and had some residue in it. The eight drums that had been empty before; now had the lids clamped on and felt full. The clamping bands had metal seal tags at the hinges. He decided not to disturb them. He had a pretty good idea what he would find inside. "This is enough goat shit to create one hell of an explosion" he said aloud. He left everything as he found it and returned to his car. He pulled out and headed toward Little Falls to find a motel and called Jake. "The place was deserted as before, but I found eight drums of goat shit in the barn. Enough to do some real damage somewhere." He told Jake. "Stay close and keep an eye on the road to the farm, don't let anyone know we're on to them. Ty is watching Abraham, so we'll know if he heads your way. No word on our friend Mustafa so far." Jake said.

Saturday and Sunday passed without anyone going near the farm. Mel rented a Harley for a few days and rode to a tavern near the crossroads where the dirt road to the farms left the main road. He hung out at the tavern, playing pool with the regulars for awhile and sitting at the crude tables outside drinking beer and watching the road. At first the locals were wary of him but after a while they accepted him when he told them he was looking for part time work on the farms. He made a couple of trips down the dirt road, toward the small farms each day and returned to the tavern.

CHAPTER EIGHTEEN

Ty had two uneventful days watching Abraham. He rotated with Nate and Ron listening in on business calls and following him between the office and his condo and a couple of restaurants. Most of the calls were conducted in English and seemed to only coordinate

the sale and shipping of goods between the US and various Mediterranean ports. They recorded all the calls and Ron translated the Arabic ones. No mention of Mustafa or anything remotely connected to him.

The highway patrols had come up empty on the suspected vans from Florida and had nothing on the mysterious motorcycle rider either.

Monday evening Mel had just arrived at the tavern and was eating fish and chips outside and chatting with a couple of his new acquaintances when he noticed a rusty looking white van. It had gone past the dirt road and then stopped for a second before backing up and turning down the road toward the farms. "Somebody's lost" the man next to Mel said. Mel just grunted. A short time later a rusty blue van turned down the dirt road. Mel got up and said "later boys, I got to turn in, I may have a job tomorrow the other side of Little Falls" with that he fired up the rented bike and headed off toward his motel. He hurried to his room and got on the phone to Jake. "I just saw two rusty old vans heading down the road toward the farm, neither looked familiar and one acted like he was lost" he said. "Could be our Miami suspects, Mel. Ty just called. He's following the Mercedes across into New Jersey as we speak. You keep out of sight away from the farm until we get up there. What ever is going down may be happening tonight. I want all of us there with plenty of firepower before we move on them" Jake said. "Meet me at the super market between Little Falls and the crossroads, call me when you get there" Mel instructed. "I'm going in for a closer look, they won't know I'm there" he added. As he pulled out of the motel Ty called on the radio and said he was about 30 minutes from the farm. Mel told him to follow the Mercedes until it turned off on the dirt road and then u-turn back to the supermarket and wait for him and the others. Mel rode to the woods

bordering the last farm before the Esco property and hid the bike in the trees. He walked through the woods and used his night vision goggles to scope out the farm. The Mercedes was in the driveway, but no other vehicles were in sight. Lights were on in the barn so he crept over to the side and tried to look through the windows. He couldn't see anything inside except the glow of the lights through the smeared old windows. He moved around to the back doors and laid down on his stomach so he could look through the crack between the big doors. Inside he saw two men rolling a drum up two planks into the white van and could only partly tell that the same thing was happening further ahead with the blue van. He could make out Mustafa and Abraham watching the operation from one side. He backed slowly out of position and headed back into the woods. Inside, Mustafa and Yousef were going over the final plan. "The practice runs showed that it will be difficult to go into the Holland tunnel from both ends during rush hour, it's just too congested to get the vans and get away cars in place at the same time." Mustafa said.

"What is the better plan then" Yousef asked. "Do you think one van will be enough to bring down the tunnel?" Mustafa asked. "Possibly, I can only estimate the effect. What do you have in mind?" Yousef asked. "I want to send one car and van into the Holland as planned, from the Manhattan side and the other car and van through the Lincoln tunnel at about the same time. That way we can blow up both tunnels and escape through New Jersey. The escape car will be directly ahead of the van so the driver can park the van and jump into the escape car. When they are safely out we can detonate the vans. We won't have to be really close to the tunnels to make the detonators work, will we?" Mustafa asked, his eyes gleaming. "We will have to be in line with the mouth of the tunnels to be certain the signal can reach the detonators. I have tested the reception in the Holland

tunnel and have the frequency and amplitude adjusted to make certain the receiver will get the signal. I don't know about the Lincoln tunnel but it should work the same" Yousef said, with some hesitation. "We will leave early enough to get to the Manhattan side in plenty of time to get in line on the west bound entrance to the tunnels during the morning rush hour. I will lead Muhammad's van through the Lincoln tunnel and you will lead Malik's van through the Holland tunnel" Mustafa explained. "Did you get the getaway cars ready, Mustafa?" Yousef asked. "We stole two older sedans and parked them near the university, just off of Houston street. We can meet there and pick them up before heading to the tunnels". The boys were pushing the last of the drums into the vans where they tied them down with heavy cargo straps when Yousef handed Mustafa an old style bag phone. He told him it was programmed for the receivers in Muhammad's van and was much more powerful than the new small phones. "I have programmed the numbers into speed dial number one. Just turn it on, push number one and press send, the rest is in God's hands, my friend" With that he said he would be leaving first and for the others to wait at least one hour before leaving and to space their departures by twenty minutes each. "Death to the infidels" he said in Arabic as he went out the side door to his car.

"Allahu Akbar!" echoed from the others.

CHAPTER NINETEEN

When Mel arrived at the supermarket everyone was there. He explained to the group what he had seen in the barn. They listened in grim silence while he laid out the plan.

"We'll hide the cars in the woods and proceed on foot to the farm. When we get there we can take up positions across from the front of the barn and wait for them to start out of the doors. Ron will take out the first van with a rocket propelled grenade when the doors

open. That should explode both rigs. We'll let the smoke clear and then inspect whatever's left."

All agreed it was the safest plan. Jake said "We can't afford for them to leave here with those bombs. If there are any survivors after the blast lets try and take one alive". He couldn't help think what a relief it was to have that kind of authority. Regular law enforcement could never operate in this manner. They were authorized to get the job done with whatever means they deemed necessary and then get out of dodge and let the other agencies clean up the mess and/or take the credit. They were like Mel, just puffs of smoke. They had just arrived at the farm and had taken up their positions when Abraham appeared out of the side of the barn and got into his car. He backed out and took off down the road at normal speed. "Shit," Jake said "where the hell is he going?" "Ty, get to your car and try to follow him" The brake lights came on at the back of the Mercedes just as the barn exploded into a huge fireball. The blast knocked Jake off his feet and debris rained down on all of them. Then the propane tank between the house and barn added a second explosion and lit the house on fire. When they regained their senses the Mercedes was gone. Ty took off on a dead run up the road to his car, while the others skirted around to look at what was left of the barn and the burning house. Finding no one, they headed back for the cars and quickly left the area. They were back near the supermarket when the first fire truck and rescue unit flew by with lights and sirens blaring. They regrouped at the market and waited for word from Ty. He soon called and told them he had caught up with the Mercedes. He said it was traveling at the speed limit and appeared to be headed back to Manhattan. "Do I force him off the road or should I just follow him and we can take him at his home?" He asked Jake "He must not have seen us at the farm,

just follow him and report when he gets home, if that's where he goes. Don't alert him.

We're heading back and will meet you near his place. Keep in touch." Jake said. They got in their cars and headed back to the city.

CHAPTER TWENTY

It was nearly dawn when they pulled into the parking lot a block from Abraham's condo and met up with Ty. "How do you want to play it?" Ty asked Jake.

"Let's disarm the main alarm and go in quietly. When we get to his door, just knock and say you are from the condo association. If he opens it we jump in and grab him quietly, if not, we break it down and grab him anyway." They went down opposite sides of the street while Ty made his way to the condo garage to disable the alarm. It wasn't necessary. It was nearing 8 am and cars were leaving the garage, causing the gate to remain open and making it easy for them to enter unnoticed. Ty went up the elevator to the fourth floor while the others came up the stairs to avoid the tenants coming out of the elevator. Mel stayed behind to check out Abraham's car. They waited behind the stairway door while Ty knocked on the apartment door. It opened slightly and Ty shoved his way in and grabbed Abraham, clamping his hand over the man's mouth to keep him quiet.

The others came in and closed the door behind them. Jake held a gun to the man's neck when Ty let go of him. Jake moved him to a chair and told him to sit. "Who are you men?

What do you want?" He asked, too calmly. The door opened and Mel entered carrying a black object. It was the bag phone Abraham had used to detonate the bombs. Ty slipped behind the man and wrapped a strip of duct tape across his mouth. Then he stood him up and pulled his arms behind his back and bound his hands with a plastic wire tie. Mel went out first and checked the hallway and the stairs. No one was around so they put Abraham

between Jake and Ty and moved on down the stairs to the garage. Mel checked the garage and waited while a white Cadillac left. He motioned for the others to follow and went to Abraham's Mercedes. Mel got behind the wheel while Nate and Ty jammed Abraham into the back seat between them. Jake sat in the passenger seat and handed a black hood to Nate who quickly put it over Abraham's head and pushed him down, out of sight. Mel pulled out of the garage and drove back to the lot where the other vehicles were. They moved Abraham to the rear seat of Jake's suburban. He left immediately, with Ty and Nate holding Abraham out of sight. Mel took the Mercedes back to the garage, entered using Abraham's remote gate device and then walked back to his own car. He kept the remote for later use. He headed for the safe house where they were going to interrogate Mr. Abraham. On the way he turned on the news radio. The broadcast led with the story of a large explosion in rural New Jersey. "Local police and firemen are investigating an explosion that occurred at a small farm in northern New Jersey early this morning. No word on what caused the massive explosion and police have not released the name of the farm's owner. Local police say that people from neighboring farms were awakened by the blast and saw the glow from the fire over the nearby woods that separate the farm from the nearest neighbor, nearly five miles to the west. More on this later." Mel called Jake and told him he was going to go to

Abraham's office to catch any phone calls that might come in from the police or media. Sooner or later the police or FBI would discover the ownership of the farm and trace it to Abraham, just as Ty had done.

CHAPTER TWENTY ONE

When the hood was removed, Joseph Abraham found himself in a room with gray concrete walls and no windows. He was seated at a table facing two men directly across

from him. The tape had been removed from his mouth, leaving a stinging abrasion on his lower lip. "If I am under arrest, I demand to call my attorney" he said as he rubbed his lips with the back of his hand. "You don't seem to get it, pal. You are a terrorist. You have no rights. We can do whatever we want with you." The stocky man who seemed to be in charge said as he leaned close to Joseph's face. "Don't waste our time denying it, we were at your farm last night." The other man said. "We want to know everything you know about terrorist groups in this country and how you came to be involved with Mustafa, for starters." "What were you planning to blow up with your home made bombs, before they accidentally sent your friends to terrorist hell?" the other man demanded. "That was no accident. I planned to blow those scum off the earth from the beginning" he blurted out. Stunned, Jake and Ty stared at each other as the man went on.

"I am not a terrorist. Fuckers like those killed my entire family. My wife, my baby boy, my beloved brother and my parents who were in our office in the south tower on the day of the 911 attacks" he sobbed. "I have thought of nothing but how to get revenge since 911" he added. "And you just happened to own a farm and knew a few terrorists and knew how to build a bomb? You don't expect us to believe that, do you? Jake asked sarcastically. "I bought that farm as a surprise for my wife after our baby was born. She was raised on a small farm like that, in northern California. We planned to use it for weekend getaways until we could build a new house and live there. Our condo in Manhattan was going to become too small. We planned to have many more children. The name Esco Farms represents Elaine and our son, Samuel. I have a degree in chemical engineering, so constructing a crude bomb from simple materials was easy for me. As for Mustafa, I began frequenting a mosque known to be sympathetic to radical Islamic views

to see if I could become acquainted with people who could lead me to some of the terrorists. I used my Arabic name, Yousef Ibrahim and did not let anyone know my home address or what my business was. I very slowly gravitated to the most radical members of the mosque and professed a similar hatred for Infidels. Eventually I was approached by a visiting Imam preaching radical ideas who asked me if I would be interested in meeting with some others who shared my views. I met a man from somewhere near Buffalo, a teacher, I believe, who talked to me a few times about different acts of Jihad that had appeared in the media. After several of these conversations he introduced me to the man you call Mustafa, at the mosque. I asked him how I could be of service to the cause of Allah. He quizzed me about my skills and I explained that I was a chemist and could possibly be useful in making explosive devices." When was this? Jake asked. "About six weeks ago. After a second meeting at the mosque, Mustafa asked me to join him at a motel in Trenton where I met him and four young Muslim students. They told me of a plan they were making to create panic in New York City. A great disaster to punish the infidels. He told me he needed to build one or two portable bombs of great power, similar to the one used in Oklahoma City. They asked me to swear allegiance to their great leader, Osama bin Laden whose idea it was for the plan. After pledging my loyalty, I suggested that I could provide similar bombs, easily, because I owned a small farm that would allow me to purchase the materials I needed and it would be an ideal place to do the work out of sight." "Did they tell you what they planned to do with the bombs?" Ty asked "Not right then, but later after we met at the farm. They wanted to destroy the Holland tunnel during rush hour." He added. "Holy shit!" Jake exclaimed. Then he told Josef he was going to have him take a polygraph test before they went any further. Joseph willingly agreed. They decided to take a break while Nate went to get the polygraph equipment. They had been video taping the interrogation the entire time and would go over it later to study Abraham's body language. For now they had coffee and sandwiches brought in and adopted a relaxed atmosphere. When Nate returned with the polygraph, Jake and Ty went out to another room while he set it up. Joseph was allowed to stretch his legs and walk about the room until Nate was ready to hook him up to the machine.

"Think he is for real? Or is this an elaborate story to cover his ass?" Jake asked Ty as they watched the video monitor. "We can check most of it out pretty quickly. Mel is at Abraham's office probably going through the files while he poses as Joseph's assistant.

Let's get the rest of his story after Nate applies the polygraph test. We need to see how much he knows about the terrorist network in this area. Maybe he can lead us to someone higher up we can squeeze" Ty said. Nate was an expert at applying lie detector tests and interpreting the results. When he finished with Joseph he came out and told the others.

"Either he is telling the truth or he is very good at fooling the machine. I really put him through the wringer and he never faltered." They returned to the room and asked Joseph to go on with his statement. He began again. "It was about then when I got the idea of how to get my revenge. It was perfect. Their own paranoid desire for secrecy allowed me to build the bombs and set them up so I could detonate them while they were busy in the barn. Their practice of always leaving a meeting place one by one at intervals made it easy for me to leave them and then detonate the bomb safely from down the road. I gave Mustafa a bag phone and told him it was programmed to operate one half of the bombs.

You see, he had decided to split them up and have one bomb at the Holland tunnel and the other at the Lincoln tunnel. What the fool didn't know was that the explosives were too small to do any major damage to either tunnel, even if he was successful at setting them off." "How do you know they wouldn't collapse the tunnels?" Jake asked "Check your history, in May of 1949 a truck loaded with 80 drums of carbon disulphide exploded and burned in the tunnel. It burned and damaged 600 feet of tile but didn't scratch the massive cast iron rings that make up the main support for the tunnel. Four drums of Anfo in a panel van would make a lot of noise, cause some damage and generally fuck up traffic but would never collapse the tunnel. Besides, I only used 30% of the ammonium nitrate I could have put in each drum. Enough for my purpose, to kill those assholes, but still confined to a relatively small and safe area on my own farm." He explained. "Did you plan the propane tank to blow and burn your house down as well? Ty asked. "I wasn't aware that that happened" he said. "I guess I forgot about the propane tank." "Do you think you can identify that Imam or the teacher from Buffalo or any of the radicals you met at the mosque?" Jake asked. "They are very secretive; I don't know where to find them except at the mosque. I can give you the names that they gave me but I doubt any of them are genuine at least not the ones that would be involved in any illegal activities" He said.

"How did Mustafa get around? Did he come to the farm with the others?" Jake asked.

"I think he used a motorcycle, I never saw it but he wore clothing that looked like what a motorcycle rider would use. He always appeared on foot and left the same way. I never saw him in any other clothing. I assumed he left it in the woods near the house but I couldn't risk asking him or looking for it. I did notice one time that he had a key in his hand with a BMW insignia on it." They asked him about the other men and were told he only knew them by first names and didn't know where they came from. He also told them

about the stolen cars Mustafa said he left in New York. "What are we going to do with him Jake?" Nate asked "We can't let the FBI or the police connect him with the terrorists or we will have a hard time explaining what happened to him" he added. "I have an idea, at least for the short term. We'll put him back into his home and office, like nothing happened and keep Mel with him at all times while we check out his story and figure out how to get the most out of him." Jake replied. "Who are you guys?" Joseph asked, encouraged by the relaxed atmosphere in the room when Jake and Nate returned. "We're the good guys. That's all you need to know for now. We are going to make you a little proposition. We will return you to your home, today, but you will have our associate with you at all times while we check out your story. When the police or FBI trace the farm ownership to you, you tell them that you were out of town and didn't know about the fire until you returned. Mel will act as your executive assistant and help you deal with them.

When things return to normal we will decide what happens next. We are going to blindfold you while we return you to your home. No one gets to know this location and you can never tell anyone about today. If you attempt to cross us in any way you will disappear forever. Understand?" "Yes, I understand completely" Joseph replied. They replaced the hood over his head and lead him out to one of the SUV's. Ty put him in the rear seat and told him to lie down out of sight. Some time later he told him to take off the hood and sit up. They were back in Manhattan and nearly back to Joseph's condo. At a nearby parking lot Mel was waiting in Joseph's Mercedes. Ty introduced them and Mel handed Joseph the keys and then got into the passenger seat and told him to drive on home. Jake had called ahead and filled Mel in on the developments and the new temporary plan. Mel told Jake he had found death certificates for Joseph's wife, son,

brother and parents. They had indeed been killed in the 911 attack. At least that much of the story was true. They rode the elevator in silence and went into Joseph's condo. Mel started by saying. "What you did took real balls, my friend. Do you have any idea what Mustafa and the others would have done to you if they caught on?" "After what happened to my family, I really didn't care what happened to me. All I could think of was to exact revenge any way I could. These extremists are insane, they don't care who they murder.

They are a stain on normal Muslims everywhere. It has nothing to do with religion.

That's all bullshit." "Are you really a Christian, Joseph?" "Yes, my brother and I were raised as Muslim's but we had childhood friends who were the son's of Christian missionaries, we spent many happy times with them and their family. My father and uncle were furious when Tariq and I converted to the Christian faith while at University here in America. For a while father refused to acknowledge us. That's when we changed our names to the English version and applied for US citizenship. When my wife Elaine found out she was pregnant, I pleaded with father to accept us and come to see his grand child. He really wanted grandchildren and finally decided to forgive us for changing our religion. He was always more of a businessman than a religious Muslim anyway. I guess he decided family was more important to him as he grew older. I never got the chance to make up with him in person. I had to go to a meeting in Toronto the day before they arrived. He and mother had gone from the airport directly to our office when they arrived.

They had slept on the long flight from Dubai. I was booked to return by two in the afternoon. You know the rest." He turned away to hide the tears welling up in his eyes.

He was exhausted; he had been up since early the day before and had not had a good night's sleep since planning to kill Mustafa and the others. Mel told him to go ahead and

turn in unless he was hungry. He went to his bedroom and collapsed on the bed, fully clothed. Mel watched the lights of the city from the window for a while and then turned on the T.V. news. Local New Jersey firefighters had reported that the explosion at the small farm near Little Falls had been caused by a leaky propane tank. There was no mention of any terrorist plot suspicions. The next morning Mel had coffee, scrambled eggs and toast ready when Josef appeared freshly showered and fully dressed. They ate their breakfast and then drove to Josef's office. Shortly after they arrived, a call came from the Little Falls, New

Jersey police. The officer on the phone asked for Mr. Abraham and informed him of the fire at his farm. He asked him if he could come out to the farm today and answer some questions. Joseph agreed and said he could be there by one o'clock. The officer said he would meet him there at that time. "What do you think they will do?" he asked Mel. "Let's get up there a little early and have a look around. You stick to the story that you had no idea that the fire had happened until they called this morning. If it's just small town police and arson, not the FBI, it should go away shortly.

Do you have any insurance on the property?" "Yes, a minimal policy on the house and barn. Should I call the agent?" "That's a good idea. Do that while we drive." Mel said.

They arrived at the farm around eleven and found police tape strung across the front of the driveway, from the trees to the mailbox and to the fence. They ducked under it and walked over toward the barn. None of the structure was visible, just gray ashes and the partial remains of the vans. Mel could tell the arson guys had been poking around. The house had not fared any better, there was only ashes and the low foundation left. "How will we explain the vans?" Joseph asked. "Just tell them they were old work vans left by the previous owner when you bought the place" Mel told him. The tractor had been far

enough from the barn that it was still intact, a small wonder. The corn appeared to be prospering. "Let's check the trees and brush on both sides. We should find Mustafa's car or motorcycle somewhere." Mel said. He went into the brush near the house and Joseph walked over to the other side of the barn area and into the trees. "Over here," Mel shouted to Joseph. When Joseph found Mel he was on one knee looking at motorcycle tracks. They could see where someone had spun a bike around in the soft duff between the trees. The tracks led off to the north on what appeared to be a deer trail. "It looks like our mysterious Mustafa has nine lives. Unless these tracks are from a previous visit, he got out of the barn before you blew it up" He said. Joseph stared at Mel in stunned silence. "He was standing by the back of the rear van when I left through the side door. I can't believe he left before I detonated the bombs" He said, visibly shaken. "Unless you tipped him off." Mel thought to himself.

They walked back to the car in silence, to wait for the police to arrive. A few minutes after 1:00 an unmarked police car and a red and white fire department car arrived. Joseph gave them a statement as instructed earlier by Mel. They seemed satisfied for now and left right away. Mel and Joseph waited a while longer before the insurance agent arrived.

After a brief discussion, Mel and Joseph drove off, leaving the agent at the scene.

CHAPTER TWENTY TWO

Back at the office in Greenwich Village Jake and the others were going over the names Joseph had given them and replayed all the video from the mosque. Jake sent an encrypted report on the entire operation to Doug Small. On the way Mel asked Joseph how much Mustafa or any of the others knew about where he worked or lived. Joseph said he had given no one his American name or his actual address. They all appeared to

operate with as little knowledge of each other as possible to prevent discovery if any one were captured and interrogated. Mel said he would have the videos from the mosque brought over to the condo so they could try to identify the radicals that Joseph had had contact with. He wasn't ready to risk letting Joseph know where the office in the Village was located, at least not yet. When they arrived back at Joseph's office, Mel made a discreet call to Jake and told him that it appeared Mustafa had somehow managed to escape before the blast. Jake asked if he thought Joseph had tipped him off. Mel said it occurred to him, but Joseph had appeared visibly shaken when they discovered the motorcycle was not in the woods. It was possible that Mustafa had arrived in one of the vans, but Joseph was adamant that he had been in the barn before the vans arrived.

"Didn't Abraham say that he saw a BMW key in Mustafa's hand?" Ron asked. "That's right" Jake replied. "Let's get the highway patrol to check for any stolen BMW

motorcycles in the Tri-State area. He could have grabbed one anywhere." He continued.

CHAPTER TWENTY THREE

Asrar was shocked when her brother Fayez arrived at her door after dark. He told her to pack what she could fit in one bag and come with him to the car. She was more shocked when she slid into the backseat of the Chevy wagon and discovered her lover, Karim. He pulled her close, kissed her lightly and whispered "My work is finished here for now, we are leaving". She wept with excitement as Fayez pulled out and headed for Buffalo. They got out at the bus station and boarded a bus for Toronto. Mustafa used Fayez' passport and they traveled as brother and sister through Canadian customs at the Peace Bridge. It couldn't have been easier.

CHAPTER TWENTY FOUR

Joseph studied the videos with Mel and Jake at his condo and one by one identified a few of the men from the mosque. "The only one I don't see here is the teacher." He said. "I know the visiting Imam came in from Buffalo and I believe the teacher, the name he gave was Fayez. No one ever gives their full name. They came together every time I saw the teacher." He said "I'll have Ron and Nate check out the colleges in the Buffalo area for any Arabic faculty, maybe we'll get lucky." Jake said. With that, they broke up for the evening, leaving Mel behind to baby sit Joseph. A couple of days passed without any news on the motorcycle or their suspect. Finally, Ron came up with the name of a professor Fayez Al-Sayiid at the Buffalo campus of New York State University. A search of motor vehicle records showed that professor Al-Sayiid owned a Chevy station wagon and a 1995 BMW motorcycle. "Get up there and nose around. Don't alert the professor but let's check him out." Jake told Ron. "See if you can get a picture of him from the driver's license bureau, Nate and show it to Abraham to see if it is the guy he met with."

He added. Ty was checking up on the professor with immigration when he discovered that professor Al-Sayiid had a sister that had come with him from England on a visitor's visa and had never left. He decided to check with US and Canadian customs to see if she had ever gone back through Canada. US customs had no record of her leaving the US at any port of entry, only that she accompanied Fayez Al-Sayiid when he arrived from England on British Airways one year ago. Then Ron got a hit from Canadian customs.

They said Al-Sayiid and his sister Asrar had entered Canada at the Peace Bridge port of entry on a tour bus headed for Toronto two days ago. He decided to check out the airlines in Toronto for any flights they may have taken out of the country. This would be a slow

process; he needed to go through Doug Small to get passenger lists from Canadian based airlines. He sent an urgent request to Doug and waited for a reply. Meanwhile, Nate got a drivers license photo of professor Al-Sayiid and forwarded it to Mel. Joseph identified the picture as the man he knew as Fayez. Mel called Jake and told him Joseph had confirmed the professor's identity. Jake called Ron, who was on his way to Buffalo and gave him the update, including the home address from the license. When Ron arrived in Buffalo he drove to the professor's address. It was a low rent apartment complex with car ports behind the buildings. He drove through the alley and checked out the carports.

There was a BMW motorcycle in the car port that matched the professor's apartment number; the space next to the bike was empty. It was nearing 5:00 o'clock so he went out to the main street and parked at the Burger King to grab a bite and watch the turn off to the apartments. According to Jake's update the professor was supposed to be gone to Toronto, but he could have returned by now. It was about 5:45 when a Chevy station wagon with one man in it came down the block and turned into the apartment complex.

Ron waited until he thought the man had time to park the car and go into his apartment before driving down the alley again. He found the wagon parked next to the motorcycle and checked the plate. It matched the one Jake had given him. He went back out by the Burger King and phoned Jake with the news. Nate had come up with an address for the sister in Lackawanna which Jake gave to Ron. Ron decided to drive by and have a look at the sister's place. When he arrived it was getting dark and there were no lights on in the apartment. He parked and watched for a while and then decided to knock on the door. No one answered. He tried the door and found it unlocked. He quickly slipped inside and closed the door. With his penlight he moved through the small apartment that had only a

kitchenette and a living room with a hide-a-bed couch and a small bathroom. There were some clothes still in the closet, mostly old sweaters and some socks on the floor near the two open drawers built into the closet. It looked like someone had left in a hurry. The apartment smelled of garlic and onions and there were dirty dishes in the sink. He peeked out the window and seeing no one outside, he slipped out and back to his car. He called Jake and told him what he had found. "Stick around until tomorrow and then phone the University and ask for the professor. If he's there, hang up and go check out the apartment. He is supposed to have a wife there so don't go up to the door unless you can tell no one is home. I want a bug in that apartment as soon as you can get in there." He instructed. There was a truck stop and motel not far from the Burger King so Ron got a room and settled in for the night. In the morning, he walked down by the apartments and watched the professor leave on the motorcycle. He could see a woman in the doorway just as the professor rode past and waved to her. He waited a while and then went to the car port. He found the station wagon unlocked and slipped a mini transmitter under the dash and a satellite tracking device under the rear fender. He went around the other end of the building and walked over to the Burger King. He got coffee and watched for about an hour and then went back to the motel. Around noon he decided to go back and check out the apartments again. When he got to the alley he saw that the station wagon was gone. He parked in the empty car port and walked around to the front of the building. The professor's apartment was on the end, on the ground floor. He walked right up and knocked. When no one answered he quickly picked the lock and let himself in. He went directly to the only telephone he found and inserted a bug in the handset. He checked

outside and then walked out the door and back to his car. He called Jake and told him what he had done. Jake told him to lay low and keep an eye on the professor for now.

CHAPTER TWENTY FIVE

Back at the office Jake told Nate and Ty that Ron had found the professor. "He can't be in two places at once. I bet our man Mustafa is traveling on the professor's passport with the sister for cover." Ty said. "Any word from Doug, on the flights out of Toronto?" Jake asked, looking at the computer monitor. "Not yet. Maybe we should fill him in and see if he can speed up the Canucks. We should also have him alert Interpol to watch for them at the major European airports. British secret service has an interest in Mustafa; we should have Doug alert them too." Ty said. Jake decided to call Doug on the secure phone and talk to him personally. It might not be too late to grab Mustafa before he disappears again. If they could find them on a flight that hadn't landed there was still a chance.

Nate had been checking into professor Al-Sayiid's finances while this was going on. "I just found a transaction on the professor's American express card where he booked two tickets on an Air Canada flight from Toronto to London, yesterday." He said. "I have Doug on the line now; he says can get that information to the British right away." Jake said. A short while later a message from Doug came back saying that British immigration reported that the professor and his sister had passed through customs at Gatwick airport in London on the last Toronto flight yesterday. "Too fucking late! Again." Jake screamed in frustration. "Well at least now the Brits can look for him over there." He added with a heavy sigh.

CHAPTER TWENTY SIX

He then called Mel at Abraham's condo and filled him in. Mel explained it all to Joseph to get his reaction. He still wasn't convinced that Joseph hadn't tipped Mustafa off. "You mean it was all for nothing? I killed those boys and the bastard that planned this got away?" He said. He was so angry he was shaking. Then he sat down and put his head in his hands. "Cheer up" Mel told him. "You stopped what would have been a disaster in the tunnels and probably saved many lives. The information you have given us will help us track down his network here and probably prevent some other scheme that we don't know about yet. All in all you have done a great service for this country. You should feel good about that." "Do you think the others will suspect me as a traitor and come after me?" Joseph asked. "I don't know maybe we could have you go back to the mosque and blame the accident on the inexperienced young men. Even Mustafa might believe it was an accident. You said he wasn't all that knowledgeable about explosives and the dummy bag phone you gave him should have shown him that you trusted him. Let me talk to Jake and see what he thinks." Mel answered.   .

Mel called Jake and told him. "I have to believe he is for real, Jake. We could wire him up and send him back into the mosque with Nate as backup. If the Imam and the professor accept his claim that it was all an accident there is no telling what kind of inside man he could become." "Do you think he is willing and able to pull it off?" Jake wondered. "You saw how calm he was when we grabbed him. It took a hell of a set of balls to do what he did. He hates these bastards like they hate us. Knowing we have his every move covered should give him some confidence especially with Nate in the mosque with him. He could be the best informer we could have ever hoped for if this works out." Mel said. "Get him over here if you believe he's the real deal. Our radical

friends will get suspicious if he doesn't show up pretty soon. If we are going to try this, let's do it now" Jake said. Mel hung up and went over to Joseph. "We have decided to trust you, Joseph. If you are willing to work with us to uncover these terrorists we will do everything in our power to protect you, but you must understand the risk. These guys don't play around. If they discover you are a traitor to their evil cause, we may not be able to save you. We won't always be able to be right with you." He said, looking him straight in the eye. "It will be worth any risk to avenge my family" Joseph replied, with fire in his eyes. They left Joseph's car in the garage and walked up the block to retrieve Mel's from the parking lot. When they arrived at the office Jake and Nate were going over the FBI reports from the previous few days. "There is nothing here about the farm; I guess the locals didn't bring anyone else into their investigation." Nate said. "Let's hope it stays that way." Jake said. Mel formally introduced Joseph to the group and said.

"Gentlemen, Joseph has agreed to join us and go undercover to investigate potential terrorist threats."

"Welcome, Joseph, I hope you know what you're getting into" Jake said. Mel explained Joseph's reasons for his actions and told the group he had promised him they would do whatever they could to back him up. "We can wire him up so that we can monitor him from outside the mosque and get Nate in there for close-up protection if things go badly."

Jake said. "Joseph, do you have any training or experience in self defense?" Ty asked.

"Not really but I am fairly athletic and spent many hours wrestling with my brother while we were growing up." He replied. "If things go alright, he shouldn't need to defend himself inside the mosque. I doubt anyone would try anything in the holy place, anyway." Nate said. Ty brought in the necessary components to wire Joseph for sound

and video and had him remove his shirt. Since it was the latest CIA gear it was small enough and slim enough to go under a normal shirt without being noticed. Joseph said it wasn't uncomfortable at all, in fact, barely noticeable. They had him walk down the stairs to the restroom and say a few words while they checked the audio and video transmissions. Everything worked as expected and Ty was satisfied. The plan was for Mel to drop Joseph at his home to get the Mercedes and drive to the mosque in time for afternoon prayers. Nate got into his undercover clothes and picked up his prayer rug at his apartment and then rode to the mosque area with Mel. He was wired up the same as Joseph and had an ear piece that went deep in his ear, out of sight, that allowed him to get instructions from the others if needed. Mel dropped Nate at the familiar bus stop and drove to a street two blocks west of the Mosque to meet the others. Mel took off on foot and walked to the area north of the Mosque's parking lot and sat on a bench where he could get to the mosque in hurry if needed, but remain out of sight. Ty stayed in his SUV

with Jake and monitored the feed from Joseph while Jake did the same for Nate. They could get to the mosque in seconds if it became necessary. Ty fed regular reports on Joseph's whereabouts to Mel's earpiece. Nate was already inside when Joseph arrived.

He stood near a small group where he could survey the room. He saw Joseph come in and walk toward the Imam. Two men fell in beside Joseph and walked with him to meet the Imam. Joseph appeared relaxed and greeted the men warmly. After the brief greeting they took their places among the throng of people preparing for the prayers. "So far, so good Ty said. "They didn't jump him about the failed attempt on the tunnels. Maybe they don't know exactly when it was supposed to happen or even what the exact target was" He added. "They will when they hear from the professor. Ron says he hasn't left Buffalo and

he hasn't made or received any calls since it happened. He may not want to report a failure or just won't risk a phone call." Jake said. When the prayers were finished Joseph, the two other men and the Imam walked into a side room. Nate moved over near the doorway, trying not to look conspicuous. Ty listened while Joseph explained in Arabic what had happened at the farm. The men were shocked. One of them asked how it could happen. Joseph explained that the dynamite he had to use to detonate the explosives was old and unstable and probably went off when the vans started to leave. "What about Mustafa?" the Imam asked.

Joseph told him that he believed he was killed with the others. He told them that the plan was for them to leave separately at irregular intervals and proceed to the target by separate routes. "By the grace of God, I was a mile of so down the road when it happened or I would have not been here today" Joseph told them.

"You were indeed lucky my friend. Perhaps you were meant to live to carry on God's work." one of the men said. "I have dedicated my life to God's glorious cause. Tell me what I can do to honor his will." Joseph said solemnly. "Please continue to attend services here. If Allah has more plans for you we will soon know." The Imam replied.

"Allahu Akbar" (God is great) they all repeated quietly and began leaving the room.

Inside the main room Nate watched them leave and then went out and over to the bus stop across the street. When Joseph started his car and drove away Mel sat up in the back seat and instructed him to drive to where the others were waiting. They all drove out of the area and met at a diner where they went in for coffee to discuss what had happened.

"I got a little worried when you left the main room, Joseph." Nate said. "That was too risky. We need to give you a way to protect yourself when you are alone from now on. I want Mel to give you some training and a weapon before you go in again." Jake said.

"I'll take him to a gun range and teach him to shoot close up for now. I can give him a small pistol and teach him how to get at it quickly for starters. Have you ever fired a gun Joseph?" Mel asked. "I have never even held one. But I'm a fast learner." He replied.

"Maybe Mel can teach you a few of his deadly bare handed techniques" Ty said, only half kidding. They decided to go back to the office and go over the recordings to see if they could identify the men that met Joseph at the mosque. "I'll keep Ron monitoring the professor in Buffalo and have Nate continue to go to the mosque while we get Joseph prepared for his next visit." Jake said. Mel and Joseph took Mel's car and headed to a gun club on Long island. The place was nearly empty at that time of day and Mel took his time explaining the operation of the little Walther PPK he brought with them. He showed Joseph not only how to load and fire it but how to dismantle it quickly and how to clean it. "You want to be so familiar with this weapon that it becomes like a part of you. Your life may depend on it and you want to know that it will work when you need it." He instructed. "I'll show you the standard pistol stance and aiming procedure first. You will fire and reload many times until you can hit a man-sized target with some accuracy at 25

feet. When you have mastered that and gotten comfortable with the sound and recoil of the weapon we'll go into close range techniques and start again." He said. He left Joseph to his practicing and stepped into the next stall. With one swift motion he pulled another PPK from behind his back and rapid fired the full clip into the face of his target in a three inch pattern. Then he reloaded and repeated the move, this time grouping the shots in the chest area of the target, firing from waist high with his arm parallel to the ground. He would spend the next several days teaching this to Joseph. Joseph turned out to be a natural with the pistol. His standard aiming stance produced acceptable accuracy almost

immediately. After watching Mel in amazement he began to learn the slick way that Mel got the pistol out from the small of his back, from under a jacket and into firing position.

Many times his first shots went high or wide and he never got the close patterns that Mel did but he was learning at an amazing rate. At the end of the second week with hundreds of rounds fired, Mel took him to an outdoor range with multiple targets and had him practice firing two shots each into several targets in rapid succession. He excelled at this also and Mel pronounced him ready for action. "He's turning into a regular James Bond or Wyatt Earp" He told the others back at the office.

CHAPTER TWENTY SEVEN

Things had stayed quiet and Ron was getting sick of Buffalo when he followed the professor to a Mosque near his home. There the professor met the Imam and they drove off together in the professor's Chevy. They drove up to a rest area on Grand Island while discussing Mustafa's escape and the disaster at the farm. The Imam asked if Fayez had heard from Mustafa or Asrar. The professor said he had had no word form either of them.

The Imam asked if Mustafa thought he had been betrayed by Yousef. "He said it appeared to be an accident. He said he had escaped only because he was leaving through the woods on the motorcycle and did not need to wait after Yousef had left by the road.

He wants us to keep an eye on Yousef, though. If he doesn't return to the Mosque we'll know he has something to hide." The professor said. "Imam ABD-Al-Azziz phoned me and said he met with Yousef at the mosque a couple of days after the accident. He gave a reasonable explanation for what had happened and did not seem to be nervous about returning to the mosque. He expressed a desire to try again if needed." Imam ABD-Al-

Allah confided. They both decided to stay away from Brooklyn until word came from Mustafa or someone else with a new scheme.

CHAPTER TWENTY EIGHT

Ron phoned Jake with the news and was told he could come on back. They would keep an eye on the professor's whereabouts with the satellite locator. Glad to get out of Buffalo, Ron went back to his motel, gathered his equipment and drove back to the City.

Joseph and Nate made three more visits to the mosque over the next two weeks but no one had approached Joseph and he made no effort to communicate with the others even though he saw them at least one more time. Neither of the two men were found on any of the existing terrorist watch lists. Jake sent their photos and names to Doug Small and had them added to all the watch lists. They had decided not confront the professor but to use him to track Mustafa if he returned and generally keep an eye on him for any suspicious movements. During this quiet period Joseph and Mel continued Joseph's training with the weapon and added some useful self defense moves and knife techniques. Joseph worked hard to master the training and was quickly gaining the respect of his teacher for his efforts. They decided to take a break and go have a look at the farm. When they arrived at the farm the yellow police tape had mostly blown away or had been broken by sightseers.

Bart Klepner, the hired farmer, had phoned Joseph to ask if he should continue to irrigate and otherwise maintain the corn. Joseph instructed him to go ahead and to forward his time to the office for progress payments. Joseph intended to have the corn crop harvested and donate the proceeds to a local church group when sold. He and Mel went to the area where the motorcycle had been parked and walked the trail to see how Mustafa had

escaped. They came out of the woods and found a dirt road leading to a cross road at the north end of the row of farms. It had to be how Mustafa escaped unnoticed.

At the office in Greenwich Village Jake had received word from Doug that the British secret service had missed Mustafa at Gatwick and were combing the London area looking for him. He seemed to have vanished again. There was no sign of Asrar either.

They had either left London or were being well hidden by local sympathizers.

CHAPTER TWENTY NINE

Joseph returned to his office and went back to running his business. He never knew his home and office were bugged and that Mel kept an eye on him. He went back to the gun club and practiced regularly with the PPK. Some time later he received a letter from his uncle Hafid saying that he needed him to come to Dubai as soon as possible. In the letter he said he had an offer to sell the business and wanted to discuss it with Yousef. Joseph phoned Jake and explained that he needed to go Dubai. Of course Mel was nearby and heard the call to Jake. When Joseph rang off Mel called Jake to discuss the arrangements.

"Ron is probably the best choice to go with Joseph. He's familiar with Dubai and knows the local languages better than Nate does. He'll be able to know what's going on around them and I don't think Joseph knows that he speaks fluent Arabic." Mel suggested. Jake agreed and said he was sending Ron over to Joseph's and he wanted Mel to explain to Joseph why he needed a traveling companion. Mel told Joseph that Ron would be going with him for his protection. "Why aren't you coming instead of this other person?"

Joseph asked. Mel explained that Ron Pierce had some connections in Dubai that they wanted him to contact regarding Mustafa. "Don't worry, you'll like Ron. He'll be more fun to travel with than I am. I tend to get a little cranky on long flights. He'll watch your

back just the same as I would. "This is strictly a business trip for me. I will eventually inherit the family business and all the assets of my father and my uncle. Uncle Hafid never had any children and his wife died years ago. I am all that is left of the Ibrahim tribe. I don't expect to get in any trouble." Joseph protested. "We don't know where Mustafa is or who he may have watching you. There could be trouble waiting in Dubai.

We can't take the chance that something may happen to you on the way or after you arrive. Besides, I'm getting used to having you around and I don't want all that training to go to waste." Mel said, with a smile. "Bullshit Mel, your guys still don't trust me. What do they think I will do? Run off and join Osama? If I wasn't on your side I would have built a proper bomb and finished what Mustafa came here to do. What is it going to take to convince you people?" He asked. His frustration showing for the first time. "OK, you're partly right Joseph. I'll level with you. We are still being cautious. There is a lot at stake. Ron is the one coming along because he knows the area and speaks most of the languages. If anything does come up he is better prepared than I would be and he is equally capable protecting you. He has saved my butt many times. You can't carry a weapon on an airline, but he can provide both of you with one when you get to Dubai.

I'm not kidding about the potential danger, these snakes have operatives everywhere and you could very well be a target. When Ron arrived he and Joseph went over the planned itinerary. Joseph insisted on paying all the expenses for the trip and booked two first class tickets on Air France out of JFK for the next morning. He also got reservations at the Hyatt Regency in Dubai City. He explained that it was the closest good hotel to his family's business offices in Port Rashid. Ron said he remembered it as being about 15

minutes from the airport and right on the way to Port Rashid. Mel told them to watch

their backs and have a good trip as he was leaving. Their flight was uneventful; they both slept for the last few hours before landing at Dubai City. Since it was too early to check into the hotel they decided to get a car and drive up to Port Rashid and visit the family business offices. On the way Ron asked Joseph to stop at the outdoor fruit and vegetable market on Al Khaleej road. They parked and took a walk down through the stalls along the street. It was good to stretch their legs after the long flight. A mixture of exotic spices and sweet fruits filled the air. "This brings back many memories." Joseph said. "For me too, I haven't been here for several years." Ron added. As they walked along a man came out of a doorway and fell in behind them. Ron guided Joseph gently by the arm into the next alleyway and the other man followed them. Out of sight of the thoroughfare, in the shade of the buildings, Ron stopped and turned to the man following them. Without a word the man removed a small package from under his arm and handed it to Ron. Then he walked past them down the alley and out of sight. Ron tucked the small package under his arm and started out the way they had come in. "What was all that about?" Joseph asked quietly. "You'll see when we get in the car."

Ron replied. They retraced their path and returned to the rental car ignoring the vendors who tried to sell them goods from open sacks. Back in the car Ron opened the package and removed two Walther PPK hand guns and two extra clips. These he slipped into the glove box. Joseph didn't bother to ask how this had been arranged. He just stared at Ron for a second and shook his head. "Do you really think we will need those?" He finally asked. "I hope not but I like to be prepared. Mel said you handled one of these pretty well. Did he show you any of his scary shit with a knife?" "Yes, he tried to but I will never be able to move like he does."

"Don't feel bad about it. There aren't a handful of people on the planet who can" Ron

told him. Before long they could see the blue water of the port shimmering in the morning sun. They passed through the Shindagha Tunnel and arrived at a four story white stucco building on the waterfront. There were about a dozen cars in the parking lot.

"This is where my father and uncle have been running the family business for the past ten years. They started in a smaller building on this site almost 50 years ago. When they outgrew it they tore it down and had this one built. They had the foresight to buy quite a bit of waterfront property here in the port when it was relatively cheap. He decided not to enter the offices for now and headed on down to Jumeriah Beach road to pass by the family home before going to meet uncle Hafid and the lawyers. Joseph pulled up to a gated entry with a guard post. He showed his passport to the guard and the gate opened.

There was one fairly large pink stucco two story house. A circular drive made of brick serviced the entry. Both Joseph's parents and his uncle's families had occupied the house Joseph explained. The main house was not large compared to the huge villas and mansions visible in the area, but it was probably about eight thousand square feet. A small, formally dressed, Hindu man came out of the house and hurried up to Joseph.

"Mahesh, my old friend it is wonderful to see you." Joseph greeted him warmly. "Oh Sahib, it is with very great sadness that I must greet you. A thousand sorrows for your loss." He said. Not acknowledging Ron. "Mahesh has been running this home for as long as I can remember." He told Ron. "He rules the servants with an iron hand and is totally devoted to uncle Hafid and my parents." As the small man led them into the entry Ron asked why they went to a hotel instead of staying here. "You'll see in a moment" He said with a small grin. Inside there were ceiling fans but no air conditioning. It was cooler than outside and the fans kept the air moving, which helped. "My father and Hafid lived

their early lives in tents. They never wanted or needed air conditioning. I on the other hand have been spoiled by my life in America and rather appreciate the comfort of a good hotel until I get used to this heat again." He said with a rare chuckle. Mahesh disappeared for a few moments and then returned with the entire staff of housekeepers, gardeners and the cook. Only the cook, who was Mahesh's wife, recognized Joseph. The others had been hired after he and his brother had left. "Are you going to remain in Dubai and help Hafid run the business?" Mahesh asked. Ron tapped his watch and told Joseph it was time to go meet with his uncle. They left with Mahesh and crew bowing and waving as they drove out of the gate. They were to meet uncle Hafid at his attorney's office in the business area near the first interchange and it took about twenty minutes to drive there.

When they entered the modern air conditioned building they nodded at each other as the cool air hit them. The office was on the third floor. When they stepped off the elevator they were met at the reception area by a young woman dressed in western business attire.

She asked if they had an appointment in English while glancing at Ron's graying blond hair and blue eyes. Joseph answered her in Arabic and she told them to follow her in the same language. Joseph's uncle and two other men, Ron assumed they were attorneys, were seated at a round glass table. After a short hesitation on both their parts, Joseph and uncle Hafid embraced each other warmly, releasing the visible tension in the room.

Joseph introduced Ron to his uncle and the others as his assistant. Ron asked how long the meeting might last. A good two or three hours was the reply. In English Ron told Joseph that he thought he should let him have the meeting privately unless he needed him to remain. Joseph thanked him and said he appreciated it. Ron told him he would go to the hotel and check them in and for Joseph to call him when he was ready to leave. Ron

excused himself and left. He took the rental car and drove to the US embassy where he showed his passport and was let inside the reception area. A few moments later the man he had met earlier in the alley came out and shook his hand and led him to an office on the second floor. Sean Moore had an official title as "Press Liaison" for the embassy but was in fact head of station for the CIA in the UAE area. "I couldn't believe it when Doug Small told me you were coming. Who exactly are you working for? I heard you left the NSA some time ago." He said. "I'm more or less freelancing for Homeland Security, but you didn't hear that from me." Ron replied. "I'm babysitting a witness while he clears up some family business here." He added. "Do you need my help with anything here; besides what I gave you this morning?" Moore asked. He and Ron went back many years and Ron had saved his life in Afghanistan. "I don't know yet. I need to check it out but my friend is going to be here longer than I want to be. He has family business here and he may have his hands full for quite a while. Would you be able to keep an eye on him if I get the OK to leave him here?" Ron asked looking him in the eye. "I'll do anything you need if it's within my power. I owe you that." He said taking Ron's hand in his firm grip.

Ron filled him in on Joseph's identity and where he would be while in Dubai. He avoided telling him anything about the task force in New York. Sean knew all of the guys except Ty but did not have the "need to know" about the task force. Ron headed to the hotel and checked in. They had sent his and Joseph's bags ahead from the airport and their rooms were on the same floor on opposite sides of the hall. He connected his laptop to his satellite uplink and sent an encrypted message to Jake. Jake replied that he wanted Ron to stay a couple more days until he felt comfortable that no one was in Dubai that would cause Joseph any harm. He agreed that Moore was reliable and should keep an eye on

things. Ron ordered a light lunch from room service and then dozed off on the couch until the desk phone rang. Joseph said his uncle's driver was bringing him back to the hotel so Ron should wait for him there. Joseph rang up again when he got to his room. He told Ron he wanted to take a shower and shave and would meet him in the lobby in an hour so they could go get some dinner. Ron decided to do the same. "How does some real Indian curry sound for dinner?" Joseph asked when they met in the lobby. "Fine by me. Do you have a favorite local spot in mind?" Ron asked. Joseph nodded his reply. They got in the car and Joseph drove them up to the port district near the family's business office. He parked in a lot half a block from the office. They walked between some low buildings and arrived at a small restaurant on the waterfront. It was the kind of place a tourist would never find. The salt air was filled with the delicious smell of garlic and spices and they sat at an outdoor table. They were about to order from a waiter wearing a Fez when a man in an apron rushed out of the door. He came directly over to Joseph who stood immediately and embraced him. "This is Mahesh's brother-in-law Niraj." He told Ron.

"He cooks just like his sister, the best curry in Dubai." "May I order for both of you?"

Niraj asked "Absolutely" Ron and Joseph said in unison. Niraj asked if Joseph was back in Dubai to stay. Joseph said he hadn't decided yet. Niraj offered his condolences for Joseph's losses. The dinner came in continuous courses of small but exquisite dishes.

Each dish was served at precisely the proper temperature just as they finished the one before. Afterwards they lingered over Turkish coffee and enjoyed the sea breeze before returning to the hotel. On the way Ron told Joseph that he only planned to stay until he was satisfied that there was no imminent danger. He also gave him a direct phone number for Sean Moore at the US embassy and told him he could call him if he needed help.

"He's the man who gave us the guns. He doesn't know about the task force and you can't tell him about it or about the men we work with. Officially he doesn't know me or you.

He is an old friend of mine you can trust. If someone comes after you he can get you into the embassy and out of the country if need be. I think you are safe here for now but I'm going to hang around and make certain of it before I leave." "What if I decide to remain here?" Joseph asked. "That's entirely up to you. We can't stop you and I wouldn't blame you if you did. You have to do what you feel is best for you. We can use your help at home but as far as Jake and the rest of us are concerned you already made your bones when you stopped Mustafa's plan." Ron assured him. Then he asked how the meeting went today. Joseph explained that his uncle was considering selling the business to a corporation from Abu Dhabi. "My father had left his portion of the business to my uncle and vice versa when my brother and I moved to America. Father's will was never changed, but he told Hafid that he was going to amend it when he returned from New York. Uncle Hafid has changed his will to leave everything to me when he dies. I think he really wants me to join him and help run the business until he can't do it any more and then have me carry it on from there. But he is too proud to ask it." Joseph explained.

"Why don't you want to stay here and work with him? He's all the family you have now." Ron asked. "I'll have to spend some time here with him before I can make that decision. I haven't had much enthusiasm for business or any desire for much of anything except revenge since 911. Maybe if I had succeeded in killing Mustafa I could have put some closure on it. I just don't know. We have thirty days to respond to the offer. By then I should know whether I can put my anger aside and run the business or sell out and come back to New York." He said, finally.

Ron met with Moore one more time and spent two days checking with informants and other agents to see if anyone in the area appeared to be interested in Yousef Ibrahim.

Nothing suspicious turned up and Ron prepared to leave for New York. Joseph invited him to dinner at the family home where they spent a pleasant evening talking with Joseph's uncle Hafid. Hafid Ibrahim was a tall man with a stately air about him. At work he wore Saville Row suits and Gucci loafers. At home he was dressed in a traditional Muslim Jalabiya, off-white with gold trim and sandals. Ron liked him immediately. Hafid was impressed with Ron's command of Arabic and told him some of the family history and relived some family memories with Joseph. They were sitting on a balcony overlooking the water. Joseph remarked about all the fun he and his brother Tariq had swimming and scuba diving there. The next morning Ron thanked Hafid for his hospitality as the old man prepared to leave for work. Ron went over how to get in touch with Moore one more time and warned Joseph to be careful. Joseph told him not to worry and promised he would keep him informed by e-mail. He asked Ron to keep an eye on his home and office in New York for the time being.

He had had his mail forwarded before leaving New York and told Ron that he paid his utilities and so forth on line. They shook hands before Ron got in the rental car and took off for the airport. On the way he contacted Sean Moore and told him he was leaving and that he had left both handguns with Joseph. Moore told him not to worry, he would watch over Joseph "like a brother".

CHAPTER THIRTY

Ron's return flight had barely touched down when Jake contacted him on his cell phone.

"Glad you made it back. Doug is getting some flack from the FBI about the four missing

students from Miami. It seems no one has turned in a missing persons report and they have had no word on the men or those two vans." He told Ron. "How is Doug handling it with them?" Ron asked. "For now he told the FBI that the vans may have crossed into Canada, but that the information came from an unconfirmed source." Jake replied.

"Having Joseph out of the country for a while may have been a lucky break for us if they start snooping around about the farm explosion" He added. Then he told Ron to come to the office early tomorrow morning for a group meeting.

Ron and Mel had gone to Joseph's office and condo to check things out. Neither had been disturbed. In Dubai City Joseph had spent much of his time catching up on the family's business activities and ran his own business from his office on the top floor of the building. He had a marvelous view of the port and enjoyed watching the ships come and go. He was beginning to loosen up and thought maybe he could stay here. Then he got an e-mail from Ron. The British had picked up Mustafa's trail in Northern Ireland then lost him again. They had been told he might be heading back to the US by boat. So far there was no way to confirm that but Ron wanted him to know that Mustafa was on the move and to watch his back. Two sleepless nights later Joseph decided to go back to New York.

He advised Hafid that he was going to the US for a while to take care of his properties and his business. He promised to return to Dubai for good when he was finished.

He returned Ron's e-mail and told him he was coming on the next available flight. Ron relayed that message to Jake who immediately started planning to increase surveillance on the professor in Buffalo and have Nate visit the mosque in Brooklyn. Ron headed back to Buffalo to monitor the transmitters he had placed in the professor's home and car.

When he arrived he set himself up in the same motel as before and checked out the signals from the hidden transmitters. The battery had died on the one in the car but the one in the house phone was still sending. He planned to get into the car and replace the bug at his first opportunity. The satellite tracking device was still operating.

CHAPTER THIRTY ONE

In the early hours before dawn Mustafa slipped off of an old freighter and into the back streets of Marseilles. He had arranged the trip from Northern Ireland to France with the help of some IRA contacts he had in Belfast. "I need to get back to America." He told the two Algerians who were his contacts at the old port city. "We can get you close. There is a Liberian cargo ship that is traveling to Nova Scotia leaving in a few days. We can get you signed on as an oiler and you will have to work below deck in the engine room for the entire trip. We can't guarantee that you can get off the ship at Halifax but that is the only chance available right away. It will take two weeks. They transfer cargo on and off in Greenland and Iceland before turning around at Halifax." They warned. "I'm sure I can manage. I have worked on ships a little once or twice before." Mustafa informed them.

They supplied him with an Algerian passport that had a picture that he could pass for and sailor's union papers to match. He had no trouble getting hired and leaving on the ship two days later.

CHAPTER THIRTY TWO

Jake received a call from Doug saying that the British had found Asrar, the Buffalo professor's sister. She had applied to return to Toronto on a visitor's visa. They wanted to know whether to let her pass or to detain her. Jake decided that it would be better to let her return. He didn't believe that Mustafa would tell her where he was going or what his

plans were. The next day Ron intercepted a call from her to the professor's home. She told the professor that she was coming back alone. Karim had disappeared shortly after they got to London. She sounded heart broken. Ron relayed this information to Jake immediately. Jake called Doug Small and asked him if he thought it would be possible to have someone place a tracking device in her luggage when she went through Canadian customs at Toronto. That way they could see how she got across the border. Her visa had expired long ago so she couldn't just come straight through US customs. She would have to come in some other way. It would be useful to know. Doug said he would try.

CHAPTER THIRTY THREE

When Joseph arrived at JFK he was surprised to find Mel waiting for him in the terminal. "I picked up your car from long term parking right after you guys left and took it to your condo. I came to pick you up in it." Mel said, smiling. "Does this mean I'm back on a leash?" Joseph asked, only half kidding "No, it means I'm watching your butt again and even saving you some money while I'm at it. I'll take you home so you can check things out and get some rest. Tomorrow Jake would like you to come to the office if you are up to it. We have more news on Mustafa's movements." Mel replied.

When they got to the condo Mel went in first and checked the rooms. He had removed all his bugs while Joseph was in Dubai and now he scanned the rooms for anything someone else might have put there. Finding nothing he said goodbye to Joseph and left. The next morning they all welcomed Joseph back to the office and brought him up to date on the Mustafa situation. "We are watching the professor in Buffalo. His sister is coming back from London shortly. It seems that Mustafa, she calls him Karim by the way, dumped her there and took off for parts unknown. If he uses the professor to get back here we will

know it. I'd like to have you start hanging around the mosque in Brooklyn again and see if you can pick anything up. We'll wire you and get you armed this time and have Nate back you up at all times when you go inside. Mustafa is not the only terrorist we have to worry about." Jake explained. "I'd like to help Joseph brush up on his self defense moves and gun skills before he goes back in there." Mel said seriously. Jake agreed and said to make it soon because things could change in a hurry. "We'll start today if you're ready for it." Mel told Joseph. "Now is good. I need to work out the cobwebs from office work and long flights." Joseph replied. They had barely cleared the building when Ron called from Buffalo. "Our professor is on the move. His sister called from Toronto. He is going up there to get her tonight. I'm going to follow him both ways. Maybe we'll see how he gets her across the border. I guess we didn't need to have Doug negotiate that transponder set up with the Canadians after all." He said. "It was a good idea, anyway, but they refused to do it." Jake commented. Using the satellite transponder Ron could follow Abashir from a safe distance with no chance of being spotted. He followed him through the border at Lewiston and stayed a mile or so behind him all the way to Pearson International Airport. He was parked near the exit when they came out of the parking garage. The sister was sitting in the front passenger seat and remained there until they got to Niagara Falls. There the car went into a parking lot by the falls. Ron watched from up the street while she slipped into the rear of the station wagon under a blanket. They drove a cross the bridge into Niagara Falls on the US side. The professor showed his papers and went straight through customs. No one looked in the back of the wagon. It was a busy night and there was a steady stream of traffic both ways at the border. "So much for our secure borders." Ron said to himself. He called Jake and told him what he had seen and

followed them back to Buffalo at a safe distance. The next few days Mel and Joseph spent time at the outdoor gun range and in a gym working on self defense. Satisfied that Joseph could probably hold his own if he had to fight his way out of the mosque, especially with Nate close by, they returned to the office ready to start. They made two visits to the mosque on consecutive days without incident. Joseph didn't try to make contact with anyone in particular and no one came up to him. By the third visit the local Imam came up to Joseph after prayers and invited him to join him for tea. Joseph accepted and went into the same side room as before. There he met the two men he had talked with before the accident at the farm. "We missed you around here for a while one of them said." Joseph told them he had gone out of the country on business and had just returned. He remained calm and did not elaborate. "Allah may have need of your services again. Are you still willing to serve him?" The Imam asked. "Of course, I would be honored. But are you certain you want my help? It did not go well last time." He said. "It was God's will. We can't question His wisdom. Perhaps he has a bigger plan for you."

The Imam replied. "I swear I will do anything in my power. Allahu Akbar" Joseph said.

"God is Great" they all repeated. He was told to continue coming to the mosque whenever he could and they would let him know when he was needed. They finished their tea and then Joseph left back through the main room. Nate followed outside a few minutes later. He spotted a man in an older VW watching Joseph's car pull out. He alerted Mel who was across the street. "He picked up a tail; an orange VW is following him." He said. Mel called Joseph on his cell and told him he was being followed. He advised him not to do anything different or look around. "Go to the diner over on Flatbush. Go in and sit at the counter and order some food. Don't look around or get

nervous. We've got you covered." Joseph did what he was told. The VW went on past the diner and pulled into an alley. The man got out and walked back to the diner. He sat in a small booth and looked at the menu while pretending not to look at Joseph. He finally ordered a sandwich and coffee. Joseph went to the restroom and called Mel. Mel told him to finish his meal and then drive on home. Joseph finished his food, paid the tab and walked out to his car. When he drove off the man came out and went quickly to the alley.

His car had been "gangster tagged" with black spray paint and all four wheels were gone.

It was sitting on the frame. He kicked the door in frustration and pulled out his cell phone. He called the Imam and told him what had happened. It was a rough neighborhood known for gang violence. Mel called Joseph and told him what had happened. It was amazing what you could arrange for fifty bucks in this part of town.

"They won't know if it was a gang thing or not, but they have your license plate and will eventually find your home address if they don't have it already. They may just be checking you out before letting you in on any more of their plans. If they were on to you they probably would have grabbed you at the mosque. We'll know if they come looking for you." "Maybe this means that something is definitely in the works. I think we should keep going to the mosque as if nothing has changed and see what develops." Joseph said.

"I agree, but it's getting a little spooky. Did you notice if the room you went in has an outside entrance by any chance?" Mel asked. "There is a side door but I don't know where it goes." Joseph replied. "We'll check it out before you go in again. I'd like to know if there is a way for me to get in there if things go sideways." Mel said. He decided to check for an outside entrance on the north side of the mosque before their next visit.

He went online and looked for a floor plan for that style mosque. He found several plans

that resembled the one in Brooklyn. Off the main prayer room for men there were two offices. Both had doors leading to a hallway. There was no direct access to the outside from the offices but there was an entrance to the hallway from the parking lot. He decided to go over to the mosque and have a look for himself. He got off the metro bus and walked over to the Mosque. He had a 35mm camera on a strap around his neck and he was dressed like a tourist. He found that they gave walking tours on Tuesdays and fell in with some other tourists and took the tour. He went out to the parking lot and took several pictures of the building. When no one was nearby he walked over to the side door and found it unlocked. He opened it a ways and looked inside. No one was in the hallway. Satisfied, he fell back in with the other tourists and then went to the bus stop.

Back at the office he told the others what he had found. It was decided that Mel would stay close to the parking lot whenever Joseph was inside from now on. That way Mel could get in quickly if anything went wrong and Nate could enter from the prayer room.

Hopefully that would prevent any attempt to kidnap Joseph and take him out of the mosque.

CHAPTER THIRTY FOUR

The old Liberian freighter had made it to Halifax and was off-loading goods when Mustafa simply went ashore with the other sailors. Canadian customs had an officer come aboard and check all the papers for the crew and then they were allowed to leave the ship.

No one paid any attention to Mustafa and the others as they made their way to the waterfront taverns. Mustafa told his companions that he was going to visit friends in town and would see them later. He went back to the port area and talked a delivery truck driver into giving him a ride to Port Royal where he boarded the ferry and crossed over to St.

John, New Brunswick. He went to a bar on the waterfront and used the pay phone to call the number the Algerians had given him. A short time later two men came in wearing the Toronto Maple Leaf hats he was told to watch for. He joined them in a booth where they ordered a pitcher of beer and acted like old friends. He had given up pretending to be a devout Muslim long ago and drank beer with the others. They finished their beers and walked out together after leaving some money on the table. They all climbed into a van and drove down to the marina at St. George. When they arrived at the docks one of the men pointed out a forty foot cabin cruiser at the far end of the row of boats. "He will take you to Rockland, Maine where you will find a green Mazda car in the parking lot of the café next to the marina. Here are the keys." With that the men turned and left him there.

He walked down to the boat and climbed aboard. The trip was
pleasant and the water was calm. When they arrived at Rockland
marina the boat's captain handed Mustafa some fishing clothes,
two old poles with reels and a net. "Put those on and take the
fishing gear to the car with you." He instructed. No one paid any
attention as Mustafa walked over to the car and put the fishing
gear in the trunk. He could see the boat backing out of the dock as
he pulled out of the parking lot. The car was registered to a Max
Werner with an address in Portland and had Maine license plates.
In the back seat was a suitcase with a couple of changes of clothes,
a shaving kit and a cell phone. In the glove compartment he found
a folding knife along with a small.25 caliber semi-automatic pistol
and a box of ammunition. Grinning to himself he decided the
money he had paid the Algerians was worth every franc.

CHAPTER THIRTY FIVE

Jake decided it was time for another visit to the mosque. This time
they would have Mel go in closer. Just in case. Again, the visit
went without incident until Joseph left the mosque. This time they
allowed a car to follow Joseph back to his condo. There were two
men in a green Pontiac. They parked up the street and watched
Joseph go into the parking garage. After a short while they took
off and headed back toward Brooklyn, unaware that Ty was
following them. When Joseph opened the door to his condo he was
shocked to find Mel just inside against the wall next to the door.
"Shit! You scared the hell out of me" Joseph gasped. Mel laughed
and told him to relax. The men who followed him home were
gone. "Well, now we know for certain that they know where you
live but we don't know what they are up to. Ty is following them
to see where they go. We'll be watching you at all times from now
on in case they make some kind of move toward you." Mel told
him. "Do you think they suspect me or are just being cautious?"
Joseph asked. "We won't know until they either let you in on
another plot or try to take you out. All we can do is watch your
back and wait for them to do something." Mel replied. Ty called
and said he had followed the men to an apartment complex in
Brooklyn not far from the mosque in a neighborhood with a large
Islamic population. Jake ran the plate and found that the owner

was not on any of the watch lists. His name was Abdul Al-Kalifa a naturalized American citizen who owned a Halal meat market in Brooklyn. The men from the car were too young to have been him. Ty said he would have Nate check out the store later and see who else was around. Mel told Joseph he intended to set up a safe house as a way for him to get to and from the task force office without being followed.

"Just go to your office tomorrow and conduct business as usual until you hear from me."

Mel instructed. Then he left the condo but kept it under surveillance for another hour

before leaving the area. The next morning Mel arrived at Joseph's office a little after ten.

He was accompanied by an attractive dark haired woman wearing a white blouse and navy slacks. She was about five feet seven and very fit. Her black hair was shoulder length and she had a dazzling smile. Mel introduced the woman as Naomi Jenson. Then he explained that he had set up an apartment in Naomi's name in order to establish a place where Joseph could go on the way to the task force office. In case he was followed he would park in front of the building and go into Naomi's apartment. From there they would go down to the underground garage and get into a mini van with no side windows.

He would sit in back out of sight and she would drive them to the office. Ty had installed hidden surveillance cameras to watch the garage and the front and rear entrance on monitors in the apartment. That way they could safely go into the garage if no one was watching. Mel explained that Naomi was ex-CIA and could lose anyone that attempted to follow them. "Is all this really necessary?" Joseph asked. "We can't afford for anyone to connect you with us, friend or foe. If they decide to follow you from your office to ours we can't take that chance. This way you can pretend you have a lady friend that you visit from time to time and we can watch to see if they are on to you. If they check up on Naomi they will run into a well prepared cover story. If anyone tries to get to you, through her, God help'em. She's as deadly as anyone of us." Mel assured him. Naomi went over the procedures with Joseph on how to contact her whenever he needed to go to the task force office or to meet with any of the others without being seen. "We're going to make another visit to the mosque tomorrow. That will give us a chance to test this out and see if they are still following you when you leave. When you leave the mosque this

time, call Naomi on the way and go directly to the safe house. Stay at least one hour before going home." Mel instructed, before leaving with Naomi.

CHAPTER THIRTY SIX

Early the next day Ron called from Buffalo and told Jake that the professor had picked up the Imam and they were headed for Brooklyn. "The reception from their car is pretty poor at times but they have mentioned Yousef and Brooklyn" Ron told Jake. "We're going to the mosque for afternoon prayers. Do you think they will be here in time or should we wait for the evening session?" Jake asked. "They're driving pretty fast. I think we will get there in plenty of time for the afternoon session." Ron replied. Jake called everyone and told them what was happening and directed them to go to the mosque for afternoon prayers. This time Mel would get close to the side entrance of the mosque before Joseph and Nate went in. Jake, Ty and Ron would spread out to cover the outside of the building from all sides. This time Jake had Naomi wire Joseph up at his office before he left for the mosque. She fit him with an earpiece that was virtually invisible without shining a light in his right ear. Jake wanted to be able to warn him if something changed on the outside. Everyone except Ron was in place when he called and told them that the pair from Buffalo had arrived and were pulling in to the parking lot. Jake told him to take a position on the north side, out of sight. Nate went in first and took up a position where he could watch the main room and the side doors. Joseph arrived and walked into the main room. Nothing happened until after the prayers were finished. Joseph was about to leave when the local Imam motioned for him to follow and went into the side room. Nate waited a few seconds and spoke softly as he shuffled toward the side room. "Joseph has gone inside with the local Imam. I haven't seen the professor or the Buffalo Imam

anywhere." He told the others outside. Joseph greeted each man with a handshake and spoke their names as he did. This allowed Jake to know how many were in the room.

This time there were only the two Imams, the professor and Joseph. After the initial greetings and small talk professor Al-Sayiid asked Joseph if he knew anything about poisons that would be stable and effective in drinking water. Joseph said that he did but would have to do some research to estimate the amount it would take to be effective in a large volume of water. "How much volume are we talking about? I will need a fairly accurate estimate of not only the amount of water, the temperature and how long it will need to last in order to do the proper calculations." He said. "If you can give me the location and a few days to inspect it I can speed up the process. There are many chemicals that could possibly be used but choosing the right combination will be critical." He added. "We don't have a specific target at this time but we need to know you can do this if we need you." Professor Al-Sayiid replied. "I understand. Maybe you could give me a couple of possible sites that I could look into so I can work out some calculations. Then you could decide on the best one. Bear in mind that some chemicals are harder to obtain than others. If you want it to be lethal for anyone who drinks it then that is a completely different problem than just making the supply unusable. There are many ways to contaminate a reservoir and make it look like an industrial accident. But to put enough of any poison in a large volume of water that would be strong enough to cause death in one dose would be nearly impossible. If I know what the target is I may be able to come up with a solution." Joseph explained. "Thank you for that information, Yousef, perhaps Allah will provide us with the guidance we seek." Fayez Al-Sayiid said.

"I am His humble servant as always and willing to give any help that I can." Joseph replied. He bid them goodbye and went out to the main room and on out to his car. In his ear piece he heard Jake tell him to go home instead of to Naomi's and wait for his call.

This time no one followed Joseph's car and Mel checked out the area around the condo and found no one watching the place. He picked up Joseph and drove over to meet Jake at the office. Jake wanted to talk to Joseph about the feasibility of terrorists poisoning a large water supply, like New York's. When they arrived Jake asked Joseph if he thought there was any way to effectively poison New York's water supply. "If they could isolate a small enough area of the system; maybe. But I believe they are testing me. The idea of killing large numbers of people with poisoned water is a terrorist pipe dream. I can't think of anything that they could use that wouldn't be diluted beyond effectiveness in millions of gallons of water. We can be certain that I'm not the only one who knows this.

I think I have to tell them that I looked into it and decided it was not practical and then see what they are really up to." Joseph replied. "I think Joseph is right. He should go back in a week or so and tell them he could not come up with anything that would do the job and then wait and see their reaction." Mel said. "Ron is still watching the professor's car.

Maybe when they get in it again he will pick up something useful." Jake added. They didn't have to wait for long. Professor Al-Sayiid and Imam ABD-Al-Allah left for Buffalo that same day. Ron tailed them again, trying to stay closer so he could get more of their conversations. This time he was more successful for the first part of the journey.

He got a clear recording of much of their conversation but was surprised he didn't fully understand their words. They were speaking in a dialect that he was not familiar with.

When they got to the area where he began losing reception he decided to turn around and get the recordings back to the office. Maybe Nate or Joseph could translate the parts he didn't understand. He called Jake told him what he had in mind. Jake said he would get Joseph to meet Ron at Naomi's and the three of them could try to translate it. Naomi was very good at several Arabic variations. "It's Iranian or Pakistani. These guys must be from the same area near the Pakistan border. They are mixing Arabic with Urdu" Joseph said. "My father traded with leather merchants from Pakistan that spoke this combination of Urdu and Arabic. They could have come from either country, but near the border." He added. "He's right, I ran into this before when we captured some guys in Afghanistan. It took us a while to work it out." Naomi added. "Thanks for the geography lesson. What the hell are they talking about?" Jake demanded. "Most of it is about waiting for Mustafa to return. They think he is coming back with a new plan from al Qaeda. Apparently they want to try again on the tunnels. They don't seem to have any idea about where and when he will show up. They also discussed my reaction to their water supply question. I'm certain it's just a way to test my sincerity. After the first disaster they're still not convinced I'm on the level." Joseph said. "They have done some research and know that he does have a degree in chemical engineering and that his business is in international trading. There was no mention of his family being killed or that his office was originally in the World Trade Center." Naomi added. Jake told Ron to go back to Buffalo and continue watching them. "If Mustafa comes back they are our best chance to hear about it before he does anything." Jake added.

CHAPTER THIRTY SEVEN

Jake got a message the following day from Commander Mulligan detailing what was learned from their detainee in Alamogordo. The intended goal of the plan to shoot down an airliner in Los Angeles had an interesting twist. It seems they had intended to go up

near the Mount Wilson observatory to launch the attack. The effective range for a stinger missile fired from ground level is about 11,000 feet. Anything below that altitude is dead meat. In order to get a shot at an airliner traveling under 11,000 feet they would have to be near an airport and shoot it down during take off or landing. Getting close to LAX

undetected and then getting away would be very difficult. Airplanes coming in from the east are descending as they enter the San Gabriel Valley. Mount Wilson is about 5,700

feet high. A stinger fired from that altitude could conceivably hit an airliner descending to the landing pattern for LAX. The net effect would be much greater because the resulting crash would happen over a highly populated area. Jake relayed this information to Doug Small at Homeland Security. "We'd better get someone to look into this possibility. This extends the watch zone for ground to air opportunities exponentially.

Any airport with high terrain near it could be a target. We don't have enough people to cover all the likely spots near our major airfields let alone all the damn mountains in their flight paths." Small said to Jake. He intended to go to the president with this himself. He couldn't risk this leaking to the news media. Mulligan also said they had discovered the source of the stingers. They were US made. They had been sent to Afghanistan during the war against the Russians. The remaining Taliban forces had stores of this type of weapon hidden all over between Afghanistan and Pakistan. Their prisoner did not know the exact method used to get them out of Pakistan. He had been given them in Syria. He named the people in Syria who supplied them to him. Jake sent this information to the CIA. He didn't ask what was going to happen to the prisoner. He didn't need to know. Other leads from Doug Small included one where some supposed Cuban refugees had capsized near the Florida Keys. When the Coast Guard picked them up they discovered that two of

them were not Cubans but Saudis. They were being held on a Coast Guard cutter anchored just off Key West. They hadn't confessed anything and claimed they were sailors traveling with the Cubans because they had been prisoners there after a ship they were working on went aground in Cuban waters. They spoke very little heavily accented English and no Spanish. Jake wanted to interrogate them and maybe try to find the boat they had been on. The Coast Guard said they had the approximate location of where it sunk, based on where they had picked up the survivors. Doug Small arranged for Jake and his men to get on board as Homeland Security officers. Jake approached Joseph about going along. "Ron tells me you are an experienced diver. How would you like to get away for a few days and travel to Florida with Mel and I? We may get in a little diving while we're there." "Nothing seems to be happening here for the time being. Let's do it." Joseph replied. On the way Jake explained that he wanted Joseph to talk to the Saudi sailors. If they looked genuine they would let them go with the Cubans when they were deported. If they looked suspicious they would keep them on the cutter and go diving for the boat they came on. After two and a half hours of questioning, Joseph told Jake and Mel that these guys were not Arab sailors. They knew nothing of the Red Sea or Arabian Sea ports and shipping companies. They were faking it. Jake told the Coast Guard Commander to hold them until further notice and then asked him for a boat and crew to aid them in the dive for the wreck. It was too late to dive that day so they went in to Key West for the night. The next morning they were met by two young seamen from the cutter who led them to a forty foot dive boat. They headed out to the area to begin a search for the wreck. It took most of the morning to locate a likely looking wreck in about 100 feet of water. Mel went down first to get a closer look. He came right back up

and said it was a new wreck. Nothing old was growing on it yet. Jake and Joseph got into their gear with the help of Seaman First Class, Glen Becker. Seaman Charlie Parsons kept the boat turned to the waves. The wreck was an older Wellcraft fifty footer. It appeared to have no visible hull damage that would have caused it to sink. The Coast Guard had said there had been a squall line that probably caused it to capsize. Inside the cabin they found some surprisingly new navigational and communications equipment. One look in the forward section told the real story. It was packed with plastic wrapped bundles of drugs each about twelve inches square and four inches thick. And two crates of semtex plastic explosives. Another box had an assortment of automatic weapons and ammunition. They were nearing the end of their air and started back up. After their required safety stops they reached the surface and boarded the boat. Mel brought up one bag of dope which they quickly opened. Seaman Becker produced a kit and tested the white substance. "It's definitely high purity heroin." He said excitedly. "How much of that is down there?" The other seaman asked. "Enough to overload that old tub in rough water." Jake told him.

They radioed the cutter and reported the find to the commander. He told them to remain there until he arrived. Jake, Joseph and Mel got dressed and headed below on the cutter for another visit with the prisoners. They told the two Saudi men that they had found the boat and its cargo. They refused to talk to Joseph about where they were going with the explosives or where they had gotten them. Jake left them and took the alleged Cubans into a room one by one. He told them he had no interest in them and would trade their freedom for information on the Saudis. They weren't Cubans but Salvadoran drug smugglers who had been hired to get the two Saudis into Florida. The interesting thing was that they had been hired by Castro's secret service men and had picked up the

Saudi's in Cuba along with their cargo. They didn't know what the pair were planning and didn't care. They had been supplied with thirty pounds of pure Afghan heroin for their efforts, which they had added to their own supply. The Coast Guard commander wanted to know what to do with the prisoners. Jake told him to turn the Salvadorans over to the DEA, along with the drug evidence. Lying to them about letting them go was standard procedure. Then he told him to make sure the two Saudis got a vacation at "Club Gitmo" for the time being.

When the diving crew had finished searching the wreck they found a plastic pouch belonging to the Saudis. It had several pages of handwritten Arabic script in it. Joseph set to work translating it. He read it twice and then told the others. "This is part of a detailed plan for the next attempt on the tunnel. They were supposed to meet someone in Miami that would take them to meet Mustafa in

Brooklyn and give him the semtex. There is a name and cell number here for a Doctor Abashir." "That's the professor that supplied the vans for the first attempt." Jake said. "The FBI has his home phone tapped, but nobody has had this cell number before." He added. "Chances are good that he has never met either of these guys. We could have Joseph call him and pretend to be one of them. He could say he was coming alone and get the professor to meet him. It would be interesting to see how they planned to get the semtex to New York. We could grab the professor and then go to meet Mustafa. The professor must know when he is coming or how to contact him." Mel suggested. They took the dive boat back to Key West and picked up their rental car then headed for Miami to set up a surprise for the professor. They booked into a hotel near the airport and then had Joseph make the call. Jake had learned the names of the two from the Salvadorans who heard them talking to each other during the trip. When

the professor answered Joseph said he was Ali Al-Asam. The professor told him there had been an accident and the men who were to pick him up had disappeared. "How are we supposed to deliver this gift to the chosen one then?" Joseph demanded. "I will have to take you in my car I suppose." Dr. Abashir replied. "This is a fairly large gift it may not fit in a car." Joseph said. "I will have my wife bring our other car. We will have to separate the gifts into two vehicles. It is the only way at this time." The professor added.

"We are not at the original pick up place. There was no safe place to park. Come to the marina at this address, tonight at ten o'clock when it is dark." Joseph instructed. He closed up the phone and told Jake "I think he bought it. He and his wife will bring two cars." "Perfect, we can grab them both and have the FBI hold them while we set up our trap for Mustafa and the rest of this network." Jake said. Mel went down to the marina and rented a cabin cruiser for the next week. It was docked at the last slip in the marina.

There was a large metal building in front of the boat slips for boat storage that would give them a place to stay out of sight until Joseph had them in position. He went back to the hotel and went over the layout with the troops and made final plans for snatching Dr.

Abashir and his wife. "We need to make certain he has the cell phone on him when he arrives. You call him when he gets out of the car." He told Joseph. By nine thirty Joseph was on the boat, Mel and Jake took up positions on either side of the walkway next to the boat storage building and a tool shed. The night air was humid but a nice breeze came off the water making it very pleasant to be in the marina. Faint sounds of reggae music from the nearby nightclub came and went with the breeze. Precisely at ten o'clock a tan Volvo wagon and an old corolla pulled into the mostly empty parking lot. Professor Abashir got out of the Volvo and glanced around furtively and then started up the walkway. His wife

stayed in the corolla. When he had gone about ten feet up the walkway he stopped and pulled his cell phone out of his pocket. It was Joseph telling him to bring his wife to the boat because it wasn't safe to leave her in the car. He turned and motioned for the woman to come with him. As they walked slowly toward the boat Mel and Jake slipped in behind them. As they approached the end of the slip Joseph got out of the boat and motioned for them to get on board. He helped the woman over the gunwale then the professor. Joseph pointed a pistol at them and told them to be silent as Jake and Mel came aboard. They stared at the men in wide eyed fear. Mel said. "We are not going to hurt you. Be quiet.

You are under arrest for aiding terrorists." Then he reached inside the professor's jacket and removed the cell phone. "Stand up. I am going to search you for weapons." He told the man. Jake frisked him and then pulled his arms back and placed him in handcuffs.

Mel took the woman by one arm and stood her up. He handcuffed her and then looked through her handbag. No weapons only a cell phone. "Put them below and keep them quiet." Jake told Mel. Then he and Joseph untied the boat. Jake pulled out of the boat slip and idled out of the Marina. He headed toward Key Biscayne and then shut off the motor and let the boat drift. He went below and addressed the prisoners. "I'll make this very simple. You will tell us where to meet Mustafa and everything you know about your connections to terrorists in this country; or I will feed your wife to the fishes." He told the man. The woman screamed and struggled against the seat. The professor told her to be quiet and said to Jake. "You can't do that. We demand to see an attorney immediately. I know our rights" "You people amaze me. You want to destroy this country and its way of life and then you demand to have the same rights as the men and women who have fought and died to provide them." Joseph said in English. Then he told them in Arabic.

"For you it is Qiyamah, the day of judgment. These men will show you no mercy if you do not cooperate fully. You will be treated fairly under American law if you tell them what they want."

The woman began pleading with her husband to cooperate. He shrunk into his seat as though the air had been let out of him. Head bowed, he agreed to tell them what he knew.

"Mustafa never gives any information in advance. He uses disposable cell phones and changes them regularly. I get cell phone calls telling me to call a certain number at a certain time. These come from Imam ABD-Al-Azziz in Brooklyn. I do not have a working number for Mustafa at this time. I never know exactly when he is coming here."

"What were the explosive intended for?" Jake asked. "I don't know what the plan is; I was just supposed to help get the men and materials to Brooklyn. Originally two of my students were to arrange delivery. But they have disappeared." He answered. "Give me the names to go with the cell numbers of anyone connected with you in this." Jake demanded. "The numbers are in speed dial on my phone." He listed them by their speed dial position. They included ABD-Al-Azziz in Brooklyn and ABD-Al-Allah in Buffalo.

The others were for the missing students. Mel took over questioning the man while Jake started the boat and headed back to the marina. Jake called Doug Small and asked what he should do with the prisoners. "Take them over to Homestead Air Force base. I'll set it up with the head of base security. They can hold them until we sort out the rest of this mess. Ask for Major John Sample when you get to the gate." "What about my job? I will be missed. I have classes tomorrow." The professor blurted out, suddenly aware that his life was never going to be the same. "We'll call the school and tell them you had a family emergency and had to leave town." Jake told him. The man and woman both remained

silent on the ride to Homestead. When they reached the entrance they found Major Sample waiting just inside. The guard waved them through the gate. The Major came over to the car and told Jake to follow him. They fell in behind his car and were led to a restricted area away from the airplanes and hangars. "This building used to be the brig until we outgrew it. We can keep your guests here indefinitely if need be." He told Jake as they entered through the heavily reinforced front door. "They are Muslims so try to keep them fed accordingly." Jake instructed. Mel removed their cuffs and told them to follow the Major. They were both taken to the same cell. It was set up for two people with iron bunks, one desk and chair and a toilet and sink behind a partition. Jake thanked the Major and then left with the others.

CHAPTER THIRTY EIGHT

They returned the rental car at the airport and boarded a red eye back to JFK. It was after two am when they landed. They were in Mel's car headed out of the airport area when the professor's phone vibrated in Jake's pocket. He handed it to Joseph who opened it and listened without speaking. He then explained that he had the package and was driving up from Florida. He was told to go to an address in Trenton, New Jersey and then call back on the same number. "Who was the caller?" Jake asked. "Imam ABD-Al-Azziz" Joseph replied. "I recognized his voice. I hope he didn't recognize mine. He gave me this address and said to call him back when I get there." He wrote down the address and handed it to Jake. "We've got to decide whether to fake the explosives and go to this address or to just stake it out and grab whoever shows up." Jake said. "It would be very risky to try and fool them with a fake set of explosives. Besides, some of them know Joseph. I think we should go check out the location first. They think the delivery is on its way from Miami.

That gives us two days to check out the location ahead of time." Mel suggested. "This address has to be close to where I met Mustafa at the motel the first time. There are some warehouses and industrial buildings in that area. Maybe they have a place to hide the explosives near the motel." Joseph added. "Why don't we go to the mosque today and see what happens. They don't know Joseph is supposed to be the one driving the explosives up from Miami." Mel suggested. "Good plan. I'll have Ty go by that address in Trenton today while we go to the mosque." Jake said. Then he told everyone to go get some rest and then they would make it for evening prayers at the mosque. "I'll call Ron in a while and see what's happening with our Buffalo suspects." Jake added. "Meet me at Naomi's about four o'clock so I can wire you up." Mel told Joseph. Everyone headed home for a few hours rest.

Ty drove down to Trenton on Highway 95. He stopped at the truck stop where Joseph had met Mustafa and looked around the surrounding neighborhood. His gps unit located the exact location of the small industrial park where the explosives were supposed to go.

It was only a few blocks from the interstate and the truck stop. It was a typical industrial layout with low concrete buildings. There were three rows of connected low rise concrete buildings with a paved driveway and parking area the rows. The front row of shops had small offices and large roll up doors. The other two rows were just warehouse bays with roll up doors and no windows. Ty found number 310 at the far end of the third row. He parked near the end of the second row of buildings next to the dumpster and walked over by the door at 309.

There were no cars at that end of the strip and all the doors were closed. He banged on 309 and listened for activity inside. No one answered. Then a man backed a car out of the next bay in line number 308 and parked in the driveway. Ty walked over to the man as he got out of the car. He was dressed in greasy coveralls and wore a quilted black welder's cap sitting slightly askew on his head. "What can I do for you?" He asked as Ty approached. "Are any of these bays for rent?" Ty asked. "309 has been empty for a while but you'd have to ask the landlord if it's available. He's in the first office by the street, right where you turned in." He said. Ty thanked him and walked back toward his car.

There was a six foot high chain link fence with angled barbed wire at the top bordering the property. A narrow dirt alley ran between this fence and the back of a similar concrete building parallel to it on he other side. It had the same kind of fence running the length of the alley. He got in his car and drove out to the front street then went to the right until he came to the next cross street. He went down it to the alley and then drove up the alley to where he could see the back of the buildings where 310 was located. There was an old apparently abandoned house in an over grown yard behind the industrial buildings. The continuation of the cyclone fence separated it from the rear of the concrete building.

There were two large old willow trees, the remains of a rabbit hutch and some miscellaneous junk in the yard all the windows were covered in plywood. A gravel driveway led from the alley to the detached single car garage next to the decrepit house.

Ty made note of the rest of the surrounding area as he drove up the alley. Then he went back to see the landlord at the first office. There was a small sign about one foot square with vinyl letters stuck on that gave the name and office hours on the door. Ty tried the door and found it open. There was no one in the office so he stepped into the shop area.

There was a pristine red and white1955 Chevy sitting there with the hood up. A man was bent over the fender working on something. He turned around when he heard Ty walk over. "Nice ride." Ty said. Then he added "I'm looking for a shop to rent." "All I have available is a single stall warehouse with no office. It rents for twelve hundred a month on a one year lease." The man replied. "I really need an office. Could I rent the warehouse by the month until you get a vacancy on one with an office?" Ty asked. "You give me two months rent in advance and I can do it, I guess." The man replied. "I'd like to see inside first. Do these units have three phase power?" Ty asked further. "Yeah, they do and there's a wash room in the warehouse units as well. We can go take a look if you want. I have time right now. My name's Dave." He said. He grabbed they key for unit number 309 and led Ty out the door. They walked over to the unit and opened the small door. Once inside Dave opened the big roll up door and turned on the overhead lights.

There was a workbench at the rear and an electrical panel on the far wall. On the wall adjacent to the next unit, 310, there was a small washroom with a sink and a toilet. Ty said "OK I'll take it. I have to go get the cash though. My name is Ralph Baker, I restore antique motorcycles." They went back to the office where Dave wrote up a rental agreement while Ty left to get some cash. He went to a local bank and withdrew $2,400

from his MasterCard. He returned right away, signed the agreement and picked up the keys to the unit. He went back and opened the small door to the unit. He checked out the washroom again and found that the wall between the two units was just two by fours and drywall in the washrooms. He poked two small holes in the wall next to the sink and inserted his penlight in one and peeked through the other. He could see that the room was identical to the one he was in. Satisfied, he went back to his car and headed back out to the truck stop café to wait for dark. About nine o'clock he went back to the unit. He parked his car inside and then went to the small door on unit 310. He picked the lock and

let himself in. There were two assault rifles under some rags on the work bench at the rear of the bay. He found six extra clips of ammunition under the bench. He walked to the wash room and checked for the two holes he had made earlier. They were nearly invisible unless you knew they were there. Before he left he decided to remove the firing pins from the two rifles. He did this expertly and then placed them back under the rags as before.

Then he installed a small closed circuit camera and audio transmitter under the bench.

Neither could be seen without lying on your back under the bench. He locked the door, got his car from next door and headed back to New York.

CHAPTER THIRTY NINE

Asrar had returned to her small apartment and her job cleaning local houses and apartments. She worked strictly for cash since she had no social security card and no one paid much attention to her. Except for occasional visits with her sister-in-law she had a lonely life. She didn't dare make friends who could be curious about her and she avoided conversations with neighbors. She was asleep when Karim slipped into her apartment at two thirty in the morning. He picked the lock on the apartment door and moved silently through the kitchen and into her living room before she knew he was there. He held his hand gently over her mouth and woke her up with a whisper. "Asrar, don't be afraid, it is I Karim." She awoke with a start and nearly fainted when she realized what was happening. "Is it really you? I thought I was dreaming" She whispered back. He kissed her gently and told her he was happy to see her. She was afraid to ask where he had been or why he had disappeared in England. She was thrilled to have him near her again even if it was only temporary. "I must leave again before daylight but I had to know you were alright. Fayez does not know I have returned and you must not tell him or anyone else I

was here." He told her. It was dark in the room and she couldn't see that he had lightened his hair, it wasn't blond but several shades lighter brown. When she touched his face she realized he was clean shaven. She couldn't imagine him without a beard. They made love hungrily like before and held each other closely on the narrow couch until he slipped out without waking her around four thirty.

CHAPTER FORTY

"I rented the bay next door to the one our friends have. The partition between the two washrooms is made of wood and drywall. We could get through there if we need to but it would be noisy. The layout is good for trapping them. There is only one way in and out of the complex. The perimeter is cyclone fenced six feet high with three strands of barbed wire at the top, angled to the inside." Ty told the others as he drew a sketch of the industrial park on a white board. "This alley runs parallel to the fence and there is an abandoned house behind here." He added as he pointed to the various features on his sketch. "I had Major Sample's men pick up the professor's cars from the marina and take them to the base. I also had him overnight the license plates from the Volvo wagon. We'll grab a similar wagon here and put the Florida plates on it." Jake explained.

"Are we meeting Mustafa at the storage place tonight?" The younger man asked.

"Perhaps he will come. I do not know. One of the ways he remains free is never giving anyone more information than absolutely necessary. My instructions are to get the explosives safely inside the building and keep them there until we are told what to do next." Imam ABD-Al-Azziz replied. "The driver of the car from Florida has been instructed to call me when he is about one hour south of Trenton. We will meet him at the truck stop and let him follow us to the storage unit. That is all I know" He added. The

Imam knew that the two young men idolized Mustafa and were excited to meet him. For now he just needed them to help move the explosives into the warehouse. He would find out later if Mustafa had plans to include them in his attack on the tunnel.

Jake and Mel had concluded that they would need to construct a realistic looking explosives package and have Nate drive it to the warehouse. Jake purchased a used Volvo wagon that was nearly identical to professor Abashir's and put the Florida plates on it.

Nate called in some favors and got an empty military explosives crate and some of the waxed paper wrappers from C-4 explosives. He and Joseph cut some modeling clay into bricks and wrapped them in the C-4 wrappers. They made enough for two layers on top of an olive green waxed paper partition that hid a carton of clay made up to simulate the weight of the C-4. Joseph came up with another idea that met with everyone's approval.

"Why not put a padlock on the lid and tell the others that only Mustafa has the key. If he isn't there they can't open it. If he is there, Nate can just open it for them." He suggested.

"These wrappers make the clay smell just like the real thing. If any of them know what C-4 is supposed to smell like they'll believe it's authentic." Mel added. They closed the crate, installed a padlock and then loaded it into the Volvo wagon under a blanket. The plan was to have Ty and Mel hide in the rented bay and monitor the bug he had planted earlier. Jake and Joseph would stake out the alley until everyone arrived and then block the exit from the complex with Jake's SUV. If things went sideways Ty and Mel would come in through the wash room wall and then Jake and Joseph would come in the front door. Nate would have a pistol hidden in the small of his back under his jacket and a knife in his right boot. Just in case. "Any word from Ron?" Mel asked. "He called earlier and said all his bugs were still working but no one had contacted professor Sayiid. I'd

like to have him here but we need him to stay in Buffalo in case Mustafa shows up there." Jake said. "We could bring Naomi in place of Ron if you think we need more back up." Mel suggested. "Not a bad idea, but I think we have it covered. They probably won't have more than two or three guys if they are just expecting to unload the explosives tonight." Jake replied. "We'd better get moving. I want Ty in place long before anyone else arrives and he needs to set up the rest of his monitoring equipment.

Nate, you take the Volvo and go south of the truck stop a few miles and wait at the north bound rest area on 95. We'll call you when it's time to come up to the truck stop. It was getting dark when Nate passed the truck stop, heading south. Jake cruised by the industrial complex and then drove slowly up the alley checking to see if anyone was watching the shop or was parked there. It appeared to be clear so he and Joseph dropped Ty and Mel off at the rented shop and drove back to the truck stop. Ty set up his monitoring equipment on the bench and settled into one of the folding canvas chairs Mel brought with them. They checked their guns and equipment one more time and then did a communications check with Jake and Nate. So far everything worked fine. The lights were off next door but the video showed a little stream of light around the large entrance door. It was about ten pm when Joseph made his call. "I am about thirty minutes from Trenton coming north on highway 95. Where should we meet?" He asked. "Stay on the highway until you see the large truck stop on the left. Pull in to the café at the truck stop and we will meet you. What car are you driving?" "It is a tan colored Volvo wagon with Florida plates." Joseph replied. We will watch for you from the café. When you pull in and park, flash your lights two times and then come inside." Jake called Nate and relayed

the message to him at the rest stop. Then he alerted Ty and Mel. "Nate is giving it 20

minutes and then he will drive up to the truck stop. We'll watch him from the parking lot then call you when they leave. Is everything working OK?" "We removed the drywall from our side of the bathroom wall and have cut most of the way through the two by fours. One good push and we are inside. The audio and video are working perfectly so far." Ty said. Nate arrived at the café and found a spot right near the door. He blinked the headlights as instructed and then walked inside. He was met at the door by a young man in jeans and sweat shirt who led him to a booth where one other young man and the Imam were seated. Nate and the Imam both had full beards. The younger men were clean shaven and could have passed for local students. When Nate sat down the Imam motioned for the waitress to come over. He asked

Nate if he was hungry after the long drive. Nate nodded and then asked the waitress for a chicken sandwich and coffee. They made small talk while waiting for his food to arrive, speaking English all the while. The café was crowded and noisy and no one paid any attention to them. When they finished the Imam paid the check and they all went out to the parking lot together. One of the younger men got into the Volvo with Nate. The other two got into a green Pontiac and backed out. They left the café and headed for the industrial park with Nate and his new companion close behind. "Is that the same car that followed me home from the mosque last time?" Joseph asked. "I believe it is." Jake concurred. The man riding with Nate asked his name but got only a glare in return. He was silent the remainder of the ride.

When they arrived at the warehouse the Pontiac pulled up by the small door, Nate turned the Volvo around and backed up to the large door. Next door Ty and Mel watched them open the door and walk inside. The younger man opened the roll up door and Nate

backed the car inside. When the door was closed Nate and his companion got out and went to the rear of the car. Nate opened the hatch and they all crowded around the opening to look at the crate as Nate removed the blanket. His passenger, Gulzar, helped Nate lift the crate and carry it to the bench. There they watched as Nate took out a key and opened the padlock to show them the contents. "This is very dangerous. Do not handle it or take any from the box. Mustafa will know what to do with it. I must return this car to Miami immediately. Allahu Akbar!" Nate told them. "Allahu Akbar!" They replied as Gulzar opened the big door. Nate bowed to the Imam and then got in the car and left. Next door Mel and Ty heaved a sigh of relief and called Jake to tell him everything was calm. They watched and listened to the conversation next door while recording it for Joseph to translate it later. Nate drove the Volvo back to the rest area and waited for word from Jake that the Pontiac had left with the Muslims aboard. When they were safely gone Jake had everyone meet at the truck stop café to go over their next move.

CHAPTER FORTY ONE

Doug Small's boss, John Worley, was livid when he returned from the Senate sub-committee meeting. "I'm getting serious pressure from a couple of our esteemed senators concerning some of the intelligence you gave me last week. They want to know how the hell we determined that Fidel Castro was aiding Islamic terrorists in getting into the US.

Since the CIA and NSA have given no concurring reports they think we are just blowing smoke up the committee's skirt. I know you have some undercover characters working on this stuff and I am going to have to come up with a plausible answer for them or this thing will get out of hand in a big ass hurry." He told Doug. "You can tell them that we

got it out of some Cuban drug smugglers during a combined DEA/Coast Guard drug bust.

There wasn't any way to corroborate their story and I told you that the source wasn't verifiable. They need to treat that kind of information as a "strong rumor" not a solid fact.

As for my "undercover characters" as you call them, we reach out to all the agencies and use their informants whenever we can. The intelligence we gain from them often leads to more substantial evidence later on. Tell them we can't risk identifying any of those sources or they will dry up instantly and we'll lose a valuable piece of the intelligence gathering puzzle. I'll get the Coast Guard man to back that up for you if need be. They should be getting on the CIA spooks to find out what's going on in Cuba instead of pestering us about how we get our info." Doug replied, his voice rising. "You're right of course but I'll have to find a diplomatic way to present that to them." John said. "You're a brilliant politician John surely you can convince a couple of weak kneed doves that national security is more important than their curiosity." Doug said, while barely keeping a straight face. He had little respect for his boss and enjoyed watching him light up under the false praise he occasionally plied him with. Secretly, Doug was getting nervous about his task force being exposed. The president had too many political enemies that would crucify him if the truth about this undercover operation were discovered. He and the president had discussed this many times and both decided it was worth the risk but Doug was getting increasingly worried. It was impossible to do what they had to do without involving key people in the other services. One leak would be a disaster. Inside, Doug felt the American public would cheer their efforts, but the mainstream press and the opposing political party would go nuclear trying to discredit the president. Maybe it was time to rethink the whole project. He decided to have another secret talk with the president as

soon as possible. He was still pondering this when the phone on his desk rang. It was FBI agent Walter Jackson from Miami. He told Doug that he had been keeping surveillance on a Professor Abashir that was suspected of having terrorist connections. When there had been no activity at the house or on the phone they had inquired at the school. The professor had told the school that he had to return to the middle east to deal with some family problems and then just disappeared. There was no record of him having purchased any plane tickets or any other evidence that he and his wife had left the country. Both of their cars were missing and he had the Florida Highway Patrol watching for them. Then there was the matter of the four Arab students who had also disappeared without a trace.

Jackson was worried that they might still be in the country and planning some terrorist attack. Doug told him he had no word on either the students or the professor but would look into it with all the other agencies. When he hung up he called the secret service to set up a meeting with the president.

CHAPTER FORTY TWO

Jake and the others met at the truck stop café and ordered dinner. "What made you decide to open the crate?" Jake asked. "I was afraid that one of them would ask Mustafa for the key before we get a line on him." Nate replied. "Anyway those guys couldn't tell C-4 from play dough and I think I put the fear of God in them about handling it." He added.

"Good move, I had hoped he would be there and we'd get it over with tonight. We'll have to keep watch on the warehouse until we know what's going down." Jake said. "I'll have to change my appearance before we go back to the mosque. They might recognize me now." Nate added. "Let's give it one more day before we go back. They might think it is too coincidental if Joseph returns right after the shipment arrives." Mel suggested.

They didn't see the green Mazda go by on it's way to the industrial park. Mustafa parked the car in front of one of the first row shops that were closed and walked quickly to the warehouse. He looked around the corner of the buildings to see if anyone was around before going to the door. He stepped inside and closed the door behind him. When he turned on the overhead lights he saw the crate sitting on the work bench. He went directly to it and then stopped suddenly. He took out a penlight and looked closely at the hinges and the space around the lid. Satisfied, he gently lifted the lid. He picked up one of the bricks and looked carefully at it. At first he hefted it a couple of times thinking it seemed a little heavy. Then he held it up to his nose for a moment and sniffed deeply. A sly grin creased his face and he replaced the brick gently in the box and closed the lid.

Jake and the others had left the café by the time Mustafa arrived at the truck stop motel.

He went inside and phoned Azziz. "Have you seen Yousef at the mosque recently?" He asked. "He comes around at irregular intervals but at least one time per week. We followed him home and have his address if you want to see him there." Azziz added.

"Give me his address. If he doesn't come to the mosque shortly I will go to him. Tell no one you have heard from me." He copied down the address and abruptly hung up.

CHAPTER FORTY THREE

Jake had just arrived at his office when Doug Small called him on the secure phone.

"Meet me at the hotel in one hour." Was all he said. Jake told the others he had to go to a meeting and instructed Ty to call Ron and get him back right away. He removed a plastic hotel room key from his locked desk drawer and left without saying another word. He knew something big was happening. Doug never saw him in person otherwise. They kept a room rented at the Wellington Hotel near 55th and Broadway for their private talks. Jake

arrived a little early and went up the stairs to avoid being noticed and to time his arrival for exactly one hour. The room was on the third floor and Jake wasn't breathing hard when he arrived at the door. He let himself in and found Doug sitting by himself with a drink in his hand. "Scotch?" he asked. Jake nodded and Doug poured him a large glass of Glenlivet, neat. "What's up?' Jake asked. "We've got problems. The FBI is nosing around about the professor in Miami and the Senate sub-committee is all over Worley about where we got the tip about Castro. I haven't said anything to the president but I'm going to have to tell him that things are heating up." Doug replied. "Mustafa is back and we've set a trap for him. It could go down in the next few days. We intercepted his explosives and substituted a fake shipment. He can't blow anything up with it but he doesn't know that yet. We can eliminate him and round up the biggest part of his network if it all works out. But unless they all disappear we will have to let the FBI in on it and have a bunch of trials including the Miami couple. What we've done so far could come out and bite us in the ass. It's your call, but I think the only thing to do is round them all up and eliminate them and hope that nobody connected to us decides to rat us out. I trust Rusty and Mulligan completely but I'm not so sure about the DEA guys, the Coast Guard guys and Major Sample. They don't know who we work for but they can identify me and my crew and possibly trace us back to you. When are you seeing the president?" "I have a meeting with him later tonight. I'm going to lay all this out for him and let him decide what our next move is. He doesn't know any of the details about our operations and I want to keep it that way. But he will have to assess the risks and decide whether to continue or not." "What should we do about Mustafa? We could just eliminate him and leave the rest in place. I think we could secretly deport the Miami couple. They would

have to keep quiet or risk jail. Maybe we could leave the others in place and put the FBI on to them through anonymous informers. It would be a shame to end this right when we are beginning to make real progress, but if the risks are too high we have no choice." Jake said thoughtfully. "Don't do anything until I talk to the president. I'll call you as soon as I finish with him." Doug instructed. On the way back to the office Jake ran several scenarios through his mind. None of them had a happy ending. He decided to wait to tell the men until tomorrow when Ron would be there. Unknown to either man a news story was about to break that would make the president's decision much easier.

"We're live from Los Angeles with an ongoing gun battle between local police and a pair of gunmen holed up in a Jewish Synagogue in the Mar Vista district. Manny Diaz is on the scene with the City police swat team. What do we know so far Manny?" "I'm here with Captain Gerald Armstrong of the LA Special Weapons and Tactical Team. Gerald?"

"Two men purported to be Muslim extremists broke into this synagogue just as the Friday service was underway and began killing people at random with automatic weapons. A few people managed to get out of a rear door but they claim everyone inside has been slaughtered. We have the building surrounded and have been fired upon from the front entrance. The gunmen have barricaded the door area with furniture and have been firing automatic weapons. We held our fire and tried to talk to them but they appear to be intent on fighting to the end. It looks like a suicide attack. You have to move back now. We are going in." He said. The reporter and cameraman ran to the east side of the building out of the line of fire and began trying to interview survivors. "Two men came in wearing long rain coats over their clothes. Then they dropped the raincoats and began firing the guns they had hidden underneath. They were screaming in a foreign language and just killing

everyone in the room. Some of us got out by crawling on the floor to the rear door but then one of them ran to the back and locked the door behind us. It was horrible, blood everywhere and people screaming." The woman then began sobbing uncontrollably as the sound of an explosion from the front of the building distracted the reporter. The police had fired tear gas into the front door followed by flash-bang grenades. FBI snipers had arrived and were setting up on top of the swat truck trying to get a clear shot at the men inside. The firing had stopped on both sides for a moment while a cloud of smoke drifted upward from the entrance. Then there was a huge explosion as the two men detonated their suicide bomb vests. The building was immediately engulfed in flames. The fire department had arrived earlier and were standing by. They moved a pumper truck up close and began pouring water into the building. The police moved the crowd and reporters back and removed the swat van so the firemen could move in more equipment.

All the networks now had vans and reporters on the scene each trying to outdo the other with reports of the carnage. The first estimate was for 62 dead and thirty wounded. Only sixteen had escaped. It took the firemen less than thirty minutes to contain the fire so the police could get inside. When Captain Armstrong came out he was inundated by reporters and cameramen. He told them there would be a press conference in twenty minutes in the parking lot across the street. "I need everyone out of the way so we can get the ambulances and crime scene technicians in here." He said through a bull horn. The TV

cameras were able to capture the grim scene. Wounded survivors were evacuated first, every available ambulance in the metro area was on the scene. After the survivors were removed the next few hours were consumed by the removal of body bags. The City and County morgues would be overwhelmed by the number of bodies needing to be identified. Many of the dead would have to be taken to morgues at local hospitals. It was a nightmare for everyone involved. The Mayor, police commissioner and other local politicians were giving interviews to any reporter with a microphone. By six o'clock the evening news carried this story plus shots of protests being held in front of many of the mosques in the greater Los Angeles area. Several altercations had taken place near the King Fahd mosque on Jefferson. A street gang had driven past firing into a crowd trying to enter the Mosque on west Pico, killing two and wounding three more. Fearing wide spread riots the Governor was calling out the National Guard to restore order.

CHAPTER FORTY FOUR

Doug Small was with the president when the news was relayed to him. They turned on the television and watched the live report from Los Angeles. "We'll have to continue this later, Doug. There's no way in hell I'm going to call off your team. You watch, the same jokers who want to handcuff our efforts will be calling for more Homeland Security by eleven o'clock." The president said shaking his head. Doug left the oval office and went to his car. He had barely cleared the area when the national press corps descended on the white house clamoring for an interview with the president. Doug decided to go to his office instead of going home. The press would be snapping at his boss's heels and he would have to help Worley handle them. When he got to his office the parking lot was full of media vans. He went around to the side door and managed to get to his office without being seen by reporters. He buzzed the Director's office and got his assistant Madeline. She had stayed late when they heard the news from California. She told Doug that security had not let any reporters inside the building and that the boss was getting a statement ready. He went directly into the director's office where he found him in a state

of near panic. "Jesus Doug, what the hell is going on in L.A.?" was the first thing out of his mouth. Then "I need something positive to tell these reporters or we'll get murdered in the press. What have you got that I can use to get them off our necks?" "Give me a few minutes to write something up. We could give them the Castro story and tell them we intercepted the explosives that were to be used to blow up the Holland Tunnel. But it will screw up our current operation to capture Mustafa and break up his network." Doug said

"Too a big risk. What if he manages to get away and do something just as nasty? If that got out we'd be finished. There must be something else." The director pleaded. "Why don't I give them the usual song and dance about ongoing undercover operations and tell them you are working on a plan to increase border security. We'll still get some heat from the press and the Democrats will have a field day criticizing us and the administration. But it will give me time to finish our operation. Then when we get Mustafa and round up his network we can shove that success down their throats." Doug suggested. "It will have to do. I don't want to risk screwing up what you have going on.

But you'd better make it good. If this California shit gets any worse there will be hell to pay in the press." John said. Doug put a few notes on paper and got ready to face the media outside. He gave them the usual routine and finished by promising that something big was about to happen but he couldn't disclose anything about it at the present time.

They were still shouting questions at him when he got in his car and left. He phoned Jake and told him what had happened. Jake was relieved that his operation was surviving for the moment. He thanked Doug and told him he would move up the action on Mustafa as soon as possible. He decided to have a meeting with the crew tomorrow to decide what to do. He knew that his original plan to just make Mustafa and his network disappear was

becoming too risky. Sooner or later someone at the FBI would figure out that suspected terrorists were disappearing too regularly and now Doug was under pressure to make something public to show that Homeland Security was doing its job. He needed an ally in the Bureau so he could bring them in without exposing his groups past actions. He would ask his men if any of them had someone they trusted in the Bureau. He called Mel and told him to get everyone to the office tomorrow morning including Joseph and Naomi.

They were all together when Jake arrived. He gave them a detailed report on the situation and then asked them if anyone had a trustworthy contact at the FBI. They all looked at each other and then Naomi spoke up. "I have done a lot of translations and a few interrogations for them over the last couple of years. I have a pretty good relationship with deputy director Callahan. He's pretty much in favor of doing what ever it takes to get the job done. He's less political than the director and has shown a tendency to bend the rules when necessary. I think he would cooperate especially if it would get some good PR for the bureau." "See if you can set up a meeting between the two of us and him, today if possible." Jake suggested. "We need to step up the plan to trap Mustafa. I want Joseph, Mel and Nate to go over to the mosque today. Ron, you and Ty go to Trenton and have another look at the warehouse. Be careful we don't know who might be watching the place. If anyone has been there since we left, Ty's equipment should have recorded it." He added. Naomi called the FBI and left a message for Garrett Callahan. He called her back in about fifteen minutes on her cell phone. "What can I do for you Naomi?" He asked. "I need to see you today if that's possible Garrett. It has to do with Homeland Security and I need it to be private. Can we meet somewhere away from the bureau?" She asked. "I have a meeting this morning but I could meet you for lunch. Are you in the

area?" "No, I'm in New York but I could meet you by one o'clock. Shall we meet at the Plaza hotel restaurant?" "The Plaza at one o'clock will be fine. This sounds interesting.

I'm looking forward to seeing you." He replied. "If we leave now we can catch the United shuttle to DC and be in Quantico in time for the meeting." Jake told her.

CHAPTER FORTY FIVE

Ty filled Ron in on the happenings at the warehouse while they drove to Trenton. "You should have seen Nate. He had those turkeys shaking in their boots. Not only did he warn them not to touch the explosives but he gave them his best Mel impression with the intimidating stare when he told them." Ty said laughing. "I wish I had been there, Nate's usually pretty mellow unless he's really pissed. Then he even scares me. You should have seen him when he was disarming VC booby traps. Everyone would clear out and watch from a safe distance and he'd be there whistling and tapping his foot like it was nothing."

When they got to the industrial park Ty circled around the block and drove up the alley to look for anyone watching the warehouse. He didn't see anything out of place so they drove on in and parked in front of unit. They went in the small door and turned on the lights. Ty showed Ron where he and Mel had prepared the bathroom wall so they could get in if they had to. Ron gently pushed against the half sawn wood and grinned when it moved easily. "Pretty slick Ty, you could shove this in with one hand and probably be fairly quiet about it." He said. Ty set up the monitor and played back the video from next door. They watched the whole scene where Nate had warned the Muslims. "That was a great Mel type stare he gave them. Nate makes a pretty convincing bad guy. I'm glad he's on our side." Ron said. They stared in silence when the door opened and Mustafa came into the picture. At first they thought it was someone else. He had no facial hair and had a

much shorter hair style than before. "It looks like he bleached his hair too." Ty said.

"From a distance you wouldn't think he was an Arab. That's a pretty dramatic change in his appearance. We'd better show this to the others. I think I'll call Mel and tell him about this before they get to the mosque. Our boy might just fool them if they aren't prepared." Ty decided. "It looks like he went for the fake C-4. Otherwise I think he would have shown some anger unless he suspected he was being watched." Ron added.

Ty reset his equipment then they took off for New York. He called Mel and explained how Mustafa had changed his appearance. Mel passed the information to the others before they arrived at the mosque.

CHAPTER FORTY SIX

Naomi and Jake picked up a rental car at Dulles when their plane landed and drove to Virginia. They arrived in plenty of time for Naomi to get to the Plaza Hotel before Callahan. Jake drove the car to the end of the block and waited for Naomi to bring Callahan out. When Garrett arrived he walked into the lobby and found Naomi waiting by the entrance to the restaurant. She gave him a brief hug and a light kiss on the cheek and then told him to come outside with her. He was delighted to see her but was puzzled by what he thought were cloak and dagger tactics. Jake pulled the Lincoln rental car up to the curb and Naomi got in the back seat with Garrett. She introduced them as Jake pulled away and headed for the highway. "What's this all about, Naomi?" Garrett asked. "I'm sorry for kidnapping you Garrett but what you are about to learn cannot leave this car."

She told him. "I'll let Jake fill you in." She added. "We are taking a very large risk by bringing this to you Mr. Callahan and I hope you can cooperate with us. I am the head of a secret task force working for the president. We intercept and destroy terrorists before

they can unleash their weapons on American citizens. Some of our operations require us to use tactics that are beyond the law. We don't harm any innocent people only real terrorists that are in the act of planning or executing attacks on Americans. Because of this we can't take credit for our actions and we can't have public trials for the perpetrators. Before I give you any specific details I need to know we can count on your help and your absolute secrecy regarding my team and our actions." Jake explained.

"What is it you need from me and the bureau and what's in it for us?" He asked. "We need to bring the bureau into an ongoing operation that is crucial to national security. We will work together to stop a terrorist plot and round up an imbedded terror network.

The FBI can take the credit but must shield us from exposure. No one can know about my team's existence. It will require extreme secrecy on your part. You must give us people who will do what is required and not ask questions about who we are. You can tell them we are from a secret military force and that they can't know any more than that. Do you think you could make that fly?" "How many men are we talking about?" "Four at the most. Preferably veterans who can be trusted to keep silent when it's over." Jake said. "I need to know what we are talking about before I go any further. I can't have FBI men committing crimes in the line of duty." Garrett said. "I'm not asking your guys to do anything illegal. I just need them to be able to take credit for arresting the bad guys and keep silent about us. We've got to have a way to get these guys on trial and off the street without anyone discovering our existence or who we work for." Jake assured him. "I swear if you tell me the whole story I will set this up for you. I don't see that I have anything to gain by blowing the whistle on your operation. In fact I wish the bureau could have more leeway in dealing with these so called sleeper cells. Our hands are tied most of

the time." Callahan replied. He sat there in stunned silence as Jake explained who they were and what they had done on this case to date. He left out any previous operations and did not disclose anything about Joseph. "Wow, I had no idea anyone had this kind of authority. We could wipe out most of the terror networks and half of the organized crime in this country if we could operate like this. Give me 24 hours to work on it. I have a couple of guys we can trust. Can you get by with two very experienced operators?" He said when Jake was finished. "As long as you can convince everyone that these two were capable of running this operation on their own we can make it happen." Jake said. "Is anyone else hungry?' Naomi asked. "I'm starved." both men replied. Jake drove to a roadside diner where they were sure no one would recognize them. After the meal they dropped Callahan off at the Plaza and went directly back to the airport. "I hope this wasn't a mistake. I don't like bringing any more people into this but I don't see we have much choice." Jake said, staring out the window. "I really think we can trust Callahan. I just hope his guys are going to go along without asking too many questions." Naomi added.

CHAPTER FORTY SEVEN

Everyone was in place and all the communication equipment had been checked out before Joseph entered the mosque. Prayers were finished and he was about to leave when Imam Azziz motioned him to follow. They went into the side room as before and sat at the long table. There was only the Imam and two young men in the room. There was no sign of Mustafa. Azziz introduced Joseph to the boys and then asked if he was ready to do God's will. "I remain his loyal servant and am eager to do whatever I can." Joseph replied. "Do you have access to any more detonators at this time?" Azziz asked. "I have a

small quantity in my possession. How many will we require?" Joseph asked. "I do not have that information presently. Do you remember the motel we met at in New Jersey?"

Azziz asked. "I rode with others last time but if you give me the location I am sure I can find it." Joseph lied. "Meet me there tonight at nine o'clock. I should have the information you need by then." Azziz instructed and handed Joseph a slip of paper with the room number and directions on it. Joseph pretended to memorize it and handed it back to the Imam. Joseph bowed slightly and said "Allahu Akbar." The others did the same then he walked casually out the front entrance and got in his car. This time no one followed him. No one noticed the green Mazda parked at the end of the block. Joseph drove directly to Naomi's decoy apartment and let himself in. He called Mel and told him what had happened, even though he assumed Mel had heard every word. Mel told him he was watching the apartment and hadn't seen anyone following his car. Jake dropped Naomi off at her car and was about to head home when Mel called. "The Imam wants Joseph to meet him at the motel in Trenton tonight. He also asked him about detonators.

My guess is that Mustafa will be at the motel." Mel said. "Get everyone together at the office right away. I'm on my way there now." Jake instructed. "Ty, I want you and Nate to go to the warehouse right now and get set up in case this party moves from the motel to their storage unit. Take a good look around before you let anyone see you go in. I'll take Ron with me and watch the motel from the café. Mel will follow Joseph's car and monitor him from a safe distance." He instructed. "Make certain Joseph is wired up and functional before we leave here. Just go with the audio this time I don't want to risk them finding a camera on him." He told Mel. "What about the gun or a knife?" Mel asked.

"They have never searched me before. I'd feel safer with the pistol on me." Joseph added.

"If they find it he can say he always carries it for protection." Mel said. "O.K. with me as long as you think you can keep your cool if they ask about it." Jake said. It was about ten to nine when Joseph arrived at the motel. Mel had kept in touch on the way to be sure the audio transmitter was working. Ron and Jake took seats in the cafe near the window facing the motel while Mel parked on the other side of some trucks. After Joseph entered the motel Mel walked over to the dumpster by the rear entrance to the motel and waited until someone came out. He held the door for a couple who were dragging luggage and two small children and then walked inside. Joseph was to meet the Imam on the second floor in room 213 so Mel stayed on the first floor near the laundry room and vending machines. Joseph knocked softly on the door and then was let in by one of the young men he met at the mosque. Inside the Imam and the other young man were seated and had the TV turned up to mask their conversation. Mustafa was not there. "Greetings Yousef, you are exactly on time. We must wait here for a while, I am expecting a phone call." ABD

Al-Azziz told him. "I counted my remaining detonators. I used 16 and we have 34

remaining. Will that be enough for our purposes?" Joseph asked. "We will know that soon enough, God willing." Azziz replied. They made small talk in Arabic for a few minutes until the Imam's cell phone call intruded. He picked it up and listened without

speaking. "We must go now, it is time." He said when the call was
finished. They all followed him out the door and down to the
parking lot. "We will all travel in this car." He said pointing to a
Pontiac. Mel relayed the information to Jake that they were taking
Joseph in a Pontiac four door. "Don't follow them too closely,
they are most likely going to the storage unit." Jake instructed. He
phoned Ty and told him they were probably heading his way. Ty
said no one had been inside the unit so far. Mel soon called back
and

verified that the car was pulling into the industrial complex. The
Imam unlocked the small door and turned on the lights. Joseph and
the other two followed him inside. Azziz went directly to the crate
at the end of the room and slowly opened the lid. He motioned to
Joseph to look inside. Joseph sucked in a large breath and gave the
Imam a wide eyed stare. "Allah be praised!" He exclaimed
excitedly and gently lifted one of the fake bricks of explosive and
held it up to the light. Azziz and the others took a step back
remembering Nate's warning. "This will be much more reliable
than the old dynamite we used before and many times more
powerful. Do you have any idea what can be done with this much
C-4?" He asked. "Will the detonators you have work with this
material?"

Azziz inquired. "Most certainly, they will be perfect." Joseph
replied, placing the brick back in the box. "Do we have a plan
ready to go?" He asked rubbing his hands together for emphasis.
"The chosen one will inform us of Allah's mission in due time."
Azziz replied. "He is alive?" Joseph asked in mock surprise. Next
door Nate and Ty smiled nodded to each other, appreciating
Joseph's performance. "Allahu Akbar! I feared he was killed in the
explosion at the farm. It must be God's will that he lived to lead us
forward."

Joseph exclaimed. "Allahu Akbar" They all repeated reverently.
"Heads up, I believe our pal Mustafa is watching the unit from the
alley." Mel told Jake over the satcom. "He got out of a green
Mazda at the end of the alley and is walking up toward the unit."
He added. Mel was hidden in the shadows between the buildings

on the other side of the fence in the adjacent compound. "If he goes inside just keep an eye on him for now. I want Joseph in a safe place before we move in to take him." Jake told everyone. Joseph heard all of this in his hidden earpiece but didn't let on. Mustafa walked on up the alley and then turned around and went back to his car and left. Shortly afterward Joseph and

the others got back in the Pontiac and left for the motel. They dropped Joseph off at his car and told him to come to the mosque each day until they needed him. "Go in the café and order dinner." Was the instruction Joseph heard in his earpiece as he reached for the door handle of his car. It was Jake's voice. Joseph had entered the café when Mustafa drove slowly through the parking lot. He didn't stop but looked closely at Joseph's car and the others in the lot before leaving. "Do you want me to follow him?" Mel asked.

"Better not, we can't risk being spotted following him." Jake replied. They waited twenty minutes to be sure that Mustafa didn't return. Jake told Joseph to finish his meal and go on home. Mel went inside and ordered a sandwich and coffee to go without acknowledging Joseph. Mel got his food and then left shortly after Joseph. He decided to follow him home and watch for Mustafa or someone else at the condo. Jake and the others went in the café and ordered dinner. "Now that we know what he is driving it will be a little easier to keep an eye on Mr. Mustafa." Jake said. "I'd like to know how he got into the country again. He didn't use his Buffalo connections this time as far as I could tell." Ron added. "Mel got the license number on the Mazda. We can run it tomorrow and see where the car came from." Ty added. Jake decided not to tell them about the FBI involvement yet. He told them all to be at the office by 7:30 tomorrow morning.

Shortly after Jake arrived at the office Callahan called and told him he had two men who were on board and would be available today. They both worked out of the New York field office on the Hostage Rescue Team. Jake asked him to have them come to his office right away for a briefing. He decided to inform the group about the problems Doug Small had mentioned. "Before we get into planning our next move on Mustafa I have to give you all a heads up. Doug has been getting pressure from a couple of liberal Senators

about how we knew about Castro's involvement with Arab terrorists and the FBI in Miami is nosing around about the professor and the missing students. Doug is worried that they may start looking into Homeland Security's finances. If they discover us and how we are funded all hell will break loose. I'm not saying it is happening right now but we may have to wrap this operation up and fade away if things get too hot. I'm working on a way to bring the FBI into the Mustafa case and lay it off on them when it's finished.

Today we'll have two agents here that we will try to incorporate into our plans. I am promised that they will cooperate and not ask questions about us or any of our operations.

I realize it's a big gamble but we've got to cover our tracks or risk blowing our whole deal." Mel spoke first. "Are we going to let them know about Joseph?" "No, we'll tell them he is our interpreter. I'm not going to give them any background on any of us. Our contact at the bureau has assured me they won't ask." Jake replied. "These guys are from the HRT and don't want any publicity. We'll let the FBI take credit for the operation as though it was theirs from the beginning. If it works like our DEA deal did in Mexico we should be all right at least for now." He added. "These must be our guys." Nate said pointing to the monitor. There were two men in the lobby about to get into the elevator.

Jake met them when they got off the elevator and led them into the conference room. The taller man introduced himself and his partner. "I'm Ralph Huff and this is Kenji Morimoto, we call him Kenny." Jake introduced all of his men and then offered the newcomers a chair and coffee. "We have been trailing a terrorist that goes by the name of Mustafa and several local sympathizers for months. They are planning to blow up the Holland Tunnel as far as we know. We intercepted a shipment of C-4 and substituted some fake explosives. We are planning to take them down shortly and we want to tie as

many of their network into this thing as possible. When it's over we need you and the bureau to take credit for the entire operation. We must remain invisible. You have to understand that we don't exist and cannot be exposed. Are you guys willing to live with that?" Jake asked. "Kenny and I talked it over with Callahan. We knew what to expect before we got here. Don't worry about us. Can we do this thing without the media getting involved?" Ralph asked. "No one knows that there is anything happening so we should be able to pull this off without any media attention until its over." Jake replied. Mel, Joseph, Nate and Ron went to the mosque while Jake and Ty explained the set up at the warehouse. "We want to catch them in the warehouse when Mustafa is with them. If it goes smoothly you guys can call in some New Jersey or New York bureau agents to share the arrest. It's up to you how you handle that part of it. Once the suspects are neutralized we'll bow out and leave the scene. When you give me the go ahead I'll leak the story to the media. If you want to separate yourselves as well then you'll have to hand the whole thing over before I tell the media so you have time to get out before the circus arrives."

Jake instructed. "Callahan wants us to look like a special FBI task force so we'll have to be part of it. Don't worry, the New York SAC will grab all the attention. We'll be forgotten when the cameras roll." Kenny assured them. "You won't have to alert the media, believe me that will take care of itself." Ralph added giving them a knowing look.

Immediately after the midday prayers Joseph was approached by one of the men from the warehouse and led into the Imam's chambers. The Imam greeted him warmly and told him to go to the motel tonight at nine o'clock and bring all of his detonators. Joseph nodded his agreement and didn't ask any questions. When he left the mosque Mel and Ron were watching his car. No one followed him. They all met at the office to discuss

tonight's action. Jake laid out the plan and assigned the two FBI agents to be the first ones to go in the front door. Mel and Ron would break through the wall from the other unit at exactly the same time. Jake and the others would cover the perimeter and move in last. "I want everyone in place as soon as Mel gives the all clear signal. He and Ron will go to our unit and check out the area before anyone else arrives. When all the players are in the building and the perimeter is clear we'll wait for Mel's "go" signal. Joseph, I want you to get clear of Mustafa and grab one of the others and keep him in front of you when the action starts." Jake instructed "What are we going to do if Mustafa doesn't show?"

Joseph asked. "It depends on what they have planned. If it looks like he's not involved in the attack we'd better take down the rest anyway. I want this thing contained in that warehouse if at all possible." Jake replied. Joseph and Ron drove over to Joseph's storage unit and retrieved the remainder of the blasting caps. They packed them individually in paper towels so they wouldn't touch each other in transit and placed them in a canvas bag. "You okay going in there tonight?" Ron asked. "I'm a little nervous about the motel.

They may want me to ride with them again like last time. If I make it to the warehouse I think I'll be all right." Joseph replied. "Put that knife Mel gave you in this ankle sheath and wear loose pants over it. I'll show you how to get it out quickly before you go." Ron said and handed him a slim nylon knife sheath with Velcro straps. When they got to Joseph's apartment Ron wired him for sound and then waited while Joseph got dressed.

"Pull your sock down and then strap this to your ankle. Pull your sock up over it but leave the handle above the sock." Ron instructed. "Your pants hide it completely even when you walk. Now try this, use your left hand to lift your right pants leg while you grab the knife with your right. It must be done in one smooth move." He added. "I

watched Mel do this. I never saw him move and then the knife was at my throat. It scared the shit out of me." Joseph said while attempting to show Ron Mel's technique. "That was pretty good. Let's see it a couple more times." Ron told him. Joseph practiced the move until he was comfortable that he could get to the knife quickly if he had to. "Mel would be proud. You're almost as fast as he is" Ron told him. "I hope I don't have to prove it tonight." Joseph said. "Just keep your cool, we'll be listening to you the whole time and we won't be far away." Ron assured him. "If you have room, always go for the gun. Use the knife only if you are in the car or anywhere where you can't reach the gun."

He added. Mel came to pick Ron up at Joseph's condo. "We are going directly to the warehouse area to check things out. Let's do a sound check from the car before we leave.

I want to know we can hear Joseph from a distance." Mel told them. Joseph's equipment was working fine. He could hear Mel and vice versa even though he was in the condo and Mel was driving away. "He should be okay getting to the motel. If they try anything it will be there or on the way to the warehouse." Ron said. "I don't think they suspect him or they would have grabbed him at the mosque." Mel said. "We'd better record everything we can get from the motel. It may be the only evidence we get about what they are planning, unless they do it at the warehouse." Ron decided. He connected a digital recorder to the receiver in the car as he spoke. They drove to Trenton and checked out the motel and café parking lot for familiar cars or faces from before. Finding nothing suspicious they went to the industrial park and did a drive-through of the alley and the surrounding area. Finally they pulled the car inside the unit and unloaded their weapons and Kevlar vests. Mel decided to back the car into a vacant spot in the center row of buildings. This would prevent them from being trapped in the unit if they had to get away

quickly. Jake and the others took separate cars to the truck stop café. Everyone was connected by satcom and had tested satisfactorily. The two FBI agents sat at different tables away from the others and watched the motel and parking lot. Shortly before nine o'clock the Pontiac arrived with the two young men and Imam Azziz. Nate had checked out the owner of the car at the Halal meat market in Brooklyn. One of the boys was his nephew. Naomi was running down the man's finances to see if there was any connection to terror group funding. So far nothing had turned up. A few minutes later Joseph arrived and went into the motel. Nate slipped out of the café and went to the rear entrance of the motel. Some college kids were holding the door open while carrying in some cases of beer. Nate went right by them and into the motel. He took the stairs to the second floor and waited in the stairwell. He could hear Joseph talking to the Imam and the boys.

Quietly he asked if the others were receiving the same conversation. Ron replied that they were hearing clearly and recording every word. "Did you bring the detonators?" Azziz asked. "Yes, they are in the trunk of my car." Joseph replied. Jake's voice came over the satcom "Mustafa has just pulled up by the motel. He may be coming in the back way. Get off the stairs and go into the laundry room Nate." Nate turned and hurried down to the first floor and went to the vending machine area. Mustafa had a key and let himself in the rear door. He went directly up the stairs and used his key to go into the room. Joseph pretended to be shocked at the change in Mustafa's appearance and then complimented him for his expertise. Mustafa exchanged greetings with all of them and then got right to the business of planning his next attack. Nate moved up the stairs and into the second floor hallway. There was a small nook with an ice machine about halfway down the hall near the elevators. He stood by the ice machine and listened to Mustafa explain his plan

to the others. Outside Ty slipped a homing device under the rear bumper of Mustafa's Mazda. This time he would not get away so easily. "Yousef, I need you to show us how to arm the detonators and set up timing devices. We are going to set off several explosions instead of trying to blow up the tunnels. This time we will put smaller bombs in public places with large crowds and have them all go off at the same time. If we fill a large coke cup with C-4 and metal parts like screws, nails and ball bearings we can put two of them in a McDonalds bag and leave them on top of the garbage cans anywhere we want. No one will notice them; people do it all the time." Mustafa explained. He pulled out a New York City map with locations marked in red. They included Grand Central Station, subway terminals, the Grey Hound bus terminal and the Staten Island Ferry.

"How many packages can we make with the detonators you have?" Mustafa asked Joseph. "I have thirty four blasting caps. We only need one in each package so we could make thirty four such devices. Even that won't use up all of the explosives we have. We can do more later if I can get more detonators." Joseph replied. "How long will it take to get them ready?" Mustafa asked. "We will need the metal parts and some McDonalds or Burger King cups and bags. That will be easy but I will have to come up with thirty four timing devices that will fit unnoticed in the packages." Joseph answered. "I already have the metal parts in my car and a carton of cups. We could put some together tonight to see how long it takes and what they will look like." Mustafa said. "Can you use plastic watches that have alarm functions for the timers? I brought some of them along." He added. "I'll have to look at them but if we put a battery in each package we can probably make them work." Joseph replied. "Let us go to the warehouse now and see what can be done with what we have." Mustafa told the others. Nate quickly slipped into the elevator

and went down to the lobby and out the front door. Mustafa told the Imam and the boys to leave first and go directly to the warehouse. He and Joseph stayed in the room until they saw the Pontiac leave. He told Joseph to go next and he would follow in a few minutes. Nate went to the café and sat with Jake and Ty. The boys parked the Pontiac in front of the unit where Ron and Mel were hiding inside. When Joseph arrived he parked in front of the other unit and got the canvas bag out of his trunk and followed them inside. Mustafa parked his Mazda on the street by the entrance to the industrial complex and walked casually around to the unit and went in. As soon as they were all inside Mel alerted everyone that it was time to get in position. Jake and Ty parked ahead of Mustafa's car and the FBI men parked directly behind it. They all got their weapons and vests out of the cars and walked into the compound. Jake and Ty went around the north end of the buildings while Ralph and Kenny worked their way along the fence on the south end. Mustafa opened a duffel bag he brought in and showed the others the boxes of screws and ball bearings he had purchased at Home Depot. He also had a stack of generic Coke cups and a couple of fast food bags from McDonalds, Wendy's and Burger King in the duffel. Joseph opened the crate and removed a brick of clay. He unwrapped it and molded it into a column. Then he pushed screws and ball bearings into it on all sides. He also placed a layer of balls on the bottom of a cup and then shoved the clay column in on top of it. There was about two inches of space on top which he filled with more metal parts. He set that one aside while the others watched from across the room. He molded a second column like the first and shoved a blasting cap into one end leaving the wires exposed. Mustafa handed him a plastic wrist watch that had the straps cut off. Joseph asked him for a knife. Mustafa pulled the folding knife the Algerians had supplied him

from his pocket, opened it and handed it to Joseph. Joseph used it to pry off the backing plate exposing the inner workings of the watch. He set the alarm for five minutes and placed the watch face down on top of the clay. "The watch battery is not sufficient to work the detonator by itself. I will have to place a nine volt battery in series with it and attach that to the detonator wires." He explained. He then packed the column with screws and balls like the first one and placed it in the cup. He put both of them in a Wendy's bag and wrinkled the top closed like most people would do. When the alarm went off with a muffled buzz the Imam and the boys jumped back in surprise. Mustafa and Joseph laughed at their fear. "We will need more than this group to spread these bombs around to all of our targets. We won't want them to sit around for long in case someone accidentally discovers one." Joseph said. "Don't worry; I can supply plenty of couriers from our followers." Imam Azziz said excitedly. "Get some of them to purchase food and save the bags right away." Mustafa instructed. "I can get a large quantity of these watches from a wholesaler in Brooklyn." Joseph volunteered. "Batteries are no problem, but I will need time to assemble each package and solder all the connections." He added.

"Excellent, we will cause enormous panic and disrupt business as well as killing as many infidels as possible. They will know God's wrath and no one will ever feel safe again."

Mustafa exclaimed. "Allahu Akbar!" they all shouted. Mel gave the "go" signal and pushed through the bathroom wall just as Ralph and Kenny crashed against the locked front door. Unfortunately the door did not give way on the first try. Mustafa pulled a pistol and began firing at Mel and Ron. The two younger Muslims grabbed for the AK-47's under the bench just as the front door gave way. Joseph pulled the knife from his ankle and grabbed Mustafa around the neck from behind. Mustafa fired wildly and

struggled against Joseph's grip. Joseph plunged the knife into Mustafa's abdomen and then into his right kidney using moves he learned from Mel. Mustafa dropped the gun and grabbed at the knife as Joseph slashed the artery inside Mustafa's right thigh. Mustafa twisted around to look into Joseph's eyes as he slumped to the floor. Surprise and hatred flashed in Mustafa's eyes for a brief instant when he recognized Joseph. Then he was gone. The Imam had pulled a knife from somewhere and attacked Ron with it. Ron broke the Imam's forearm with one quick move and then immobilized him with a chop to the throat. He reversed the knife, still in the Imam's hand and plunged it into his diaphragm.

He died instantly. Kenny and Ralph took out the two younger men as they struggled with the assault rifles. They hadn't known that Ty had disabled the rifles earlier. "You'll have to explain that you thought had Mustafa and the Imam safely in custody when they pulled out knives causing a fight that ended in their deaths." Jake told Ralph. "I'll tell them Kenny did it. He is the expert with knives." Ralph said. Mel was talking quietly to Joseph who appeared to be in shock. "You kept him from getting any of us. Don't feel bad for that asshole. Let's get out of here. I'll drive you in your car." Mel gently guided him toward the door. Ty explained the surveillance equipment next door to Kenny and gave him a "thumbs up" as he and the rest of Jake's crew slipped out. Ralph called his special agent in charge, Kevin Dugan and told him to get some men over to Trenton ASAP. "Do you believe these guys?" Kenny asked. "My head is still spinning. I thought that front door was never going to come open. Good thing they had that side entrance thing set up or this would have been a different game altogether." Ralph replied. "Interpreter! My ass!

Did you see the way that Joseph guy handled that crazy bastard?" He added. "I was busy at the time but I did see the other guy break that Imam's arm with one karate chop or

something. Where the hell did these guys really come from? That was some amazing shit.

I thought they were a bunch of geezers when we met them at their office. We'd better get our story straight before anyone gets here." They rehearsed a plausible version of the events until they were satisfied. When Dugan showed up he had five men with him all dressed in FBI windbreakers and carrying all sorts of weaponry. "What the hell happened here?" He asked. "We've had these guys under surveillance for some time. We were about to call for

backup when they must have heard Kenny next door. I came in the
front and he broke through the bathroom wall about the time they
saw our peep hole in the wall." Ralph explained. "The guy over
there pulled a small caliber pistol and started firing at me as Ralph
came in the front door. Those two grabbed those AK's out from
somewhere. Ralph blasted them and I grabbed the guy with the
pistol. I took it away and he put his hands up over his head. Just as
Ralph reached for the older guy both of them pulled knives. We
were too close to shoot so we had to fight them off by hand."
Kenny explained, pointing to the various people and weapons
strewn around the room. "You won't believe what they were
planning to do." Ralph went on to explain the plan to set off
multiple shrapnel bombs all over New York. The television news
vans began arriving about that time along with the Trenton police.
Dugan immediately gathered the news people and held a press
conference while the others filled the Trenton police in on the
event and placed crime scene tape across the entrance to the unit.
Dugan wisely explained that the sting had been a joint effort
between the FBI and local authorities before the Trenton officers
could raise a stink about not being in on the raid. "These brave
men have foiled a heinous terror attack. I can't go into more detail
until we know if all the suspects

connected with this plot are in custody." He carried on for some
time as the coroner's wagon arrived and the crime scene
investigators swarmed into the unit.

Ty had expertly erased the video portions that exposed Joseph and
the crew. The video the FBI retained only showed the terrorists
rejoicing over their plan. When Mustafa had explained the plan the
audio remained but the video went fuzzy. When everyone was
back at Jake's office they went over the operation. Ron had two
.25 caliber bullets stuck in his vest and some bruises to match.
"It's a good thing Mustafa didn't have a bigger pistol." He said as
he rubbed at the bruises on his chest. "At that close range anything
bigger might have gone through." He added. Joseph was still
staring straight ahead and being very quiet. The shock of killing
Mustafa had unsettled him greatly. Mel put a hand on Joseph's
shoulder and said "Joseph here probably saved one or both of you

guys. If he hadn't grabbed Mustafa when he did somebody might have caught one in the head or neck." "That was a great move, Joseph. You should be proud of yourself. It is never easy to kill a human being, no matter how many times you've done it. But remember, he worked for the same people that caused the death of your family members and would have kept on killing innocent people if you hadn't stopped him." Jake told him. "I don't exactly remember going for him. It was like I was on automatic or something. I'll never forget the look in his eyes when he knew it was me that had him." Joseph said, regaining his composure. "That's what proper training does for you. You don't have time to think or plan. You just do what you've been trained for in situations like that." Ron added.

"Let's turn on the news and see what kind of BS Dugan gives the press." Ty suggested. It was the lead story on all channels. Dugan went into great detail about the investigation and capture of the terrorists. He explained the plan to use shrapnel bombs in public places

complete with appropriately shocked facial expressions. He actually gave some of the credit to information shared by other agencies including Homeland Security. They were still watching the reports when Callahan called Jake. "This won't go away easily. You know the doves will be all over us about how we spied on these guys and then managed to kill everyone during the raid." He said "What are you going to do about the Miami professor and his wife" He asked afterwards. "We'll offer to quietly deport them back to Pakistan or face life in prison. I think they'll be happy to go away." Jake said. He didn't bother telling Callahan that the real alternative to quiet deportation would be elimination.

"Should we tell the FBI about the Buffalo connection?" Ron asked. "Yes. Your surveillance video of them sneaking the woman across the border should be enough to put the professor and the sister away. You have enough on the Imam's connection with them to lock him up also. I'll give all that to Callahan and let him distribute it to the FBI field guys. No sense wasting all your Buffalo efforts. The trials will give the newsies and the libs plenty to keep them off Doug's back for the time being." Jake replied. "What happens when the FBI discovers that the explosives are fake? How are they going to explain that?" Nate asked. "Callahan knows the whole story. The plan is to say that the terrorists apparently got screwed by their suppliers if it comes out. There are a lot of unscrupulous arms dealers out there. Anyway he won't let the media know about the fakes. Ralph is going to move the explosives to a safe location for disposal instead of letting the lab boys have it. Then he will explode the crate for the cameras for dramatic effect in a few days." Jake said with a smile. "You OK to drive yourself home?" Mel asked Joseph. "Yeah, I'm OK now. I just needed a little time to accept what I did." "Try not to let tonight get the better of you, Joseph. You did the right thing." Jake said as

Joseph got up to leave. Jake soon found himself alone as everyone left for the night. He was about to leave when his phone rang. It was Kenny Morimoto. "I took a chance that you would still be at the office. I wanted you to know that Ralph managed to get the explosives removed without any problem. I also wanted to tell you that we both are ready any time you need us. Your guys are amazing and we'd be proud to work with them. We have some friends that could help out if you ever need a few more bodies. Anyway, thanks for bringing us in. We won't forget it." Jake thanked him and told him he would be in touch if he ever needed their help.

CHAPTER FORTY EIGHT

Joseph arrived at his condo completely exhausted but too wired to rest. He was about to make something to eat when someone knocked on his door. He peeked out through the security hole and was surprised to see Naomi. He quickly opened the door and let her in.

"I thought you might want some company. I remember how wired I was the first time I had to eliminate someone. It's a hollow feeling that no one who hasn't had the experience can appreciate." She said. Joseph invited her to sit in the kitchenette and asked if she would like a drink or something to eat. "You go ahead and fix something for yourself, I'm not hungry but I could use a drink." She replied. "I have some scotch that Ron left here. Will that do?" He asked. "That'll do just fine. Make it a large one with ice and you'd probably do well to join me. It will help you wind down." He poured two crystal rocks glasses about half full over ice cubes and handed one to her. They clinked their glasses together and each took a small drink. Neither spoke for a few moments. Naomi broke the silence first. "Mel called and gave me the short version of what happened. He was pretty impressed by the way you handled yourself but a little worried about how it

would affect you." She said. "Was it his idea for you to come over?" Joseph asked. "No.

And he doesn't know I'm here. He would never ask me to invade your privacy. I just felt you could use someone to talk to who would understand the emotions you are bound to feel. Besides, I really would like to get to know you." She said quietly. "This whole business has been like being in a sandstorm in the desert. Since 911 my life has been a mixture of hate and grief. I thought of nothing but revenge for months at a time. It never got any better. That's when I decided to quit thinking about revenge and start doing something about it." He told her. "Do you think you would have let it go if you had been able to kill Mustafa with the others the first time?" She asked. "I don't know. Since meeting Jake and the others I have felt like I finally have a purpose. Those guys are so dedicated and they have treated me like an equal when they could have turned me in. I know its sounds cliché, but they are like a family in many ways. I don't think I would be alive now without their help. At the time of the explosion at my farm I really didn't care if I lived or died. I just wanted to get some revenge for my loss. I don't know what is going to happen next but I think I will go back to Dubai and spend some more time with my uncle unless Jake has other plans for me." He said, visibly more relaxed. They finished their drinks and sat quietly for a few moments. Naomi got up and prepared to leave. She could see Joseph was coming down and would most likely fall asleep if he laid down.

He came over to her and took both of her hands in his. "Thank you for coming.

Are you sure you want to go home this late? You take the bedroom and I'll sleep on the couch." "Don't worry about me. I'll be fine. You get yourself some sleep. Call me later when you have rested. Maybe we can meet for lunch." She said, releasing her hands from his. When she was gone he went in the bedroom and flopped down on the bed. He was

asleep almost instantly. Naomi drove home to her real apartment, not the one Jake used to shuttle Joseph to the office. She wasn't sure what she was feeling. Her life had been pretty lonely and all about work since her fiancé was killed in Afghanistan. She liked Joseph but didn't admit it to herself at that moment.

CHAPTER FORTY NINE

As expected someone at the FBI leaked a few extra details to the press regarding the original plan to blow up the Holland tunnel and the new plan to bomb civilians in public places. The media did the usual saturation reporting and of course added their own embellishments to sensationalize the risk. The talk shows had all the usual publicity hungry politicians and so called experts giving opinions day and night. Homeland Security Chief John Worley was among the most vocal, touting the success of the operation and crediting it to cooperation between the intelligence agencies and the administration's part in creating that cooperation. The opposition spent their time criticizing the FBI for killing the Imam and failing to recognize the fact that he was the main link to Al Quaeda. They managed to ignore the fact that these terrorists, the Imam included, were planning to kill hundreds of innocent people and possibly blow up the tunnel.

Jake took advantage of the turmoil to slip down to Miami and deal with professor and his wife. They accepted his offer to be returned to Pakistan in exchange for their silence.

Jake had them prepare a letter to the university explaining that they would have to remain in Pakistan for personal reasons and wrote another for their landlord. Jake arranged for the DEA to fly them to the Bahamas and put them on a commercial flight to Karachi.

Major Sample had a wrecking company pick up the professor's cars and destroy them.

Callahan had Ralph and Kenny make a thorough search of the professor's residence before alerting the landlord that his tenant had left the country. They removed all evidence that he had lived there. Jake decided to leave the two terrorists at Gitmo for the time being.

CHAPTER FIFTY

Joseph did not call Naomi for a couple of days. He needed to catch up on some shipping contracts and decided to call his Uncle Hafid to see how things were in Dubai. Both Ron and Mel had stopped by at different times for short visits. Joseph told them he was planning to go back to Dubai for a while. They said that things were quiet for now and he should go ahead and make the trip. He finally decided to call Naomi and meet for lunch.

She agreed and met him at a Deli near where she lived. He was beginning to realize that he was attracted to her and he thought she felt the same about him. They ordered sandwiches and made small talk about the food in New York versus Dubai. "I want to drive out to the farm today. Would you care to join me?" He asked. "I'd love to. It would be nice to get out of the city for change." She replied. When they finished eating they got up and went out to Joseph's car. Naomi had walked to the Deli and said she had no need to go to her apartment first so they got into the car and headed for New Jersey. The traffic was fairly light and they made excellent time getting out of town. They looked at each other and smiled as they entered the Holland tunnel. Neither spoke of the terror plan but their eyes gave away the relief they felt as they drove through the tunnel. They rode in silence for most of the way until they reached the outskirts of the cities and entered the farm country. "It's easy to see why they call it the Garden State when you see all of these crops growing along the road." Naomi said. "Yes, it really is a nice change to get out of

the concrete canyons and see nature at work. We had planned to move out here and live at the farm. My business is mainly done on the phone and computer so I could have run it from the farm and stayed out of the city most of the time." Joseph added. She could see he was having a hard time holding back his emotions and placed her hand on his knee. He kept his eyes on the road but placed one hand over hers and gave it a gentle squeeze.

They had reached the turn off to his farm and were passing the row of small farms leading up to his property. He was unconscious of holding his breath, trying to hold back the tears that were welling up in his eyes when he stopped in the driveway. Naomi leaned over and held him tightly in a comforting embrace. He finally exhaled and began sobbing, his tears flowing down his cheeks onto her shoulder. They stayed in that position until he began to compose himself. He pulled away and began wiping the tears from his face with his shirt sleeve. Naomi reached in her purse and produced a wad of Kleenex. He took it and blew his nose, noisily and was totally embarrassed when he finally calmed down. He tried to apologize but she just pulled him to her and held him in another warm embrace. "You have never fully grieved for your family until now. Have you?" She asked "You need to let it all out before it completely takes over. I went for months without crying when Bob was killed. I walked around in a kind of trance, consumed with hate and trying to hide my sorrow. I threw myself into my work and pretended I was over it. One day I came across a woman who had been beaten to death by the Taliban. Her children were crying uncontrollably next to her body. I finally lost it and sat down and cried my eyes out with them. The next day I left Afghanistan and returned home. On the flight I began to realize that I finally felt human. I needed to release all that grief and anger and go on with my life." She went on. He pulled away from her and got out of the car. She joined him and they walked past the remains of his house and barn and stared at the corn that was now head high. "I never actually realized it until now, but I never did allow myself to cry for my family. I was so consumed with hatred for the people who robbed them of their lives that I couldn't allow myself to feel anything else.

It's a tradition in the Muslim world to grieve loudly and publicly when a loved one has died. Many people tear at their clothes and beat themselves with straps while wailing loudly for their loss. The dead are buried within 24 hours and the funerals are filled with grieving family and friends. I never really understood it until now. It's a way to release your sorrow instead of holding it in." Joseph explained. She spoke gently to him in Arabic and told him how sorry she was for his loss. He had forgotten that she was fluent in his native language and knew much about the Arab world. They stood holding hands and watching birds fly over the cornfields for what seemed like a long time before returning to the car. There they held each other and shared a gentle kiss before getting in.

Neither spoke as he turned the car around and began driving back to the city. After a while Naomi broke the silence. "When are you going to Dubai?" She asked. "I haven't made a definite plan as yet. It will depend on what is happening here." He replied "What about you? Are you working for Jake full time now?" He asked. "My leave of absence from the CIA is nearly over. I have to decide whether to continue my career with them or move on to something else. I don't know if Jake has a job for me. We haven't discussed it. I like working with his group but I don't know how much longer he can keep it going.

If the people snooping into Homeland Security get too close he will have to shut it down.

It would be a real shame if that happens, but it has been a gamble from the beginning. I don't know what will happen to his men. Except for Ty, everyone else is too old for the

FBI and they all have reasons why they can't or won't work with any other government agency. Besides, all the other agencies have their hands tied. They can't do the phone taps and other surveillance that makes this group so effective, not to mention that they couldn't eliminate threats the way Jake's group does. The very freedoms we fight to protect sometimes work against us when it comes to defending ourselves. A group like this working outside the normal constraints can fight the terrorists on more equal terms but it's a lot like the vigilantes in the old west. They get the job done but at what risk?"

She went on. "I think too many people here don't take the threat of these fanatics seriously. I can't believe how much the news media distorts the truth about what is behind these terror groups. It is already a holy war but no one seems to want to admit it.

Bin Laden is not the only force behind extremist terror. I agree he is a major factor but there are many others who don't get recognized. The money to fund it comes from Muslim countries that pretend to be our friends and I believe it starts right at the top of those governments. A basic tenet of the Islamic teaching is to kill infidels and to spread Islamic law to the entire world. Doesn't anyone realize that?" He said, his voice rising in frustration. They were nearly back to the city when Joseph got a call on his cell phone. It was Mel. He told him that Jake wanted to have a meeting this evening and would like for him to attend. Joseph agreed and asked if the meeting would include Naomi. Mel said yes it would and then Joseph explained that she was with him and they would come directly to the office. They both went silent again, alone with their thoughts, on the way to the meeting. When they arrived, Jake and the others were already in the conference room. "I want to start by congratulating all of you on the operations we have done so far. Bringing in the FBI for the last one may have bought us some more time, but it has exposed the

operation to way more people than I am comfortable with. I want everyone to take some time off for now. We'll let the media and the politicians make all the noise they want about the FBI's handling of the Mustafa case. I fear that when it all calms down the politically correct apologists will be focused on how the investigation was conducted and start hounding the FBI guys about their part in it. Jealousy and competition between departments within the agency could very well cause problems for us. We have to count on deputy director Callahan to keep them under control. I hope he can handle the pressure. Anyway, we are going to suspend our operations for a while. I am canceling the rent on this office as of the end of the month. We will keep in touch by e-mail and cell phones until further notice." Jake explained. "We can use my office for meetings if it would help." Joseph volunteered. "Thank you Joseph that may be an option when things cool down." Jake replied. "I am planning to go to Dubai for a while. You have all of my contact information if anyone needs to get a hold of me." Joseph said. "I need to go back to work at the *company* or resign by the end of this month. How long do you think we will be sidelined?" Naomi asked. "It could be a short while or it could be over. I don't know what to tell you at this time. I hope Doug will have some news for us shortly" Jake replied. There were no more questions so everyone collected their belongings and left Jake alone in the room. He decided against calling Doug and just went about closing up and removing all evidence that they had been there. "Would you like to have dinner before I take you home?" Joseph asked as they drove away. "Not tonight, thanks anyway, I'm going to be preoccupied deciding my future for a few days. Please just drop me off and I will call you when I get my head on straight." Naomi said. They rode in silence to

her block. She leaned over and kissed him on the cheek and got out without saying another word. Joseph started for home and began planning his trip while he drove.

CHAPTER FIFTY ONE

Mel, Ron, Nate and Ty met at a bar in a bowling alley in Brooklyn. The owner was an old friend of Nate's and he let them use a back room. It was set up as a card room but was not in use tonight. They ordered drinks and talked quietly about the situation.

"Jake is really upset. I haven't seen him this worried since this whole thing began." Mel said.

"He's right; there are too many people now who know just enough to cause real problems." Ron added. "We still have those two assholes stashed at Gitmo. With all the bitching about no lawyers and supposed prisoner rights we should get them out of there before somebody discovers how they got there." Nate said "Jesus, I forgot about them.

We'd better talk to Jake about it before the shit hits the fan." Ty said. "I'll call him right now." Mel said and went out the back door to the alley to use his cell phone. "Jake, it's Mel. The boys and I are down at Sherm's bowling alley in the card room. I think you'd better join us." Mel said. "I can be therein twenty minutes." Jake said and immediately hung up. "He's coming. You guys hungry? I'll get Sherm to get us some pizza and chicken wings." Mel told them. They all nodded agreement. Jake arrived in time to get in on the food and ordered a beer. "What's the emergency?" He asked somberly. "We just remembered those two tourists vacationing in Cuba and thought we should check on them. They may need different accommodations." Nate said chuckling at his humor. "Oh crap, I can't believe I forgot about them. Maybe we can get Mulligan to pick them up without too much commotion." Jake said. "Mulligan didn't have anything to do with getting them there. It was the Coast Guard or the DEA. I don't know who actually

delivered them." Mel added. "It may be a lot tougher to get them out than it was to get them in but I don't think we can afford to just ignore them. Sooner or later someone is going to want to know who they are and how they got there." Nate said. "We will have to talk to the DEA guys and find out what story they used to get them held there. For all we know the Coast Guard might have taken them there as prisoners of war." Mel added. "My guess is the Coast Guard. The DEA wouldn't normally take drug smugglers to a military compound." Jake said. "I'll contact the commander we dealt with and see if I'm right. If I am, we can probably get him to pick them back up for us or help me come up with a way to get them released to us." He added, standing up to leave. The rest finished their drinks and the remains of the pizza and then left. Jake went home and made plans to go to Key West and visit the Coast Guard. He booked the earliest flight to Miami for the next morning. He wanted to drive over and visit with major Sample before heading on down to Key West. The flight was uneventful but the drive to the air base was hectic with traffic jams and the usual morning rush. He called ahead and made sure Major Sample would be able to meet with him. When he got to the base the major was waiting for him at the guard post like before. He got in the rental car with Jake and instructed him to go back out and drive to a nearby Ihop. "I don't want anyone asking about you at the base."

he explained as they drove. "Did you get any flack about the two visitors I left with you last time?" Jake asked. "No one with any rank higher than me knew anything about that, so no worries there." He replied. When they got to the restaurant and ordered breakfast he asked Jake what was going on this time. "I had two terrorists that were involved in the previous event placed in custody at Gitmo. I need to get them out without causing any fuss. I was hoping you could assist me." Jake told him. "How did you get them in there?"

Sample asked. "The Coast Guard delivered them for me. I think I can get them to get them out of Gitmo but I need to move them to New Mexico." Jake responded. "And you want me to arrange transportation." Sample said. "That's the idea. Can you handle it without causing suspicion?" "Maybe I can arrange to get them out of Cuba and on their way to New Mexico without involving the Coast Guard. I have a good contact at the prison camp. I'll see if he can arrange the paper work. He will be glad to get them out of his hair and not have to explain where they came from or that they were even there. Do you want Mulligan to have them?" Jake was genuinely surprised that Sample knew about Mulligan. "That is exactly what I need. I won't ask how you know him." Jake replied.

"Leave it to me. You don't need to be any further involved. Will Mulligan know what you want done with them?" He asked. "He knows." Jake replied, shaking Sample's hand.

"You go on back home and leave it to me. I will have my orderly pick me up here in a little while." He ordered more coffee and opened up the morning paper as Jake walked out to the car.

"I can't believe what just happened. There are a lot more patriots in this country than I would have imagined." He thought to himself.

CHAPTER FIFTY TWO

He was greatly relieved on the way to the airport but began worrying again on the return flight. He wanted to protect Doug but didn't want to give up his operation. He knew that something ugly might happen without his team to intercept terror plots. He decided to call Doug as soon as he landed. "We need to meet. When can you be at the hotel?" Jake asked. "I can be there by three." Was Doug's answer. When Jake arrived Doug was already in the room and had poured two large drinks. "I have to cut off your funding.

Senator Hadley has stirred up a couple of other committee members and they are secretly snooping into Homeland Security's finances. They won't find anything there because I have been funding your operation from a completely different source. We can't take the risk any longer. Sooner or later they will stumble onto our operation." Doug explained. "I have already begun cleaning up. I sent the troops on vacation and cleared out the office.

As soon as the two prisoners are gone from Gitmo there will be no evidence of our operation left to worry about. I have that under control and it should be taken care of in the next few days." Jake assured him. "This will be our last meeting here. I have to make this disappear as well. We'll keep in touch the same as we have been. I may come up with another way to integrate your guys into something else later but for now we are out of business." Doug said, finishing his drink. They shook hands and left by the usual procedure. Jake decided to call everyone together and give them the news in person. He called Mel first. "I'll get everyone together. Let me call Joseph and see if we can use his place. I'll get back to

you as soon as I know." Mel told him. "Of course we can meet at
my office. Call me when you have everyone contacted. I'll call
Naomi myself." Joseph told Mel when he called. By five thirty
everyone was at Joseph's office waiting for Jake.

"I had a feeling this was about to come to and end. Otherwise,
Jake wouldn't have closed up shop." Nate said. "You're probably
right. With mid-term elections coming up Doug has to be under a
lot of pressure. Maybe he decided it's too risky to continue." Ty
added.

Jake tapped once on the door and then entered. "I guess you've all
figured out what I'm about to tell you, but here it is anyway." He
began. "As of right now we are finished.

Doug has informed me that he has to cut off our funding. I have
enough in the budget to give everyone four months pay. That
wipes out our bank account. I hate to do it but I

guess we have to fade away. I suggest everyone get out of New
York and stay away from any of our contacts in the FBI or the
other intelligence services for now. If things change after the
elections I may have something else for us. Until then, keep a low
profile and stay in contact with me by e-mail. It has been a real
pleasure to work with all of you and I know we made a difference.
You can all be proud of what we have accomplished." When he
finished he shook everyone's hand and left before anyone could
see the tears forming in his eyes. "He's taking it really hard. I've
never seen Jake this upset." Mel said to no on in particular. One by
one they shook each others hands and all hugged Naomi before
leaving.

CHAPTER FIFTY THREE

Joseph asked Ron to stay behind. He and Naomi were the last to
leave. Joseph told Naomi he would call her later. "If you don't
have any immediate plans, I want to offer you a job working with
me." He told Ron. "I don't have anything planned for now. I had
hoped this thing would last a while longer. The country needs the

kind of protection we were providing, even if they don't realize it." Ron replied. "What do you have in mind?"

He asked. "I am going to go to Dubai to spend some time with Hafid. I would like you to come along and help me reorganize the business. Hafid is ready to step down and I could really use your help. I need someone I can trust who understands both the Arab and American languages and business practices. Hafid likes you. I have never seen him warm up to a foreigner the way he did with you. He has a lot of new people working for him since my father died. I don't know any of them well enough to trust them with some of the transactions that go on in this business. I fear that extremists could infiltrate the company and Hafid would not recognize the threat. You could do background checks and

weed out anyone suspicious before they become a problem. Much of the money from the business has been set aside in safe haven banks around the world and no one but Hafid knows how to access it. If anything happens to him before he shares that information with me I would have no way to obtain those funds. I know that you have certain expertise in that area that would be very valuable to me. I can pay you much more than you have ever earned before. What do you say? Are you in?" He asked as he passed a piece of paper with a figure on it to Ron. Ron's face lit up in surprise when he saw the figure. "I'm your man, Joseph. When do you want to go?" He asked with genuine excitement. "I need to tie up some loose ends here in New York for a couple of days. Let's plan on leaving Sunday.

Pack for an extended stay. I don't know when we will be back." Joseph replied. When Ron left, Joseph phoned Naomi. "Can I pick you up for dinner around eight o'clock?" He asked. "Certainly, what should I wear?" She asked. "Something dressy, I have a table reserved at Club 24." He replied. When he arrived at her apartment Joseph was surprised at how Spartan it was. She must have noticed his surprise. "My job usually keeps me traveling so I don't do much with my living quarters." She said barely hiding her embarrassment. "You look fantastic." He said, giving her an appraising look. She did a full turn in her black sheath dress, showing off her stunning figure. "I'm as ready as I'm going to get." She said. When they arrived at the club the maitre'd had a table ready for them. Joseph and his brother had been regular diners here before 911 and kept a table reserved. "I have never been in here. Is the food as good as people claim?" She asked.

"I'm sure you will enjoy it. I have had many wonderful meals here. It was my brother's favorite place." Joseph replied. Naomi could see that the memories were causing some emotional discomfort for him. The waiter came over and took their wine order and

presented them with the menus. A second waiter recited the evening's specials. "Why don't you order for both of us?" Naomi suggested. Joseph agreed and ordered a splendid meal. They carried on a quiet conversation over their food and both began to relax.

Joseph told her about his plan to go to Dubai and that he was taking Ron with him. She was somewhat surprised but agreed that it sounded like a good idea. "Ron is very competent with computers and business arrangements besides being a great investigator."

She said. "And you couldn't ask for a better bodyguard if you ever need one." She added.

"My feelings exactly." Joseph agreed. Then he surprised her again. "Why don't you move into my condo while we are away? I'm sure Jake will have to close up your other apartment and I really don't like leaving the place vacant while I'm out of the country."

"I think you are trying to get me out of my meager lodgings. Are you trying to spoil me?"

she asked with a pleasant smile. "Maybe, just a little. I'll admit I wasn't too impressed with your present surroundings. But my motives are as stated. You keep an eye on my place while I'm away and save your rent money for other things. We both win." He said, matching her smile. "What happens to me when you return?"

She asked. "I'm sure we can work something out." He said still smiling. "Have you decided what to do about your career?" He asked. "Yes, I'm going to return to work with the CIA but I'm going to request a position here as an interpreter. I'm not ready to go into field work again.

Besides, it looks like I'm moving up in the world. I wouldn't want to travel now that I have an uptown address." She said, laughing. They finished their dessert and went out to the car. He drove her back to her place and she invited him in. When they stepped inside Naomi wrapped Joseph in a full body embrace. He returned the emotion and kissed her deeply, pressing against her and pulling her into him tightly. "Why don't you grab what

you need for morning and come with me to my place." He whispered, breathing heavily.

"All right, just let me have a moment." She replied, her voice husky with desire. She slipped some toiletries, a change of clothes and her sexiest lingerie into an overnight bag and then returned to where she left him standing. They repeated the embrace and deep kissing and then hurried out to his car. She leaned over to rest her head on his shoulder for the short drive to his condo. They both remained quiet on the ride. Joseph felt light headed and continued to breath heavily, thinking about how long it had been since he felt this way. As soon as they entered the apartment they came together again, this time the kissing was more aggressive on both parts. Naomi began undoing his shirt and Joseph whispered that he hadn't been with a woman since his wife was killed. Naomi ignored his words and continued removing his clothes and then slid the straps off her shoulders and dropped the evening dress to the floor. He slowly reached behind her and removed her bra as she stepped out of her panties. They somehow managed to make it into his bedroom and onto the bed before continuing their passionate kissing. She rolled over on top of him and guided him into her. They moaned with excitement as she gradually increased her rhythm until they were both moving at a frantic pace with him thrusting upward to meet her gyrating hip movements. They reached a soaring climax at the same time and then lay silently in each other's arms for a long while. They made love twice more without speaking and then fell into a deep sleep still in each other's arms. Joseph awoke to the smell of coffee and the sound of her rustling around in his kitchen. He grabbed a robe and stepped into the kitchen. She was facing the counter waiting for the coffee to finish brewing. She had on a sheer lacy black robe over a matching bra and thong. He slipped up behind her and wrapped his arms around her just as she turned to

meet him. They held each other in this embrace for a few moments, neither ready to speak. Finally she said "Good morning, are you ready for coffee?" "I'd love some" he said, slowly letting her go.

She poured two cups and joined him at the small round kitchen table. "Do you have any pressing plans for today?" He asked. "Not really, what do you have in mind?" She replied. "If you're up for it, I thought we could move you out of your place and into here today. Ron and I are booked to leave on Sunday so that only gives us today and tomorrow to get it done." He explained. "That works fine for me. It won't take long to pack up. I never really moved in there with the idea of staying, so there isn't much to move. I rented it furnished so it's just my personal stuff. Then we can have the rest of the day for other things." She said with a coy grin.

CHAPTER FIFTY FOUR

Ron Pierce spent the day with his sister and her family in Connecticut. He gave her the keys and the alarm code for his apartment. She had agreed to look after the place while he was away and planned to use it whenever they wanted to spend a night or a weekend in the City. Joseph and Naomi packed her belongings and made three trips to get it all into Joseph's condo. She made arrangements with the rental manager to sub-let her apartment and he had several applicants looking for a place like hers.

On Sunday Naomi drove Joseph to the airport where he found Ron waiting at the check in counter. They kept their goodbyes at the curbside short and sweet. He promised to call regularly and she did the same. He watched from the curb while she drove away in his car and then went in to greet Ron. They checked their baggage and headed for the terminal.

The flight was already boarding when they got to the gate.

CHAPTER FIFTY FIVE

"When can we test the first prototype?" Mahmoud asked through the interpreter. "It will be ready the day after tomorrow. He wants the second progress payment in cash, now."

was the reply. "I want to see how powerful it is before I give him any more money."

Mahmoud said angrily. When the interpreter relayed this information to the Chinese man, he looked Mahmoud in the eye with his face barely an inch away and said in English

"Fuck you, asshole. You pay now or get the fuck out of here!" A very large man stepped into the room and pointed an automatic rifle at Mahmoud and his two partners. The interpreter moved out of the line of fire and stood behind the large bodyguard. Rashid grabbed Mahmoud by both arms and held him still. "We are here to buy his material, not start a fight over the money with the supplier. Pay him. Now!" He rasped in his ear, tightening his grip. Mahmoud relaxed his stare and shook off Rashid's hands. He carefully reached back to get the briefcase from Ahmed who was visibly shaken. "I must have misunderstood our agreement. Here is the second payment." He said as he handed over a large envelope stuffed with money. Chen Lee took the envelope and pulled out the bills. He counted them carefully while his bodyguard continued to keep his weapon pointed at the Muslims. Without a word, only a small bow, he turned and went out to the other room. He returned seconds later with an ordinary looking hard sided suitcase. It was an exact replica of the ones sold everywhere in the world under various brand names.

"This bag is ready now but I need tomorrow to finish the detonator assembly. We will take it out to sea on my boat for the test. We cannot risk being seen with an explosive device anywhere around Shanghai. The British, Americans and Israelis all have spies here as well as many others. Have no fear; you will be pleased with the power of these

devices." With that he turned and left again. The bodyguard spoke rapidly to the interpreter in Cantonese and waved them out of the room. "We are safe to leave. He wants us to stay away tomorrow and return on Wednesday for the test." He informed the Muslims in Arabic. The three Arabs got in their rented car and drove off toward their hotel. David Wong, the interpreter went back inside to meet with Chen Lee before calling a cab for himself. "They are very evil men but they are well financed." He told Chen. "As long as they pay in cash I don't give a damn what they do. But I won't stand for any more crap about the money. They can't get what I have anywhere else. After the test we are going to raise the final price. They will agree or we will leave them to the sharks." He said without any facial expression. David Wong had worked as a go-between for Chen before and had a healthy respect for what would happen to anyone who dared cross the most powerful mob boss in Shanghai. He decided he would not warn the Arabs about the intended price increase. He was much more afraid of Chen Lee.

CHAPTER FIFTY SIX

Joseph and Ron arrived in Dubai City tired from the flight but excited abut the prospect of working together on Joseph's company. They checked into the Hyatt Regency as before and went directly to their rooms. Ron made a call to Sean Moore at the American Embassy and was told that Sean was not in. He didn't leave any message. He decided he would try again in the morning. Joseph phoned Hafid and made arrangements to meet with him at lunch time.

CHAPTER FIFTY SEVEN

Rashid was angry with Mahmoud. "You could have gotten us killed back there. We need to maintain good relations with this man. He has the technology we require to accomplish

our objective. If you ever do anything like that again I will kill you myself." He admonished. "I don't trust that infidel. How do you know he won't take our money and then murder us?" Mahmoud asked, still fuming. "We are paying him one half after the test is successful and the rest upon delivery of the entire shipment. If he wanted to kill and rob us he could have done so today. I will hear no more about it. Do you understand?

Rashid said, leaving no room for a reply. "I don't see how these things can get through the x-ray machines and explosive sniffing dogs at an airport. Won't the dogs or the machines detect the explosives? And how will he disguise the detonators or timers so the scanners won't pick them up?" Ahmed asked. "He won't tell us how it is done, only that we can check these in as luggage and then have them explode later at altitude. Perhaps we will learn how they work once we get the finished product to our safe house in London. We have experts who may be able to copy them. For now he holds all the cards." Rashid replied. They drove toward the old city and went to visit the Fuyou Lu Mosque in the Yuyuan district. "This is the oldest Mosque in Singapore" Rashid told the others. They went in for prayers and then took a tour of the premises. "I had no idea there was such a place as this among these wretched infidels." Ahmed told the others. He was visibly impressed with the holy place. They went directly back to their hotel to rest and wait for the meeting with Chen Lee. They spent the next day sightseeing around Singapore and visited the other large Mosque, Xiaotaoyuan.

CHAPTER FIFTY EIGHT

"How are you coming with the detonation circuits?" Chen Lee asked the man in the white lab coat. "I have determined the method and I am nearly ready to try it here in the lab."

He replied. "You are a true genius, Lin Yuang. No one will suspect these bags. There is

no evidence of any mechanical or electrical device inside." Chen said, looking at the x-ray screen as the prototype bag passed through. "That is because there are no mechanical or electrical parts in there. It is entirely a chemical process. When the air pressure lessens as the altitude increases the first chemical hidden here in the handle begins to migrate into this area where the chrome strips surround the perimeter. When that mixing is complete in several hours it is ready for the second chemical to enter from this handle.

This happens when the air pressure increases on the way down to the landing." He said, smiling broadly. "That means the explosions will take place over a populated area at or near the airport!" Chen exclaimed "You are correct. The pressure should be perfect to initiate the explosions when the plane is below ten thousand feet." Lin explained. "What kind of explosive power will these things have?" Chen asked. "My new, odorless explosive has about the same energy as Semtex. I am packing in about 8mm of it between the inner and outer shell of the suitcase, all the way around. One such as this will cause a huge explosion. If you place two in each airplane it should blow the fuselage apart and ignite the fuel tanks. I believe there will be total destruction of it before it reaches the ground. The fallout from the burning debris will cause untold damage on whatever it lands on." He continued. "That should be enough to satisfy these bloodthirsty Jihadists."

Chen added. "I am ready to try the detonation process now. Watch the vials in the pressure chamber." Lin said. On the bench he had constructed a pressure chamber with transparent sides made of thick Lexan. He suspended the first and second chemicals above a layer of the explosive material. He used a minute amount of explosive material.

Just enough to show how it worked without destroying the pressure chamber. While Chen watched Lin turned on the vacuum pump and simulated the pressure drop expected at

25,000 feet. As the dials reached the prescribed level, the first chemical began dripping out of its vial and started mixing with the explosive at the bottom of the chamber. Then Lin began slowly increasing the pressure to simulate the descent for landing. When the second chemical dripped onto the explosive mixture it went off with a loud "whump" and a very bright light. The sides of the chamber were left cloudy but not broken. Chen and Lin shouted and clapped with glee at the obvious success of the invention. "How are we going to simulate this for our buyers without exposing your secrets?" Chen asked. "I will mix the first chemical before the bag leaves here. You place these lead weights in the bag and throw it overboard. When it sinks to the proper depth the pressure will cause it to explode. The force will definitely impress your buyers." Lin explained. "I would like to dress as a seaman and come along for this demonstration. They won't notice me and I will get to witness the results first hand." He added. "Excellent idea Lin. You are indeed a genius." Chen said smiling.

CHAPTER FIFTY NINE

David Wong waited in the lobby for the Arabs and told them he had a car outside that would take them to the port. He drove them to the marina where Chen Lee kept his yacht.

It was a beautiful 160' ship capable of extended sea travel. It was anchored off the quay and they took a motor launch piloted by a uniformed bosun's mate out to the ship. As soon as they were aboard David led them to the main saloon where they found Chen Lee and his bodyguard waiting. "Make yourselves comfortable gentlemen. It will take about two hours to reach our destination." He told them in English. They were served Tea and sandwiches by a pair of uniformed young ladies and passed the time talking among themselves. Chen had left them in the company of the young ladies and the giant

bodyguard who totally ignored them. The sea was calm and the ride quite smooth. About two hours into the voyage Chen appeared and the boat began to slow and finally stopped.

"If you will join me at the stern we will demonstrate the product now." He explained. He led them to the fan tail where a uniformed seaman was waiting with the suitcase sitting beside him on the deck. There was a long table set up at one side with an x-ray machine and an explosive detector probe sitting on top. The seaman put the suitcase up on the table and opened it for all to see. He let them all inspect it. Rashid stuck his nose up close and tried to detect any chemical odor. Satisfied, he nodded to Chen who instructed the seaman to place the weights inside and close it up. They all watched as the man at the table passed the wand over the bag. No explosives were detected. Then he passed it through the x-ray machine for all to see. It appeared to be only a normal bag with the small weights inside. Mahmoud started to protest that the machines were rigged but Rashid stopped him with a cold stare. "You do the honors." Chen said as he handed the suitcase to Mahmoud and nodded at the rail. Mahmoud held the bag up to his nose for a few moments and then tossed it over the side. It began sinking immediately. They all watched for a few moments and then all but Chen and his men were blown off their feet by the force of the blast. Chen and company were holding onto the railing and laughing at the fallen Arabs. Rashid was the first to gain his feet. "That was very impressive Mr. Lee.

I believe we are in business." He said, bowing in oriental fashion to his host. Mahmoud helped Ahmed to his feet and they both looked at Rashid in amazement before smiling widely and slapping each other on the back. "Shall we return to the saloon and continue our arrangements then?" Chen Lee asked gesturing to them to follow the bodyguard.

Behind them at the rail Lin Yuang grinned to himself and headed down the other side of the deck.

"I believe you asked for twenty of these exquisite examples of Chinese craftsmanship."

Chen Lee began. Rashid spoke for the others. "We will require twice that many if you can provide them." He said. "Excellent. We have decided they will cost $50,000 each, above the initial deposit you have already paid. One half today in cash and the other half wired to a numbered account when the shipment has left Shanghai." Chen explained.

"That will be satisfactory, if you can provide them within thirty days." Rashid said to the amazement of Mahmoud and Ahmed. "I do not have one million in cash with me. I can arrange to have it by tomorrow if that is acceptable." He added. "Tomorrow will be fine.

You can give it to Mr. Wong by three o'clock. He will come to your hotel for it.

However, if you don't come through by three o'clock, you will not see four o'clock.

Enjoy the ride back gentlemen. It has been my pleasure to serve you." He walked out to the foredeck and boarded his helicopter for the trip back to Singapore. The extra large bodyguard remained in the saloon with them. Rashid's stone cold stare kept the others from talking. They rode the entire way back to port in silence. In the helicopter Lin Yuang and Chen Lee discussed how to get forty of the cases ready to ship in thirty days.

"I have enough chemicals on hand to make the necessary amount of explosives for this shipment and the detonation mixtures. The problem will be getting the cases modified to accept the chemicals." Lin explained. "Let me worry about that. I can push the manufacturer to get them ready in a few days. He will do as I ask." Chen said.

"I will return in a few hours. Stay in the hotel and be able to take my call if I need you."

Rashid told the others. He had to go to several banks to get the necessary cash. He would

have the funds wired in smaller amounts to make it easier to obtain cash. Chen had demanded US funds be used exclusively. He had made the calls to get the transfers underway as early as possible.

Unfortunately, it would take past noon for them to arrive in Singapore. That meant he had to wait a maddeningly long time and then cover most of metropolitan Singapore to get all the funds before three pm. He realized shortly after leaving the first bank that he was being followed. He hoped it was just Chen's men keeping an eye on him. He was completely vulnerable if they intended to rob him. He paused long enough at one bank to phone Ahmed at the hotel. He told Ahmed about being followed. Ahmed replied that he had noticed men hanging around the hotel on their floor and by all the exits. He said they had made no effort to conceal themselves or pretend they weren't watching him. "I think they are just there to reinforce Chen's threat about not getting the money on time. He probably fears that we would betray him in some way. Just mind your business and keep one of you in the room at all times. I should be there with a few minutes to spare if the taxi can get through the traffic." Rashid explained. At precisely two thirty David Wong knocked on the door to the Arab's room.

Mahmoud let him in and asked him to take a seat. "Would you like something to drink? I can have room service bring something. Rashid will be here any moment." He said.

David declined the drink and sat in a chair near the window to the balcony. "Mr. Lee is anxious to conclude your arrangement. He wanted me to inform you that the shipment will be ready in thirty days or less. However, you realize that it must be shipped by sea. It cannot be shipped by air for obvious reasons." David explained with a slight chuckle. He had barely finished his statement when Rashid entered carrying two stainless steel brief cases. He appeared calm but the sweat on his forehead betrayed the fear he had been

fighting while hurrying to get the cash back to the hotel on time. "I have the cash, in full.

Can Mr. Lee provide the product on schedule?" He asked. "I was just explaining to your associate that the product will be ready to ship in thirty days or less but will have to go by sea. You understand that he cannot ship this product by air." David repeated. "I had already assumed that. How will it get through customs in England?" Rashid asked. "Mr.

Lee ships many products from Shanghai to London. Your product will be contained within a shipment of identical items bound for his UK distributor. You will be informed when you can pick it up in the London area." He said and handed a disposable cell phone to Rashid. "The only call you will get will be on this phone. It will give you the time and location where you can receive your goods." He added. Rashid removed a bag of cash from the room safe and added it to one of the cases. "The second half of this payment will be wired when I know the product has been loaded on a ship bound for England. I have the account numbers memorized." He said as he handed over the two brief cases.

David gave them an exaggerated Asian bow and walked to the door. Mahmoud held it open for him. "Allahu Akbar" he said grinning as he went out. He was joined in the hallway by Chen's bodyguard.

CHAPTER SIXTY

Inside the room Rashid heaved a sigh of relief. "Arrogant little shit." Mahmoud said as he watched David and his big companion enter the elevator. "As long as the products do their job it is worth putting up with these wretched vermin. No one else has come up with a better way to get bombs onto airlines." Rashid said. "How do you think he made it work?" Ahmed asked. "It has to be pressure activated some way that doesn't require electrical or mechanical devices. Whoever designed it is definitely a genius." Rashid

replied. "I guess if we get them on enough planes it won't matter how they work, only that they do the job." Mahmoud added. "Imagine twenty or more planes exploding over US airports on the same day. No one will ever want to fly again. If they can't figure out how it happened there will be chaos and panic like the world has never seen." He added.

"It will take a lot of planning to get them on the right planes. If one or two go off early they will cancel all flights and start looking for the source." Ahmed reasoned. "Even if that happens, the damage to the US and UK economies will be enormous. We will probably have to send some of them to European countries in order to get as many as possible to explode at about the same time. Everyone will feel the power of Allah's warriors. We can take part of them to other airports in England as well as France and Germany. Our great leader will give us the way. We must be patient and get it right the first time." Rashid explained. "It will require a great number of martyrs and very good coordination." Mahmoud added. "We must check out now and get to the airport. I can't get away from this place soon enough." Rashid said. They quickly packed their bags and prepared to leave. Before leaving they wiped everything down to remove fingerprints.

They had barely closed the elevator door before two men slipped into the room they had just left. They quickly dusted the entire suite including the bathroom and closet. "I have several full prints and a couple of partials from the bathroom" one of the men said. "I have some partials from the chairs and the window sill here." The other replied. "They didn't find the telephone bug, it's still in here. I wonder why it didn't transmit." He added, pocketing the device. "Let's get out of here and get this stuff to the lab." The other man said as he cracked the door to look into the hallway. They left quickly by the stairs and were seen by no one. When the Muslims arrived at the airport they didn't notice the

car that had followed their cab the entire way. There were two men inside. One got out carrying a briefcase and followed the three Arabs to the ticket counter. He stayed behind a pair of tourists and watched as Rashid purchased the tickets. Satisfied he knew their destination he walked away toward the rest room. He saw that they hadn't noticed him so he turned and walked out of the terminal to where the other man was waiting in the car.

CHAPTER SIXTY ONE

136

"They're going to London. They checked their bags and didn't carry anything on that I could see." he said to the driver. "Let's check with Perry and see where their Chinese companions went" the driver said. "Perry this is Clay, are you still with them?" "They went into a restaurant in the old city. I'm sure it belongs to Chen Lee. The big guy driving is one of Lee's body guards. The other is David Wong. He works as a translator for the government when he isn't running errands for Lee." Perry replied on the two-way.

"OK let them go for now. You don't want any of Lee's men to spot you following them.

Meet us back at the consulate in an hour." Clay instructed. Clay Strong was head of station for the CIA in Singapore. His red hair and boyish freckled face made him appear years younger than his true age. He had been one of the CIA's most effective operatives during the cold war. He conducted many dangerous missions in East Germany and was fluent in German as well as Russian and Polish. His current posting in Singapore had kept him busy tracking illegal arms traffic between China and the Middle Eastern terrorists.

He had tried for years to catch Chen Lee in the act of supplying illegal arms with only moderate success. Some small shipments had been intercepted but the trail back to Lee

was never proven. Local Chinese police officials were either paid off or intimidated by the powerful gangs controlled by Lee and were no help in either case. He felt certain these Arabs were buying arms from Lee but the bug he had placed in their hotel room failed to transmit so he had no proof of what kind of deal was being made. His biggest fear was that sooner or later a nuclear device would make its way into terrorist hands. He decided to send a message to London to have the men followed when they landed. Maybe it would give them some idea where whatever they were buying would wind up. When they arrived back at the US embassy, Perry Dolan was waiting for them in the situation room on the second floor. "Let's get a list of the companies that we know are controlled by Chen Lee and see which ones have shipped anything to England, say in the last six months" Clay instructed him. "Stan, I want you to do a thorough background check on David Wong. I want to know everything we can about him and any contacts he has in England or the Middle East. Where did he learn Arabic, for instance?" He told the man who had been his driver. Stan Gumpertz had been in Singapore for years and knew his way around town as well as any foreigner could. He had formed some alliances and friendships among the local police and knew fairly well which ones would cooperate and which ones would run straight to Chen Lee if they caught him snooping around. He would do the usual computer investigations first and then do some discrete enquiries with his local contacts in person. Since the Singapore government had banned gambling except at the horse track, gangsters like Chen Lee had opened many underground gambling dens and some exclusive gambling ships. Stan spoke both Mandarin and Cantonese like a native and was able to circulate among the gambling establishments usually posing as a sailor out for a good time. Over the years he had made friends with

and was accepted by some of the seedier gamblers from the waterfront bars. He was careful not to ask questions, but just listened to the conversations around him. Most people he met did not know he spoke or understood their language. If he used Chinese he did it crudely as if he just knew a few words and expressions. He had used this tactic many times and was now able to get on board any of the gambling ships with little or no trouble. He intended to hang out on some of Chen Lee's boats to see if he could pick up anything on David Wong or any gossip concerning the Arabs.

CHAPTER SIXTY TWO

Joseph and Ron had moved into the compound at Hafid's per his request and had begun auditing the company books in preparation for Joseph to assume control. Ron was busy gathering information on the employees and doing background checks. Some of Hafid's help had been with him for years but many others had joined the company since Joseph had left. Ron started with the newest ones and worked his way down the list to the older hands. There were many different nationalities working there. The company did business worldwide, arranging trades, handling shipping and dealing in oil leases. Much of what passed through the Port of Dubai was in some way connected with the Ibrahim Trading Company. Even more business was conducted around the globe that never came anywhere near the home port. Ron was completely amazed at the volume of business handled by the company. So far most of the people he had checked out had legitimate backgrounds including education at distinguished universities in the US and Europe. He had found some that did not have such clear histories. He made a list of these and decided to go see Sean Moore at the American embassy for some help investigating them. He phoned first and made an appointment to meet Sean for lunch near the embassy. "How's

the new job going?" Sean asked. "Great. I never thought I would have a civilian job again. I'm beginning to enjoy it." Ron replied. "So what can I do for you?" Sean asked.

"I'm doing deep background checks on the employees. Most of them check out but I have a couple of names I'd like your help with." "Let me have a look at your list and any information you already have on them. I'll see what I can do. By the way, I did some looking at Ibrahim Trading's dealings after you told me you were going to work there.

Your buddy is about to become a billionaire if he takes over the whole enchilada." Sean said. "Did you find anything that looked out of place?" Ron inquired. "Nothing definite but they do a lot of trading from China to the Middle East. Some of their customers are on my watch list for illegal arms but we haven't caught them with the goods. Even if Ibrahim sets up the trades they may not know what is really in the containers when they ship. Maybe we can help each other. You keep an eye on the trading from the inside while I check out these employees. Maybe there's something going on. Maybe not." He added. When they finished lunch they went outside where Ron slipped a manila envelope into

Sean's hands as he got into his car. "Keep in touch." Ron said as he pulled his car away from the curb.

CHAPTER SIXTY THREE

Rashid, Mahmoud and Ahmed, traveling on British passports had no problem getting through customs at Heathrow. There was a car waiting for them when they exited the terminal. "Did everything go as planned?" the driver asked as he pulled away from the airport. "It all went as planned, except for them doubling the price at the end." Rashid replied. "We have much work to do to plan all the flights that we want to attack. It will be very complicated. Have you gotten all the flight schedules for planes leaving Europe for

the U.S.?" He asked. "We have most of it copied from the computer schedules listed on the internet. However there is no accounting for canceled and rescheduled flights this far in advance. I believe the larger problem will be getting the luggage safely to all the passengers first before we can purchase the tickets. Since we can't just ship them, they will have to be delivered by ground and water transport. It will be no easy task." The driver replied. Two cars behind them CIA agent Mick Randall watched from a Mini Cooper.

"I have them two cars ahead of me. They're in a blue Vauxhall sedan. The driver is wearing an Arab headdress and a full beard, probably an Imam. London police have identified the plates as belonging to Abdullah Al Rahman. His address is a mosque in Blackburn. I'll stay with them until they turn off the M6 and then you can pick them up."

He said over the radio to Rory Wells, his British counterpart several cars behind in a Fiat van. "O.K. Mick, I'll stay a mile or so behind. If you run out of cover just pull over at the next service plaza and I'll pick them up from there." Rory replied. Clay Strong had requested that Mick follow these suspects to see where they went and who they met with.

Mick had enlisted Rory to assist in the surveillance. They had worked together many times lately looking into suspected terror organizations within the Islamic community in the UK. The trip to Blackburn went agonizingly slow but uneventful. The Arabs pulled off for fuel once and a restroom stop another time. Both times Rory and Mick changed places maintaining surveillance from a safe distance. The trip ended at the Makkee Masjid mosque on North Wimberly Street, in Blackburn. Rory was nearest to them when they exited the car and entered the building. He radioed Mick and they agreed to meet at a transport café out on Preston New Road to eat dinner and decide whether to stay in

Blackburn or return to London. Mick decided to find a room for a few days and keep an eye on the mosque and the Imam's car. Rory took off for the long drive back to London.

After checking into a room near the café Mick sent an e-mail to Clay Strong in Singapore to report the location of the Arabs and request advice on what to do next. When the reply came, Clay thanked him for his work and asked him to attempt to place a gps locator on the Imam's car. Mick said he would give it a try, the car was parked in the lot by the mosque and not in a garage. After midnight he drove to an area a couple of blocks away from the mosque and walked down to the parking lot. The lighting at the mosque was aimed more at the building than the lot and he had no trouble making his way unnoticed to the car. He placed the locator under the rear bumper and walked quietly back to his car. Once inside he turned on the receiving unit and saw that the transmitter was working perfectly. Satisfied, he drove to his room and went to bed. The next two days and nights he watched the mosque from a distance and kept an eye on the locator. The car never left the lot and he never saw any of the Arabs outside the mosque. Inside the mosque Rashid and the others kept busy working on airline schedules and recruiting plans for the attack.

"Al Zwahiri insists that we coordinate the flights to maximize the effect over U.S.

airports. He adds that we must be patient and strive for perfection in our timing. When it happens is not as important as having as many planes as possible explode on the same day. If any one goes off before the others are in the air, chances are that they will cancel all other flights. If they all are airborne it won't matter. They will explode wherever they try to land. All the flights must be direct to US destinations. If we get our passengers on flights that leave at approximately the same time from European or Asian cities they all will be in the air for many hours before the first ones detonate. After that it will be too

late even if they try to cancel all the remaining flights. Every one that gets in the air will blow up somewhere when it tries to land." Rashid told the others before burning the message from Al Zwahiri.

CHAPTER SIXTY FOUR

At the request of Stan Gumpertz the computer geeks at the US Embassy in Singapore had done an exhaustive background search on David Wong and his family. "It turns out our David Wong is the son of Chinese diplomats. They lived in Baghdad for years when David and his younger brother, Dennis, were growing up. Apparently they learned Arabic while they were there. David has a job with the Chinese embassy here in Singapore as an interpreter and business liaison. He moonlights for Chen Lee on the side. He must be the connection to the Arabic world for Chen and probably the Chinese government as well.

Who knows what they are getting from China." Stan told Clay. "Where did the brother wind up?" Clay wondered. "He works for an international trading company based in Dubai, Ibrahim Trading." Stan replied. "Their parents have gone back to Beijing." He added. "I think I'll get in touch with Sean Moore in Dubai. Maybe he can see what the other Mr. Wong is up to." Clay decided. "I'll hit a few of my favorite low places and see what else I can learn about David Wong. I might be able to find him among the gamblers and follow him a while. We'll see what else he is into. Maybe I can catch him at something that will let us squeeze him for more information." Stan said. "Just be careful.

If Chen finds out we are looking at Wong, he might eliminate him or both of you. Don't underestimate the range of his power. You never know who is on his payroll or under his

influence, he has his fingers in everything around here." Clay reminded Stan. Later that evening Stan took a cab down to the harbor front area. His dark complexion and black hair allowed him to pass as a seaman of Greek or Arab ancestry. He had a full mustache and two days growth of dark beard on his rugged face. His clothes matched that of other men in the area who came off merchant ships to spend time in the port city. He slipped in and out of the bars along the harbor front area, checking out the illegal gambling dens but finding no sign of David Wong. He decided to head up to Chinatown and try his luck there. He knew it was a dangerous place to be seen snooping around and was careful not to stay too long in one place or ask any questions. He had lost a little money in some of the lower class places but still had seen no sign of Wong. His luck changed when he entered one of the newer clubs. He spotted David Wong and what appeared to be a couple of Chen's henchmen along with three young ladies. They were all dressed in nicer clothing and the women were wearing expensive jewelry. He passed by them on his way inside. They went out and got into a waiting limo. He barely glanced their way and made his way to the bar. He ordered a drink and watched the crowd for a while from his bar stool and then left the way he came in. He decided to call it a night now that he knew where to look for Wong. He would come back another time dressed more appropriately and see if he could follow his target to one of the gambling boats or another upscale nightclub.

Clay sent an inquiry about Dennis Wong to Sean Moore by diplomatic courier. Sean read it and decided to talk to Ron Pierce about Mr. Wong. When Sean called, Ron was looking into some other employee records as well as Dennis Wong's.

"Let's meet somewhere quiet this afternoon. I don't want us seen together too close to your work or the embassy.'' He told Ron. "I know just the place. Meet me in the Indian café on the back side of the market. You know the one. I'll be there about one o'clock."

Ron replied. He took copies of some of the invoices for trade from China to the Middle East that were handled by Wong over the last couple of years and packed them into a brief case. It was nearly twelve thirty so he went directly to his car and drove to the market area. He parked on the front street and walked through the souks and open air vendors to the small café on a back alley. He didn't wait long before Sean arrived and joined him at a table in the back room of the café. No one else was around except the waiter who took their order and left the room through the kitchen. He returned shortly with tea and their lunch order and then disappeared through the kitchen again. "What's your interest in Mr. Wong?" Ron asked, getting right to the point. "We've been tailing his brother in Singapore in conjunction with some kind of arms deal he appears to be involved in with some known Arab terrorists. We don't know exactly what is going down but we suspect it could be part of a terror plot against the British or us. They left Singapore on a flight to London. We tailed them to a mosque in Blackburn and are keeping an eye on them there." He replied. "I see, and you think the brother here might be part of it." "They have to get whatever it is from China or Singapore to wherever they need it and it appears that your Mr. Wong could expedite the shipping. Especially if it has to go to the Middle East or Europe." Sean went on. "I have been looking back into the files on shipments handled by Dennis Wong for the last couple of years. I made copies for you. Maybe you can cross reference the shipments with any arms deals you discovered during that time. He has had pretty much a free hand at arranging deals from

China and Malaysia while working for Ibrahim Trading. The old man extends a lot of trust to his employees. Joseph will be much more careful. That's part of why I'm here."

Ron said as he slipped a large envelope out of the briefcase and handed it to Sean under the table. Sean took it and covered it with the newspaper he was carrying. "Who is working on this in Singapore these days?" He asked. "Stan Gumpertz is doing the legwork and Clay Strong is H.O.S." Sean replied. "I remember Stan, he was one of Mel Denison's trainees. Mel thought very highly of him." Ron added. "He's a smart lad from what Clay has told me, he has good trade craft and is a genuine badass when necessary. I didn't know Mel trained him but that explains a lot." Sean added. "I'll keep an eye on our boy and see if he is working on anything from Singapore or anywhere else in Asia headed for the Middle East or England. Maybe you can intercept the shipment before they get their hands on it." Ron said as he got up to leave. Sean waited about five minutes and then paid the check and left. When Ron returned from his meeting with Sean he went into Joseph's office and closed the door. He filled Joseph in on what he had discussed with Sean. "You think Dennis Wong is mixed up with illegal arms shipping?" Joseph asked. "The CIA has been tailing his brother in Singapore in connection with a recent deal between a Chinese gangster named Chen Lee and some Arab terrorists. They don't know that Dennis has been involved but suspect that he might be helping his brother get things moved from place to place. It certainly won't hurt to keep an eye on him. How much do you know about him?" Ron asked. "He came here after I left, so I really don't know anything about him. I didn't know he had a brother in Singapore. I'm afraid my uncle didn't do much to check him out. He felt he was lucky to find someone who was fluent in Chinese, Arabic and English. His parents are or were respected diplomats.

That's about all we really know about him." Joseph said. "I supplied Sean with some old invoices so they can check out the companies that he arranged trades for in the past. They will find out whether or not he has done anything for his brother through any of Chen Lee's shell companies. We need to watch what he does for now to see if he is connected to this recent deal. Whatever it is, it will need to be shipped from one of Chen's companies to somewhere in England or maybe to the Middle East. The suspects went to England when they left Singapore so it is likely that they want the goods to arrive there."

Ron said. "All of his trades and shipping deals go through our local area network and get recorded on the mainframe in order for any deal to go through this company. If he is doing something on the side he could be using a shell company and some other computer so we wouldn't have any knowledge of it." Joseph said. "With port security tightening in Europe and the US I think he would want the deals to go through here for credibility and ease of passing though customs. Any new company would automatically be suspect, but who knows? We'll have to monitor him and see what turns up." Ron replied. He had checked the employee records and had Wong's address, so he decided he would check it out while Dennis was at work. His employment contract showed that he was single and lived in an apartment building downtown. Ron walked past Wong's work station and verified that he was there and working today then went out and drove downtown. He parked around the block from Wong's building and walked to the parking garage. He entered the building from the garage on the second floor and went directly to number 238. No one was in the hallway and he knocked lightly on the door. No sound came from within so he quickly picked the lock and let himself in. It was a small one bedroom apartment with a kitchenette, a living room and balcony overlooking the downtown area.

It was nicely furnished and had some expensive artwork and what appeared to be professional decorating evident. He went into the bedroom and found a work desk with a computer and printer on it and no paperwork of any kind. Mr. Wong was apparently very tidy. The desk was locked but Ron had no problem opening it. Inside he found a bankbook, some old photographs and a supply of printing paper. No copies of invoices or other business papers. He turned on the computer and was met with a request for a password. He didn't have time to try to bypass the password so he turned it off and went back to the living room. He peeked out into the hallway and seeing no one he quietly left the way he came in. He decided he would install a keystroke recording program on Wong's work station unit to see if he was transferring files to his home computer and would gain his password from that if he was. He was on his way back to the office when he got a call on his satellite phone. It was Jake Powell. "Jake, what's going on back there?" Ron asked, excited to hear from him. "Things have been pretty quiet since you left. The FBI is keeping a lid on the Brooklyn Mosque and the one in Buffalo as well. So far, no new activity from them. Mel and Nate went out to Idaho to hunt elk with Mel's brother and should be back tomorrow. I talked to Doug yesterday. It doesn't look good for getting the group back to work for him. He's pretty spooked about the congressional investigation into his operating budget. He's worried that without us he will get blindsided by some terror group but he can't take the chance to fund us any more. Talk about your catch 22. How is it going for you?" He finally asked. "Working with Joseph has been great and I'm getting used to living the good life here in Dubai." He said with a chuckle. "What did you really call for? You never were one to chit chat." He added.

"There has been a lot of chatter in the Muslim underground about another massive attack

having to do with commercial airplanes. It's got Doug worried and the intelligence agencies haven't come up with any good leads so far. He wondered if you could lend any assistance from your new position in the Arab world." He replied. "It may have nothing to do with it but our local CIA spook has been asking about a deal that is going down in Singapore between some Chinese gangster and some known Arab terrorists from England. It turns out that one of the guys they are watching has a brother working at Joseph's company. He has asked my help checking him out. You remember Sean Moore?

He's the local head of station and he is working with Clay Strong and Stan Gumpertz in Singapore on this thing." Ron asked. "Is that the same Gumpertz kid that Mel trained?

Mel said he was a natural and a quick learner." Jake added. "Same guy. Anyway I hear he is tailing the brother in Singapore trying to get a line on what kind of deal is in the works.

It could be connected with the recent chatter. I'll run it by Sean in case he hasn't heard any of this yet. Tell Doug we will keep in touch through you if we hear anything." Ron said and the hung up. He was back at the trading company parking lot just as the employees were leaving for the day. He waited until they all were gone before parking and going into the building. Joseph was waiting at the top of the stairs when Ron arrived.

"Come on into my office." He said and followed Ron into the room and closed the door.

"I've been watching Wong's transactions today and I found he is putting together a shipment of retail goods from Shanghai to London. It looks like department store items including luggage, toys and electronics like DVD players and computer monitors. None of it looks suspicious but I'm tracing the consignor and consignee to see if it is connected to any of Chen Lee's companies." He told Ron. "They could put anything on the invoices and ship something else entirely if no one inspects anything at customs or if they are

paying somebody off." Ron added. "Did you find anything at his apartment today?"

Joseph asked. "Nothing incriminating. He has a computer but its password blocked so I wasn't able to get in for now. I'll need to put a spy program on his work station to pick it up if he is transferring any files to home. I got a call from Jake today. Doug says there is a lot of chatter in the Arab underground about a massive attack on commercial planes and wanted to know if we had heard anything." Ron added. "Is Jake going to get the group back into action for Doug now?" Joseph asked. "He can't get any funding. Some members of congress are snooping into his budget. He had to cover his tracks for the money it took for our actions up to when we left. He has it well covered but has no way to get money now. Jake and the others will have to give it up; they can't go back to any of the other agencies without divulging what they have been doing for the last two years."

Ron explained.

CHAPTER SIXTY SIX

"Do you think they could operate with any effectiveness if private money was available?"

Joseph asked. "What are you talking about, Joseph?" Ron asked. "What if we put money into an account, offshore, that Jake could use to fund your team? Could he still get cooperation from Doug Small and the US intelligence agencies?" "I think it's possible.

They would have to be independent of the US government, but Doug could still feed information to Jake. We all have our personal contacts in the military and the spy agencies. The military will be the toughest part. It will be hard to get material and no way would we have access to military transport. It wouldn't be exactly like before." "I can pay for everything we need and you must know where to get munitions when we need them. We'll just buy whatever we need on the black market if necessary. Do you think

Jake will be interested? I can have him fly here so we can talk it over in person if you think he will go for it." "I'll contact him right now and we'll see what he says." Ron replied. They went out on the balcony from Joseph's office and Ron set up the satellite linked phone. "Jake, I have Joseph with me. He has an idea he wants to run by you. Here he is." Ron said and handed the handset to Joseph. Joseph laid out the idea for Jake and they discussed it in brief. "If you agree, I'll e-mail you a first class ticket here on the next available flight so we can make a plan and rough out a budget to get this going." Joseph said. "I'll get packed. Let me know when to leave." Jake replied. Jake was in Joseph's New York office when the call came. He couldn't believe what he was hearing but was genuinely excited at the prospect of keeping the group together and operating outside government control. Mel and Nate were back so he called them and Ty in for an emergency meeting right there and then. When they arrived Jake had just printed out his ticket and was looking at the itinerary. "What's up boss, you sounded pretty serious on the phone." Ty asked. "I have bad news and good news. The bad news is that Doug is not going to be able to get us back in action. He can't risk shuffling any more funds. The good news is that Ron and Joseph just came up with an alternate plan." Jake told them.

"Don't tease us Jake, what are they up to?" Mel asked. "Joseph wants to put up the money to run our operation. I'm going to Dubai to meet with him as soon as one of you drops me at the airport. When I get back I hope to have a plan and a way to pay for it. Are you guys up for a little independent contractor action? If we all agree we will be working on our own without any connection to any government. If anyone catches us at it, including our own people, it will get downright ugly." Jake explained. They all spoke in unison "I'm in." They said.

Jake grabbed some beers from the office fridge and they drank a toast to Joseph and the next big adventure. "What about Naomi?" Mel asked on the way to the airport. "I don't know, let me talk to Joseph and Ron before we say anything to her." Jake replied.

CHAPTER SIXTY SEVEN

Jake's flight was uneventful and he slept though most of it. Ron was waiting at the airport when he arrived. "What got into Joseph? I figured he would get into running his business and leave all this stuff for good." Jake said. "I don't think he will ever get over what happened to his family and he believes we can make a difference. He still is looking into selling the business. There is a huge offer on the table and he really doesn't care that much about the business any more. I think he is just waiting for his uncle to agree to sell before he makes a decision." Ron replied. "He picked a great time to do this. Doug is frantic to discover this latest airline plot before anything nasty happens." Jake added.

They drove to the hotel where Ron had stayed before and checked Jake into a room.

"Joseph will meet us here in about an hour. You get cleaned up and I'll wait for you in the bar downstairs." Ron said. When Joseph arrived Jake and Ron were outside the hotel entrance waiting. He picked them up in his car and they drove away toward the port district and Joseph's building. On the way they discussed the basics of how Joseph would get the money for the operation and make it accessible for Jake. "I'll set up bank accounts in various places that you can have access to by way of debit card. There will only be numbers on the cards, no name, so you can have any of the others get funds in case you are unable to do it. You will all have to memorize the pass codes. I'll get credit cards for all of you, so you will be able to use some form of identification when you need it. Get me a copy of each member's passport so I can get the credit cards issued with whatever

names you plan to use." Joseph instructed. "I met with the others before leaving New York, everyone is on board but I haven't said anything to Naomi." Jake added. "I think she'll be more valuable working for the CIA now that she is interpreting nearly everything of importance that comes out the middle east. She can keep us informed and we won't have to let the CIA officially know we exist." Ron interjected. "I'd like to be the one to tell her." Joseph said. Ron and Jake nodded their agreement. They spent the next few hours laying out a budget and then began planning their next move. "I think we should run down this possible connection between the Wong brothers, Chen Lee and those UK based Arabs as a first priority." Ron proposed. "What do we hear so far from Sean Moore about the operation in Singapore?" Jake asked. "Only that Stan Gumpertz is tailing David Wong, trying to pickup any scuttlebutt about the deal. So far he hasn't gotten anything out of it." Ron replied. "We are watching Dennis Wong's transactions to see if anything gets shipped to England from Lee's organization in the near future. The problem is that Lee has so many dummy companies and ships all kinds of stuff all the time so we might miss the important shipment among all the regular merchandize coming out of China. Our best hope is that Dennis Wong only handles the shady deals and not all of Lee's other business." Joseph said. "Sean is supposed to give me the names of the companies Lee has used in the past move illegal arms so we can cross check them against transactions handled by Dennis Wong at Ibrahim Trading." Ron added. "What are the chances Lee will use the same companies again if the CIA intercepted them before?" Jake wondered aloud. "According to Sean, they didn't go after the arms until the terrorists had received them so Lee's involvement wasn't exposed. That way they could keep an eye on them later without alerting Lee. If we're lucky he won't use a new one or if he does we

can pick it up by watching Dennis Wong. I went to his apartment and checked it out but he had his personal computer blocked with a password so we put a keystroke recorder on his work station in hopes that he will access his home unit from work. When he does I will have his password and then we can dig into his records and see what he has been up to." Ron replied. "Good move, maybe we should bring Ty here to go after his computer while you guys keep an eye on him at work." Jake said. "It might be worthwhile to send Mel and Nate to Singapore to help Stan check out with the other Wong. It wouldn't hurt to have someone watch Stan's back. I'm sure Clay is too well known in Singapore to be much help if Stan gets in a fix. Those Chinese thugs can get really nasty." Ron added.

"I'll get a hold of Doug and see if he has any more info on this airline plot and get the boys up to speed. These things usually happen pretty fast once the chatter starts." Jake said. They all stood up and shook hands, Jake thanked Joseph again and then asked Ron to get him back to the airport for the next flight home. "I'll get the funding in place and get the credit cards going as soon as you can get those passports to me." Joseph said as they walked down to Ron's car. He decided he would send Naomi an e-mail and have her call him on the satellite phone. He discovered he had a really empty feeling in his stomach as he thought about Naomi and how long it had been since they had been together. He knew that it made more sense to have her as a contact in the CIA rather than working in the field with the others. But he longed to have her with him and decided to let her make the decision whether to leave her job and join him or remain where she was.

He wanted her to know how much he missed her and he hoped that the feeling was mutual.

CHAPTER SIXTY EIGHT

Stan continued to haunt the underground gambling joints until he made friends with some of the people he had seen with David Wong that first night. He quietly kept up his gambling and refrained from asking any questions about Wong or the gambling ships until he was finally accepted by the group and got invited to join them on one of their junkets. He became friendly with one of the women who was not a prostitute. She was the sister of one of the high rollers and an enthusiastic gambler herself. They played craps and roulette together and occasionally danced. He was never totally alone with her and made no outward displays of affection. After a few hours on the boat her brother came over and suggested they all take a break have some dinner. While eating in the elegant dining room Stan saw David Wong and a small group of people enter and sit at a nearby table. Stan glanced carefully around and noticed two of Lee's men standing near the dining room entrance. He assumed they were there to protect David Wong, keep an eye on him, or both. He could tell from experience that both had weapons under their jackets.

After Stan's group finished their meal they were on their way back into the casino when David Wong stood up and greeted them. He asked how they enjoyed their meal and wished them luck at the tables. He paid no particular notice to Stan who just smiled and pretended he didn't understand the language. After they returned to the casino, Wong spoke to one of the bodyguards. "Keep an eye on the new guy with the Changs. He seems OK but let's watch him anyway." He said. Stan continued to play roulette with Janet Chang and paid no attention to David Wong or his associates for the remainder of the evening. Later when they decided to take the launch back to town, Wong and his party also got on at the same time. "How was your luck tonight?" Wong asked the group, speaking in English. "We didn't do too badly, how did you make out?" Stan replied. "I

lost more than I won, as usual." Wong replied with a shrug. "I haven't seen you around.

Do you live in Singapore? Mr...." He asked. "It's Panidas, Niko Panidas, I come here occasionally on business but this is the first time I have been to one of these fine gambling ships. Thanks to the kind invitation from Mr. Chang, I enjoyed it immensely."

Stan replied, using a slight Greek accent. "Do you own this ship? Mr. Wong" He asked.

"No, no, I work for the Chinese embassy here; I just spend more time than I should on these ships. I probably have helped finance them with my losses." He said with a laugh.

"Do you mind if I ask what business you are in?" He asked. "Not at all. I'm a broker buying Asian goods for the European markets." Stan replied. They were nearing the docks by then. David Wong handed Stan a business card as they prepared to leave the launch. "Contact me sometime at my office if you like. I may be able to aid you with doing business in China. It was nice meeting you Mr. Panidas." "Thank you Mr. Wong. I appreciate your offer. I will definitely be in contact." Stan said. Wong and his companions climbed into a waiting car as Stan bid goodbye to the Changs and got into a cab. As Stan's cab pulled away a dark Mercedes followed soon after. "He got out at the Intercontinental on Middle road, boss" the man reported to David Wong. "Wait a few minutes then go in and see if he is registered" Wong replied. Stan watched the desk from a hallway near the bar. He was certain Wong had had him followed. He had covered that base by checking in a few days before starting his surveillance on Wong. "Our Mr. Wong is indeed cautious. He had me followed to the hotel and checked to see if I was registered. I won't dare meet with you or come to the embassy until this thing is resolved.

He has invited me to contact him at the Chinese embassy to talk about potential business interests in China. I hope we have my legend well covered in Athens. I'm sure he will

check me out completely before offering any assistance." Stan told Clay on the cell phone. "Don't worry. We have your story covered. Make a few calls and e-mails to your

"Athens office" every day. We have you set up to arrange a purchase of toys from a company in Hong Kong who has a representative here. In the briefcase in your room there is everything you need to do some legitimate trading. That will get back to Chen and Wong in no time flat. We'll give him time to look you over before you make any more contact. Go ahead and continue your socializing with the Changs, but watch your back. I can't risk having anyone around you for backup. Chen has eyes everywhere."

CHAPTER SIXTY NINE

"Shouldn't we have heard from our Chinese friends by now?" Imam Abdullah Al Rahman asked. "They gave explicit instructions not to contact them and to wait until they call." Rashid answered. But inwardly he was beginning to worry. After all, they had paid dearly for the technology and up until now they had only seen a quick demonstration. He decided to investigate Chen's resources in England while waiting for word of the shipment. Later that morning he took the Imam's car and headed for London. He had done some checking on where Chen's associates had received goods before and wanted to have a look for himself. It wouldn't hurt to know where their goods would be stored when they arrived. Mick was nearly out of patience killing time around Blackburn waiting for the Muslims to make some kind of move when he realized that Al Rahman's car was on the move. He watched the GPS monitor until he was certain the car was on its way to the M6 and then got in his own car to follow at a safe distance. He phoned Rory Wells in London and advised him that that their suspect was headed to London and that he was following at a safe distance. "We've got surveillance set up on all of Chen's

known assets here and haven't seen any new shipments arrive. If anything has come in it has to be somewhere we don't know about." Rory said. "I don't know who is in the car but maybe it will lead us to where the stuff is or is headed for. Are you receiving his GPS location yet?" Stan asked. "Not yet, keep an eye on him but don't get too close. We'll pick him up when he gets into our range in London." They rang off and Mick continued to follow the tracking signal. It appeared to be the reverse of the route they had taken to get to Blackburn. Rashid pulled into a service plaza to gas up and look at the map he had made of Chen's warehouses. Noticing that the car had stopped, Mick slowed down as he approached the plaza. He pulled into the transport café parking area and watched Rashid get out of the Vauxhall at the petrol station and walk to the restroom. He decided to go inside an order a sandwich and a soft drink to give Rahman a chance to get ahead again.

"I got a look at our guy, it's the one called Rashid and he appears to be alone. He is just leaving the last petrol plaza near Heathrow." He told Rory. "We have him now. We'll take it from here. Just stay in touch in case I need you later. He can't be up to much if he is alone in that small car." Rory replied. Rashid traveled to the old warehouse district in the East End. He had learned that Chen Lee used several old warehouses in Wapping to receive goods once they cleared customs. He wasn't sure what he was looking for other than he just wanted to know where his shipment would most likely be when it arrived.

Rory Wells was tracking him and found that Rashid had gone to one of the areas he had under surveillance. Rashid had made slow drive bys at two of the three buildings that Rory was aware of. There didn't appear to be anyone around at the second location and Rashid parked around the corner and walked back to the warehouse. He tried the office door and found it locked. There were no windows on the ground floor of the warehouse

so he couldn't see anything inside. He walked back to his car and left. He apparently was not aware of the third location. After a while Rashid parked the car and entered a pub called the Rose and Crown. Rory had one of his men follow him into the pub where he ordered food and sat and ate by himself. No one came to meet him and he made a stop at the restroom and then returned to his car. "He just had a quick lunch and drank only tea.

No one paid him any attention; I don't think he has any connection to the place." The man reported when he got back into Rory's car. "He's lucky he picked the Rose and Crown. If he had gone a bit further he could have gone into one of the more dangerous ones controlled by the local gangsters." Rory mused. After leaving the pub, Rashid passed by the warehouses again and then headed back the way he came. Rory called Mick and told him what he had seen. "He must be expecting something that hasn't arrived yet. It can't be arms or explosives if he expects it to clear customs and get to these warehouses." Mick offered. "Whatever he's expecting may not arrive by normal shipping. If Chen is smuggling something to him it may come in some other way. Maybe Rashid doesn't know where it will end up yet and is fishing around hoping to find it in case Chen tries to screw him." Rory added. "You may have a point. If Chen hasn't told him where to pick up his merchandise it may not even be in the London area. He will probably wait until it's safely in England before he tells Rashid where to get it. Let's hope the boys in Singapore can get a line on what it is they are expecting and how it's being shipped. It could be air or sea. Do we know if Chen ever gets anything here by air freight?" Mick asked. "We have people watching for shipments at both Heathrow and Gatwick, just in case. But most of his cargo is large enough to go by container ship. But we don't know how big a package or packages to look for." Rory explained. "I guess I'll

have to keep watching him and hope we can get to him when his goods arrive. I'll head back for Blackburn unless he turns off for somewhere else on the way." Mick said.

CHAPTER SEVENTY

Jake met with Mel, Nate and Ty in New York and made plans to get back to Dubai. He had already forwarded their identity papers to Joseph and had received the banking ids and paper work by return courier. "I want all of us to go to Dubai for now. We'll decide whether to send help to Singapore after we meet with Sean Moore. We are going to travel as representatives of Joseph's trading company so we can meet at his offices without raising suspicion. As far as anyone in Dubai knows we have all been working here for Joseph in his American company. Sean has been led to believe we are still working for Homeland Security so no one at his embassy station or the one in Singapore will question our affiliation. Ron told him we were using Ibrahim Trading Company as our cover.

We'll split up and go on two different flights so we don't look like the American army has landed when we get to Dubai. Ty will travel with me today. You and Nate are booked on tomorrow's flight. We'll be staying at the Hyatt Regency, so just take a cab when you get there and we'll meet in the hotel." He told Mel.

CHAPTER SEVENTY ONE

"I have received a partial shipment of luggage today. The workmanship is excellent, you can't tell them from the usual junk they sell to Wal-Mart." Lin Yuang said excitedly.

"How long will it take to get them ready to ship to our friends?" Chen asked. "I need about five days to get enough of the new compound made up and installed in them. There are twenty here now and I expect the rest next week. I won't prepare the detonator assemblies until I have all of them here and the compound installed. We don't want any

of the detonator chemicals anywhere near the main compound. As you know it takes very little to set it off." Yuang replied. "Good. I have enough other products in storage to make up a 20 foot container of "harmless" merchandise going to England. It will be easy to get our "special luggage" through customs, surrounded by identical normal ones and all those other cheap items if they even pick our container to inspect." Chen said with a smirk. Secretly Lin Yuang worried that the new explosive compound or the detonator capsules would deteriorate over time and blow up prematurely. He told himself it would not happen and even if it did, they would most likely be paid in full before it did. He didn't dare let Chen Lee know there was anything to worry about.

CHAPTER SEVENTY TWO

Ron Pierce met Jake and the others at the Hyatt in Dubai. Joseph did not come with him, uncle Hafid had had a seizure at the office and had to be transported to the hospital that morning. Joseph had gone to be with him and was waiting for news at the hospital.

"Sorry to hear Joseph's uncle is sick. Do you know what his condition is?" Jake asked. "I spoke to Joseph a little while ago; the doctors think Hafid had a heart attack. He was in intensive care and still unconscious when Joseph called. It sounded pretty serious, but he is a very strong man. Hopefully he will recover. He's all Joseph has left of his family and I think he will be devastated if the old man dies." Ron replied. "Joseph said that he has the best doctors and medical team available looking after him and the hospital is very modern and well run." He added. "Have you heard anything new from Sean Moore?' Mel asked. "He will be here shortly to bring us up to speed." Ron replied. A few minutes later Sean knocked on the door. Ron let him in and stepped back to enjoy the surprise on his face when he recognized the others. "Holy shit! Where did you dig up this motley crew?

Don't answer that, I really don't want to know." He exclaimed, reaching for Jake Powell's hand. He shook hands with all the others and then flopped onto the love seat by the window; still shaking is head in amazement. "What do you hear from Singapore?"

Ron asked. "Nothing new so far, Stan is tailing David Wong in hopes of getting some drift on what the terrorists purchased from Chen Lee." Sean replied, then added "We've got people watching the Arabs in England, but that hasn't turned up anything yet. They appear to be waiting for a shipment but it looks like they don't have the final destination.

One of them looked around at some of Chen Lee's warehouse operations in east London but seemed to be just fishing at this point. That squares with Chen's past operations. He likes to keep the receiving end a secret until the last moment. He trusts no one, not even his own people. Have you turned anything up watching Wong's brother here?" "Not yet.

We were just talking about having Ty tap into Wong's home computer to see if anything is happening. We have just captured his password, so it won't take long for Ty to get inside. We'll go right at it tomorrow while Wong is at work. He may take advantage of Joseph's absence to work on his own projects." Ron answered. "What do you think of sending Mel and Nate to Singapore? They could back Stan up and maybe get a little more aggressive with Chen's people. No one knows them there except Stan, Clay has never met either of them, so they can operate without alerting anyone about CIA involvement."

Jake offered. "I like it. I'm not crazy about Stan working alone with those gangsters. Do you want to make Clay aware of them in case they need weapons or anything?" Sean wondered. "It wouldn't hurt for them to have access to a secure line to Clay, but let's leave him out of it for now. You never know where a mobster like Chen Lee might have a snitch." Jake said. "I agree, the fewer people involved; the better." Sean said. He wrote

down a number that would give them a direct secure line to Clay Strong and a cell number for Stan and gave it to Mel. He included the name and address of the hotel where Stan was staying. He shook hands all around and then walked to the door where Ron was watching the hallway. Seeing no one in the hall he left and walked to the stairs. He took the stairs up one floor and then took the elevator down to the lobby. "Did you see the look on Sean's face when he saw us?" Nate asked with a wide grin. "He has to be wondering what kind of agency would collect the likes of us for this kind of mission."

Mel added, also grinning. "I think we should wait and see what Ty comes up with before we go to Singapore. That may give us a place to start when we get there." Nate said.

CHAPTER SEVENTY THREE

Lin Yuang worked quickly to place the explosive mixture into each bag. Every one had to be perfect in order to pass through an x-ray machine undetected. Any deviation in shape could alert an x-ray technician that something was inside the hard plastic suitcase besides the normal travel clothes and supplies. As long as there was no edge exposed the x-ray would penetrate the layer of explosive as though it was part of the suitcase shell. He carefully smeared a thin layer evenly on the entire inside surface of the hard plastic suitcases. It was slow and tedious work but he trusted no one else to do it. Not even Chen Lee knew the actual composition of his new explosive paste. He obtained the raw materials from various sources so that no one could deduce his formula from the materials involved. When the epoxy-like paste was in place it took about twenty minutes to set up, then it became as hard as the suitcase and was the same color as the rest of the assembly. When this was accomplished all traces of chemical odors disappeared, making it the perfect weapon to get through airport security anywhere in the world. He wondered

if the Arabs who would fly on the planes with their bags checked would be told that they were going to die. He guessed that the leaders would not let them in on it for fear that some would lose their nerve and screw up the grand plan. Even though it was tedious placing the paste in the bags, it was perfectly safe without the detonation chemicals. The tricky part would be when he had to place the detonation chemicals in the handles and install the handles on the bags. If one drop of the detonator fluid touched the explosives during assembly, he would be vaporized along with all the bags in the room. The thought of this caused a chill to go up his spine and a knot in his stomach. He tried to shake it off and then decided to go home for the night. He wanted to be fully rested and alert when it was time to begin the installation process.

CHAPTER SEVENTY FOUR

Rashid was becoming more and more frustrated. It was a nightmare trying to arrange all the flights he wanted to get his explosive on. He studies all the published airline schedules for hours on end, feverishly making notes and trying to make sense of it. He knew that the Al Quaeda leaders wanted all the explosions to be on flights to the US and her closest allies but saying that was a whole lot easier than getting it done. He really needed someone to put all the possibilities into a database that would allow him to choose the proper times and flights in order to get as many as possible into the air at the same time. He decided he would get word to Al Zwahiri and ask if there was anyone in the organization that could assist him. They were always telling him to be patient and strive for perfection when planning an attack. This plan was far more complicated than any they had tried before. He was beginning to question his decision to purchase so many units. If he had stuck with the original plan it would have been much easier, but when he

suggested it to Al Zwahiri he was praised for his bold ambition. If he managed to pull off even a portion the entire plan he would be exalted as a hero of Islam forever. He wrote up a summary of what he had managed to plan so far and asked for help in finishing the scheduling. The choosing of the flights was only part of the problem. He had to get the units to the martyrs who would carry them onto the flights, purchase the tickets and arrange passports and visas in order for them to get accepted on the flights. This was no easy task since he couldn't use Islamic names for many of the flights. He wanted to send as many couples as possible in order to get more luggage onto each flight to ensure complete destruction of the planes. Also, couples traveling together would arouse less suspicion, especially if they took along some children whenever possible. He called to Abdullah Al Rahman to discuss getting a message delivered. "We could put the request for computer help onto the internet. The Arabic chat rooms would get the message out that we needed someone to do a computer program without having to disclose the purpose." Rahman suggested. "I don't know; it could be risky, all the intelligence agencies are watching the internet." Rashid replied. "They can't read every message that gets on the internet and this could be disguised in many ways. Job offers, student programs and game programmers flood the Arabic language internet everyday. The chances of a Western agency intercepting a message, translating it correctly and then reacting to it as a threat are pretty remote and this could look very routine."

Rahman argued. "You are probably correct my friend but I need to get some advice from our great leader concerning the total number of flights he wants and which ones he values the most.

If he gives me some room I can focus on the most important targets and increase our chance of success. I agree that it would be spectacular to have twenty or more explosions

on the same day. But only half of the intended targets were hit on 9-11 and that was considered a monumental success." Rashid went on. "All right, I'll get your message to him but I think we should try the internet idea to get a programmer going on this.

Otherwise, it will take forever." Rahman suggested.

CHAPTER SEVENTY FIVE

Mel and Nate took separate flights to Singapore. They would meet at the same hotel where Stan Gumpertz was staying. Nate used an Arabic name and a French passport while Mel traveled on an Irish passport. Each had several genuine passports to match their various aliases, left over from their time at NSA and access to very good forgeries when needed. Ty had turned up some messages from between the Wong brothers. They were not specific as to what kind of goods were being transported or exact shipping times. David had asked Dennis to look into shipping a couple of containers to England in the near future. His request was vague and somewhat cryptic as though he was worried about someone intercepting it. Whatever it was, David did not want the order to go through normal channels. He would send more information when the goods were ready to go. He promised a large commission for handling this shipment confidentially. Ty had read the message before Dennis had seen it so there was no response in the outgoing message box. Now that Ty had access to Wong's computer they would keep track of everything that came in or went out. He had given this information to Mel before he and Nate left for Singapore. They were convinced that whatever Chen Lee was selling to the Arabs he would have the shipping arranged by the Wong brothers. At least that would give them a target to focus on in Singapore. They arrived in Singapore a few hours apart on the same day and checked into the Intercontinental where they knew Stan was staying.

They had agreed earlier to meet in a small café a few blocks from the hotel. There were only a few customers in the place and they sat in a booth away from the windows where they could watch the door. They exchanged room numbers and determined that they were on the same floor at opposite ends of the hallway and one floor above where Stan was staying. "Have you made contact with Stan yet?" Nate asked. "No, I'm a little hesitant to call him until I know he's alone. I checked his room before you got in and he wasn't there." Mel answered. "I think I'll call him now. If he doesn't answer I'll leave this number and a fake business name so he can return the call when he is alone." He dialed the number and waited. It went to message right away. "Mr. Panidas, my name is Ian Cleland with Erin Imports. Please return my call at your convenience. I will be staying in Singapore for a few days and have some potential business to discuss. Thank you." Was the message Mel left. "Do you think he will recognize your voice?" Nate asked. "It's possible but it has been a few years." Mel answered. They didn't wait long until Mel's phone rang. "Ian here." he answered on the third ring. "Niko Panidas, returning your call, Mr. Cleland. What can I do for you?" "Are you alone, Stan?" "Yes, I'm alone in a cab. Is this Mel Denison?" He asked in a low voice. "In the flesh, my friend. We need to talk.

When you get to your hotel room make sure no one is watching you and take the stairs up one floor and go to room 631." "I'll be there in twenty minutes." He said and rang off.

Stan was excited and confused at the same time. Mel had to know what he was up to or he wouldn't have had the cell number. He couldn't imagine how Mel got involved unless he had somehow been recruited by the CIA. He was anxious to see his old friend but

wondered what it all meant. When he arrived at the hotel he removed his golf clubs from the cab and took the elevator to his floor. He dropped the golf clubs in the closet and checked his "tattletales" to see if anyone had been in the room. None were disturbed but he assumed the room was bugged by now. He was always cautious and practiced the tradecraft he had learned from Mel. It had saved his butt more than once in the years since he had last seen his mentor. He went into the bathroom and washed his face and then changed his polo shirt for a loose silk Hawaiian print like the tourists wore. He walked to the elevator and pushed the down button. When the door opened he stepped in and pushed number 2 before stepping out and heading for the stairs. The hallway was empty as was the stairwell so he took the steps two at a time up to the sixth floor. He checked the hallway through the glass on the door before entering and then walked casually to number 631. He knocked softly on the door and it opened immediately. When he stepped inside he saw Mel seated in a chair across the room grinning from ear to ear.

Nate closed the door and checked the hall through the peep hole one more time. "We swept the room. We're ok for now." Mel said grabbing Stan by the hand and arm as he stood up. Stan had met Nate years earlier and recognized him right away. "There must be a God somewhere if the two of you are still alive and kicking." He said as he stood back to look at them. "What are you doing here?" "We heard you were playing in the wrong sandbox and thought you might use a little help." Mel replied. "How we got here is a long story and probably better off left untold. Your boss doesn't know we are here; we got onto your situation through another old friend. Anyway, we are here to help. We believe that this transaction between Chen Lee and the Arabs may have something to do with all the chatter about a new airline attack. It must have to do with explosives or other

weaponry that Lee can provide." He added. "I haven't gotten anything close to a lead so far. I have to be very careful not to arouse Lee's suspicion. I've been working on getting close to David Wong. He is the go-between for Chen Lee in this deal and many others involving Islamic extremists. He has had me followed and knows I'm staying here and has checked out my cover story in Athens. My cover is pretty air tight but I don't want to move too fast and get myself in a jackpot." Stan explained. "Mel and I have been formulating a plan to get closer to David Wong without getting you any deeper in this thing alone." Nate said. "What if you ask Wong if he knows anyone who would be interested in talking to one of your business contacts. You can tell him that you only know of this person through a mutual friend and haven't mentioned Wong's name to him.

Just tell him that the man is interested in buying some Chinese items that you don't have access to. Let him take it from there. If he's as greedy as we believe him to be, he'll want to find out what kind of deal might be in the works. I'm guessing that he would check it out himself before going to Chen Lee about it." Mel offered. "It will be risky, but I don't see how else I'm going to get any information. David Wong is smart and very careful. He has some of Lee's goons around him anytime he's out away from the Chinese embassy. I have been using my acquaintance with some friends of his named Chang. We play golf together and I've been on one of Lee's gambling ships with them. That's how I was able to meet Wong in the first place. He has invited me to call on him at the embassy if I want to do business in China; he says he can be of assistance." Stan explained. "That's perfect, get an appointment to see him at the embassy and ask about buying electronics for a distributor you have in England. See if he can line up some big name knock offs on video games and dvd players. We'll get our connection to organize the funds and get you an

address to send it to. Tell him you will need to store it for a time while you separate it for several customers. That way we can see where he ships to in case he has some facilities in England we don't know about. When you finish that transaction, see if you can get him out to dinner or golf or gambling where you can bring up the idea that you need someone to get some "delicate" items from China for another client. Nate will pose as a well financed Arab looking for weapons. Maybe our friend Mr. Wong will offer him whatever the others have ordered." Mel explained. "I'll set up a meeting with Wong. How fast can you get your end arranged?" Stan asked. "Two days should do it. See if you can call the embassy and set up an appointment two days from now. We'll get our part organized right away." Mel replied. Nate was checking the hall through the peep hole and then stepped out to look around. Seeing no one, he motioned for Stan to leave. Stan looked Mel straight in the eye and then left without saying a word. He took the stairs down to his floor and went straight to his room. He wasn't sure if he was relieved to have help or scared shitless about what might happen. He knew that Mel would have his back and that was comforting, but he also knew they were playing in Chen Lee's sandbox. One wrong move and death would be the easiest part.

Mel called Jake and told him what they needed. Jake got with Joseph and worked up an order for some somewhat shady electronic items. They wired money to Stan's Athens cover company so he could pay Wong with a wire transfer that would come from Greece.

Ty had been monitoring Dennis Wong's computer transmissions and reported that nothing new had passed between the brothers. By the next morning everything was in place for Stan's meeting with David Wong. Stan called the Chinese embassy and left a

message for David Wong. A secretary returned the call a short time later and said that Mr. Wong would be free to meet him at ten Thursday morning.

CHAPTER SEVENTY SIX

Lin Yuang was smiling. He had finished all but ten of the suitcases. The last ten had to wait for the paste to set up and then he could assemble the detonator handles. Chen Lee was standing nearby talking on a cell phone. He had arrived just as Lin Yuang had closed up the thirtieth bag. He snapped the phone shut and looked over at Lin's collection of finished bags. "My friend you have done well. You can finish these tomorrow, let's go out to the Jade Queen for dinner and some relaxation for now." He said "Just give me a minute to lock up." Lin replied. "Go ahead and wash up here first, then we'll go straight to the launch" Chen said. Lin Yuang was nervous, he didn't like Chen or his men to be alone in the lab. Keeping the chemical recipe's secret was his best insurance. But he quickly complied and went into the locker room to wash up and change clothes. As soon as he was out of the room, Lee opened the door and allowed another man inside. He quickly opened Yuang's files and began copying invoices with a tiny camera. He finished quickly and ducked out before Lin Yuang returned. Chen Lee went out to the limo and waited for the scientist to lock up and come out. Lin appeared moments later dressed in a sport jacket and white shirt with a Mandarin collar. He tried not to look nervous and smiled as he got into the car. "Tomorrow we will have the entire order ready to pack up.

It will take most of the day to put the bags onto pallets and surround them with normal luggage and get the packaging prepared but we will be ready to ship in one more day at the most." He told Lee as they drove off. "It may take a few more days for the shipping arrangements to be finalized but go ahead and get everything ready to ship. I want their

money as soon as the boat leaves the port." Chen explained. He planned to meet David Wong on the ship later and let him know it was time to get the container ready and get it on a ship to England as soon as possible. He was thinking that he would like to have more such customers before the attacks took place in case the authorities determined what caused the explosions. He decided to have Wong look for other buyers.

CHAPTER SEVENTYSEVEN

"W e need to get some weapons in case things get sticky." Nate said. "I was thinking the same thing. Maybe we should get in touch with Clay Strong and see if he can supply us.

I'm afraid to go after any black market stuff here. We don't have any other sources here and Chen Lee would very likely find out if some stranger was trying to purchase illegal guns." Mel replied. "Maybe we should have Jake contact Sean and see if he can arrange a drop box somewhere here where Clay could leave something for us." Nate offered.

"Good plan, I'll call Jake right now and see if he can set it up."
Mel agreed. "Jake, we could use some firepower. Stan is afraid to
carry anything for fear of alerting Wong and we weren't able to
bring anything along on the commercial flights. What do you think
about having Sean get with Clay and set up a drop box for us?"
"My only worry is that we'll have to explain to Clay who we are
and what we're doing. We don't know if he has any leaks in his
operation. Maybe there's another way. Let me get back to you."
Jake told him. Two hours later Jake phoned back. "Take the ferry
to Bintan tomorrow then take a cab to the Banyan Tree Resort.
Rent some clubs and get a tee time for one o'clock. When you get
to the eighth hole there is a restroom. Go inside and lift the lid on
the toilet in the last stall. You'll find what you need." "Thanks
boss, sometimes you amaze even me."

Mel said and rang off. "Ready for some R&R? We're playing golf
tomorrow on Bintan; Jake has us covered as usual." Nate just
grinned and shook his head, nothing Jake did surprised him
anymore.

Stan went down to the front desk to see if he had any messages.
The desk clerk handed him a Fedex envelope. He thanked her and
headed back up to his room. The return address was from his cover
company in Athens. When he opened it he found a detailed order
for electronic gadgets, shipping destination and routing numbers
for arranging a wire transfer for the deposit on the order. He put
the contents in his briefcase and purposely left the envelope in the
waste paper can under the desk. It was nearly time for his meeting
with David Wong so he called down to arrange a cab and left for
the elevator.

He arrived at the Chinese embassy and was escorted to a waiting
room where Wong's assistant met him. "Good morning Mr.
Panidas, Mr. Wong will be with you shortly.

Would you care for coffee or tea while you wait? He won't be
long." She said smiling and bowing slightly. "No thank you, I'll be
fine." He had the feeling he was being watched and assumed there
were cameras in the room. In a few minutes Wong's assistant

returned and motioned for him to follow her. "Mr. Wong, thank you for seeing me." Stan greeted him. "Please, call me David, there is no need for formality here. What can I do for you Niko?" He said, motioning to a chair at the long conference table. "I have customers who would like to obtain some merchandize from China. I have here a detailed order for the items they desire." He said, opening his briefcase to remove the order form.

He slid it over to Wong and waited for his reaction. "I see. There should be no problem arranging a purchase for you. Most of these items are available in these quantities. Of course if they want genuine brand names it will cost much more and take longer than if

they would accept similar items from a different source." He said. "I believe they could get genuine brand name merchandize through normal trade channels. I had a feeling you could arrange some comparable items for a much better price. That's why I came to you."

Stan said, looking him straight in the eye. "Then leave it in my hands and I will see what I can do." Wong replied, reaching for Stan's hand. They stood up and shook hands briefly. Before leaving Wong invited him to have dinner aboard the Jade Queen. Stan accepted and agreed to meet Wong at the boat launch at seven. He grabbed one of the cabs that circle the embassies hoping for a fare and went back to the hotel. On the way he dialed Mel's phone and hung up after two rings. It was a prearranged signal to let Mel know that he was finished with the meeting with David Wong. Mel was just getting back in the golf cart when the phone buzzed. He checked it after a minute and saw that Stan had called. "Stan's had his meeting with Wong." He told Nate. "This is the eighth hole coming up and there's the restroom building." He told Mel and motioned to the small building to left of the cart path. Nate walked over to the door and looked inside. Mel waited near the door appearing to watch the foursome ahead of them tee off. Nate went inside and quickly checked the stalls. No one was inside so he went in the end stall and closed the door behind him. He lifted the lid to the toilet tank and found a small zip lock plastic bag inside. He opened it and found a key and a note on flash paper that had a locker number for a public locker at the ferry terminal. He replaced the lid and lit the flash paper with his lighter and then flushed the plastic bag down the toilet. He paused to wash his hands and then went outside. He nodded at Mel who went in and used the facilities before returning to the cart. When they were out of the cart and on the tee box he told Mel about the key. The finished the eighth and ninth holes and returned the cart

and clubs to the pro shop and took a cab back to the ferry terminal. Mel went into the gift shop while Nate went to find the locker. He carefully opened it and found a duffel bag with the Golf resort's logo printed on the sides. It had a zippered closure and loop handles. Nate didn't bother opening it and went to find Mel just outside the gift shop. Mel didn't even look at the bag Nate carried and they walked onto the ferry for the ride back to Singapore. Nate noticed that many of the tourists had similar duffels and placed the bag on the floor by his feet. When they returned to the hotel Mel went up first and checked both rooms while Nate bought a paper in the hotel gift shop. He sat in the lobby and read the paper for a few minutes and then headed to the elevator and up to his room.

Mel was waiting when he got inside. "Still no bugs, it's ok to talk." Mel said as Nate placed the bag on the bed and opened it. Inside he found four pistols, two silencers, ammunition and two Ka Bar knives under some gym clothes and a beach towel.

"Whoever Jake knows in Indonesia, knows how to supply our kind of toys." He said as he laid the items out on the bed. Mel picked up one of the PPK's and checked the magazine. It was loaded and there were extra clips for each of the four guns. "No serial numbers and these appear to be nearly new." He said. There was a soft tap on the door and Nate looked through the peep hole before opening it. Stan stepped in and stared at the equipment on the bed. "I'm not going to ask how you got this stuff but I feel better knowing you have it." He said. Mel nodded and asked how the meeting went with Wong.

"I'm going to meet him at seven to go out to one of Chen Lee's gambling ships for dinner. He took the order from me and said to leave it to him. I suspect he will ask me for a deposit or finders fee tonight at dinner. If things go smoothly I'll see if he has any interest in doing some more business with one of my acquaintances." Stan replied. "Is

there any chance we could get on that ship tonight?" Mel asked. "There is a launch that leaves every half hour from the docks but you need to be invited or recognized to get on one the first time. That's why I cultivated a friendship with the Changs. You could try going into some of the underground gambling dens and getting mixed in with a crowd that is going to the ship. It took me quite a while to work my way into that. I don't know if you can pull it off in one day. If you create suspicion it might hinder what we are doing. I think you'd better let me find a way to get a meeting arranged on my own." Stan replied. He gave them a description of where he had gone to work his way into the "in crowd" and then left to get ready for his dinner with Wong. After Stan left, Mel and Nate decided to at least have a look around tonight at some of the spots Stan described. "Stan said he saw many of the gamblers on the ship arrive with high class prostitutes. Maybe we should look for a way to connect with some of Chen Lee's hookers at one of the night clubs uptown. They might be able to get us onto his gambling boat." Nate suggested. "It's worth a try. A couple of business men looking for a good time shouldn't cause any suspicion with Chen Lee. He has to get his customers from somewhere; they can't all be his personal friends." Mel added. They dressed in business suits and called down for a cab. When they got in the cab Nate asked the cab driver where they could find some girls who liked to party and gamble. As he asked he handed a twenty dollar bill over the seat to the driver. The driver, an Indonesian man in his twenties with a pencil thin mustache grinned widely and told Nate he would take them to a good place for what they wanted.

He headed up to the nightclub district and pulled up at a place called the Emerald Palace.

They didn't know it at the time, but it was the same place where Stan had originally spotted David Wong. The driver called someone on his cell phone and then told them to

go into the bar and take a table near the bandstand, on the far left. Nate gave him another twenty and they went inside. Since it was still early there was no one on the stage and the lights above the bandstand were off. They sat down and ordered drinks from the waiter.

When the drinks arrived, the waiter nodded to two girls at the bar who came over and sat down with Nate and Mel. The waiter introduced them as April and May. Nate introduced himself and Mel as Ian and Abdul. The girls ordered drinks and sat smiling at the men while they waited. "Do you ladies know where we can go for some gambling? I heard it is illegal here." Nate asked "There is a ship outside Singapore that offers gambling and other entertainment. It is possible we could arrange to go there." The one calling herself April said. "That sounds like fun. How do we get there?" Mel asked. "It is very exclusive and a bit expensive, but we can arrange it if you give me a few minutes." She replied. She excused herself and went through a curtain to a back room. Nate kept a small conversation going with May while April was gone. When April returned she said it had been taken care of. "When do we leave?" Nate asked excitedly. "As soon as we settle the bar bill and call for a cab." She replied. The waiter came back and handed Nate a bar tab for twelve hundred US dollars, He pulled out a money clip and peeled it off in cash and palmed a hundred dollar bill to the waiter. "All right, ladies, lets go have some fun." He said. They rose and walked out to the curb where a limo was waiting. A valet opened the rear door on either side and they all got in with the two girls in the center. The limo had a fully stocked bar and Mel made drinks for all of them. They didn't talk much, just sipped their drinks on the short ride to the docks. When they arrived the launch had just returned and was unloading a few early birds who must have been through for the night. They got on board with several other couples and some single men for the ride out to the ship. It was just after nine so they figured Stan would already be on board when they arrived.

Nate asked the girls if they wanted to have dinner before trying their luck and they both agreed. They went directly to the elegant dining room and ordered drinks and dinner.

They paid close attention to the girls and appeared to be having a good time even though they both took in their surroundings and looked for Stan. They didn't see Stan in the dining room at that time and they took their time with dinner and wine before heading for the gaming tables. Nate and April went to a baccarat table while Mel and May decided to give roulette a try. They had been gambling with varied success for about an hour when they finally saw Stan enter from another room. He was accompanied by David Wong, two Chinese men and four large bodyguards. Stan and Wong went over to a craps table and began playing. The other Chinese men walked slowly through the room, It took them a while because the taller man seemed to know everyone and made many stops to greet people. Mel guessed it was Chen Lee, but wondered about the shorter, older man with him who seemed to just follow behind without being acknowledged by the other guests.

The bodyguards spread out in a relaxed but vigilant formation. They were obviously well trained professionals. If Stan noticed Mel and Nate he did not let on and they paid no visible notice of Chen Lee and his troupe. After another hour or so, Wong and Stan left for the Launch. They appeared to have been having an enjoyable evening even though both were on the losing side of the gambling. Nate had managed to break even at baccarat and his date came out a little ahead. Mel and his date lost more than they won at roulette but seemed to be having fun. They waited until the next launch to return to port.

Somewhat surprisingly the same limo was waiting when they arrived to take the back to the Emerald Palace. The limo driver was surprised when Mel asked him to drop the ladies off and take him and Nate back to their hotel. Nate gave each of the girls a wad of bills and thanked them for the evening. They just smiled and went inside. Back at the hotel they went into the bar for a drink before going up to their rooms. Stan was alone at a table in the corner and watched them leave. He nursed his drink a while and then went to the elevator and up to his room. He checked his tattletales and saw that the room had been gone over. The Fedex envelope was gone along with the other trash. He waited about twenty minutes and then took the stairs up to Mel's room. Nate let him in and told him it was ok to talk. "How the hell did you two manage to get on the gambling boat tonight?"

Stan asked laughing. "Smooth talking Nate and plenty of Joseph's cash." Replied Mel, also laughing. "Who was the older guy with Chen Lee?" Nate asked. "His name is Lin Yuang. I gathered he is some kind of scientist. Didn't say much, just grinned a lot. He and Chen seemed to be celebrating something. They spoke to each other in Chinese, a mix of Cantonese and Mandarin. I caught most of it, but not everything. I'm pretty sure it has to do with the Arab deal. Some kind of explosive device that the little guy must have made for them. Nothing about nuclear or bio that I could hear." Stan replied. "Did you get a chance to propose a meeting with another client?" Mel asked. "That was a little surprising. After I got the bank transfer numbers for a deposit on the gadget order, one of Chen's men brought in a laptop and had me enter the wire transfer. After that they seemed to warm up considerably so I got Wong aside and asked if he was interested in other business. He spoke to Chen and they agreed to hear my idea. I told them I had a contact who was interested in buying fireworks and they agreed immediately. Wong said he would contact me here tomorrow to work out the details. I told them I had not met the contact person and that I only had a name and number given to me by a mutual

associate." Stan explained. "Good, that way it won't matter that we were on the boat and didn't make contact with each other. I'm certain we were checked out before we left the Emerald Palace." Nate added. "When we meet them, you should speak Arabic with Wong for the real details. He is fluent in Arabic, Chen is not, as far as I know. They will probably converse with each other in

Chinese, believing that we won't know what they are saying." Stan added. "Be sure to ask Wong for a finders fee. He'll probably be more willing to trust you if he believes you are in this business strictly for the money." Mel reminded him. Stan left for his room and Mel called Jake to report in. He explained the plan they were trying and asked Jake if the other Wong had moved any merchandize. "He hasn't sent anything to his home computer in a few days and Ron is keeping track of his orders at the company. So far it has been no help." Jake explained. "Something may be happening now." Mel said, then explained what Stan had learned on the ship. "Whatever Chen is supplying for the Muslims has to do with some sort of explosive device. We hope to get him to offer it to us as well." He added. "Well, we are pretty certain it will be sent to England, so we'll try to track anything that Wong sends by air or sea in that direction."

Jake explained. They rang off after that and Nate headed for his own room while Mel checked his hiding place to see if the guns had been discovered. Nothing had been disturbed so he decided to get some sleep.

CHAPTER SEVENTY EIGHT

Lin Yuang was relieved; he had finally finished all the bags. All that was left to do was to place them in the printed boxes and then get them on pallets. He had enough regular bags in-house to make up a couple of pallets. The special ones would be surrounded by normal ones and they all had the same Wal-Mart, UK packaging. They would get plastic shrink

wrap applied before loading them into the truck to take them to the container port for shipping. He had just finished when Chen Lee showed up in his limo. "We can ship these now and collect the money." He told Chen. "Good work. I have the shipping arrangements underway as we speak. The truck can take the pallets to the port right away.

One more day and the rest of the container will be full. There is a ship leaving in three days. These will be on it." He said. "When can you make another sample?" He asked. "I don't have enough material to make any right now. Do you have another customer?" Lin asked. "Possibly, I may know soon. You must get ready another sample right away in case we need to do another demonstration." Chen instructed, his tone emphasizing the urgency. "When they doubled their order it took all the material I had to fill it. I must go to Shanghai right away to get my ingredients." Lin replied. "Then go now. I'll have my plane ready when you get to the airport." Chen demanded. Lin went back inside and returned with a briefcase then climbed into his car and left. Chen phoned the airfield and had the pilot get his Lear ready immediately. Then he and his body guard went into Yuang's lab and rifled through the files again. "He did not take the papers that I photographed before. They are still in the file." He said. "No matter, we'll get what we need when he returns this time." Chen spat, shaking his fist. He did not like the old man keeping secrets from him. He let him feel like he was safe by keeping the recipe a secret, but Chen knew he could force it out of him if he needed to. For now he just wanted to make as much money as possible on the project. If the Arabs were successful this time, he could charge anything he wanted for the next batch or just sell the formula to the highest bidder. He phoned Wong to see if he had set up another prospective buyer. "Mr.

Panidas has suggested we meet with a third party to discuss a similar transaction. Of

course he doesn't know about the special luggage but I believe his buyer is in the market for something similar. I told him I would arrange a meeting with this person today. If he checks out, we could have him come to your yacht for a more specific proposition. He gave me the name Abdul Latiff and a number to reach him here in Singapore. I have our people checking his background. He appears to have come from Morocco on a French passport, via Dubai and is staying here in Singapore at the same hotel as Mr. Panidas.

Panidas says he hasn't met him and he may not know he is in the same hotel. Our people are looking into that." Wong explained.

"Let's get on with it. Have Panidas and this Abdul meet us at the boat launch. They can meet each other there before we go out to the ship for the meeting. If it looks fishy we'll just dispose of both of them." Chen instructed.

Wong phoned the number Stan gave him and Nate answered in Arabic. Wong told him he should take a cab to the boat launch at five o'clock and gave him the directions in the same language. Then Wong phoned Stan and told him they would meet at the boat launch at five o'clock. Stan agreed and then told Wong he expected a five percent fee for bringing in new business. Wong agreed and rang off. Stan dialed Mel's number and hung up after two rings. "It's on for five o'clock at the boat launch." He told Nate. "No one has mentioned me so I think I'll get down there earlier and scope it out. It won't hurt to have some firepower in the area in case they smell a rat." He added. "How good is your boy Stan, if we have to fight our way out?" Nate asked, looking Mel in the eye. "Well, you'll both be unarmed and Chen has some big help, but I'd say Stan is as good as they come.

I'd let him watch my back anytime." Mel answered. Nate nodded as if to say "that's good enough for me". Mel loaded two of the PPK's and stuck one in his pocket and the other in the small of his back under his jacket. He wrapped two extra clips in paper towels to

keep them from rattling in his other pocket and went out. This time he strolled down the block to where he and Nate had stopped in the café the first day. He went in and ordered coffee and picked up an English newspaper from the kiosk on the sidewalk. He killed a few minutes reading the paper and drinking his coffee while watching the street for anyone following him. He crossed the street and went around to the next block before finding a cab and going down toward the docks. He got out a few blocks from the waterfront and went into a building and watched the cab disappear before coming back out and walking toward the boat launch area. It was nearly four thirty when he got to the docks. He went into a tourist trap gift shop across the street where he had a good view of the docks. He casually poked around the souvenirs and tourist junk for a while then purchased a straw hat, sunglasses and a couple of tee shirts. The clerk put the tee shirts in a large shopping bag with the store name on it. Mel paid in cash and then put the hat and sunglasses on and walked outside. Two doors down there was a sidewalk café with umbrella tables where they served sandwiches and cold drinks. He sat down where he could watch the boat launch and ordered iced tea and a sandwich. He pretended to look at the stuff in his shopping bag while he slipped one of the guns into it. Nate arrived in a cab precisely at five o'clock, carrying a newspaper under his left arm as instructed. The launch returned to the dock at almost the same instant. Another cab arrived and Stan got out and walked over to the launch where he met David Wong coming off the boat. He walked right past Nate who stood waiting for Wong to make a move. Stan and David Wong shook hands and exchanged greetings while one of Chen's bodyguards circled around behind Nate. Nate pretended not to notice and then David Wong walked over and asked if he was Abdul. Nate nodded and then shook hands with Wong. David then

introduced him to Stan and motioned them to get into the boat. The bodyguard followed them in and the launch took off. Mel decided he couldn't be any more help so he hailed a cab and went back to the hotel. When he got back he called Jake and filled him in. Now they just had to wait and hope things went smoothly for Nate and Stan.

Stan was surprised when they went a different direction after leaving the docks. He was expecting to go back to the gambling ship. Instead they pulled alongside Chen's beautiful yacht anchored a couple of miles east. Chen's helicopter was already on the deck when they got there and he was waiting in the saloon. David Wong introduced Nate to Chen and Stan greeted Chen with a smile and a handshake. "What can we do for you Mr.

Latiff?" Chen asked, getting right to the point. "I represent a group who desire to have access to explosive devices that can be carried on or checked onto an airplane, undetected." He replied. "And what makes you think we can provide such and item?"

Wong asked. "The Jihad is worldwide, many rumors abound. When one entity discovers something useful, others always wish to take advantage also. If I am misinformed, please accept my apologies. If you are just being cautious I fully understand. My group is anxious to obtain what we need and are willing to pay handsomely for the privilege." He replied. "How reliable is this group?" Chen asked Stan. Stan replied "I have no specific knowledge of Mr. Latiff or his group. He was referred to me by a customer who has been reliable for me in the past. He assured me they were able to pay any amount needed to get what they want. That's all I know. I prefer not to have any more information than necessary, for obvious reasons." Chen and Wong spoke to each other in Chinese for a few moments. "Do you want to offer to describe the product to him?" Wong asked. "Yes, but we will ask for a deposit first. Have Mr. Panidas leave us while we discuss it." Chen

replied. "Niko, would you mind excusing yourself for a while? We would like to talk with Mr. Latiff in private." "Certainly, I would love to have a small tour of your beautiful ship, Mr. Chen." Stan replied. "Excellent. Take Mr. Panidas for a tour of the boat. I will call you when we are finished." Chen told his bodyguard. "Are you prepared to produce a cash deposit in advance of what we will tell you?" Wong asked. "Yes. If the amount is not more than I have in here." He said, patting his briefcase. "I think $50,000 would be a reasonable deposit." Chen replied. Nate opened the briefcase and handed over five packets of bills, each packet wrapped with a $10,000 label. "Just what have you heard about our product?" Wong asked. "Only that you are able to get explosives past airline security." Nate replied. "What we have is the technology to place an explosive device in the baggage compartment, completely undetectable and able to self detonate when the plane is descending for a landing. A passenger can check in a bag containing the device, undetected, as regular luggage. He doesn't even have to know he is going to die with it."

Chen said with a wide grin and a nod at Wong. Nate's reaction of wide eyed amazement looked genuine because it truly was. He took in a deep breath and looked at both men, excitement apparent on his face. "How can it be detonated by the passenger without his knowledge?" Nate asked. "A very special device arms it when the airplane reaches cruising altitude and then detonates when the plane is back down to about ten thousand feet. The passenger has nothing to do with it. It is fully automatic and requires nothing from the outside once it is on board the plane. It is the perfect weapon." Chen explained.

"And what will be the price for such a weapon?" Nate asked. "We will require one million dollars for the privilege of purchasing plus two hundred fifty thousand dollars per device." Chen explained. "For that price my group will want proof that the device works

as described and is powerful enough to bring down a large plane. If we are satisfied with your proof, the price will be acceptable." Nate replied. "Mr. Wong will contact you when we are ready to demonstrate the product. Thank you for coming Mr. Latiff." With that Chen got up and left with one of his bodyguards. Wong picked up his cell phone to let the other bodyguard know that Stan could return to the saloon. When Stan got back they all went down to the launch and started back to the docks. As they were shoving off they heard Chen's helicopter rev up and take off. "How long will it take before I can see a demonstration?" Nate asked. "Only a few days, I trust. Mr. Lee has other interests to attend to. I will let you know as soon as he returns and is ready for you." Wong replied Stan remained quiet throughout the ride until they reached the docks and Nate left in a taxi. "I take it Mr. Chen is willing to do business with Mr. Latiff. Has a price been agreed to?" He asked Wong. "Relax, you'll get your fee when the deal is done. Chen Lee always pays well for successful ventures. It should be quite a large sum. I will contact you when it's time for you to get paid." He said, shaking Stan's hand before returning to the boat.

Stan grabbed the next available cab and went back to the hotel. He went into the hotel bar for a drink and to wait a while before contacting Mel. He was certain he was being watched. But, he was anxious to hear what Nate had learned. Finally he went up to his room and dialed Mel. "Come on up." was all he heard when Mel answered. Even though he was curious to hear the news, he took the usual precautions and went up the stairs.

Nate let him into Mel's room and nodded that it was still ok to talk there. "Did they tell you what the Arabs bought?" He asked. "Not entirely, they said it was an explosive device that could pass airport security and was fully automatic. They claim it doesn't need any outside input to detonate it." He replied. "Christ, if that's true they can get the

damn things onto any airline. I wonder how many they are getting." Stan said. "Chen also indicated that the person carrying the luggage and checking it in would not have to know it had a bomb in it. That means the thing has to be very cleverly disguised as well as non-detectable to dogs or chemical sniffer equipment. It has to look like something a person would normally have in their bag when traveling." Nate added. "I just hope we find out what it is before the Arabs get theirs." Mel added. "We need to get some details on anything Chen's companies are shipping. Shit, they could make these things look like regular merchandize and go right through customs unnoticed." He continued. "We'd better alert Jake and get this info to Sean right away. Maybe Ty or Ron can get a list of what kind of goods are going from Singapore to England." Nate said. "If they actually ship the stuff from here. It might come from somewhere else. They may make the deal here and make the actual devices elsewhere. Chen has connections everywhere in China and Asia." Stan added. "You're right. Ron needs to check on everything Dennis Wong handles. There is no guarantee that the shipment will originate in Singapore." Mel agreed.

"I'll contact him right away." He added.

CHAPTER SEVENTY NINE

"We have a couple of prospects for our programming dilemma." Imam, Abdullah Al Rahman, told Rashid. "It is about time. I'm getting more confused every time I try to get them all in the air at the same time." Rashid replied. "When will we be able to speak to them?" He asked. "I have one of them coming by today. He is a graduate student, right here at Blackburn College. His major is computer science." Rahman replied. "Do we know anything about his background or where his loyalties are placed?" Rashid asked.

"He was born in England but his parents came from Indonesia. His brother is in Iraq

fighting with Al Quaeda. He is sympathetic to our cause." "Good, good, I want to see him as soon as possible." "He will be here within the hour. I'll bring him right in when he arrives." Rashid was relieved. He had worked himself into a state of near madness trying to get all the possibilities refined. He was fairly certain the packages would be shipping soon and he wanted to be ready when they arrived. It still would be a huge task to get all the pieces in place and the cases to all the intended passengers. He thought maybe the programmer could help with that puzzle also.

"What do you think a mosque would need a computer programmer for in Blackburn?"

Rory wondered. The intelligence people had picked up some chatter about the Imam advertising on the internet chat rooms for an experienced programmer. They had used the mosque and the known suspects as keywords for their watchdog program. When it picked up multiple transmissions involving the Makkee Masjid mosque and Imam Al Rahman they routed the messages to Rory Wells. He called Mick Randall and posed the question to him. "I'd bet they are trying to combine some airline schedules for the attack they are planning. It must be huge if they need a programmer to sort it out. We know they planned to get six flights all to explode on flights to the US on the same day, at least once before.

This could be bigger than that." Mick answered. "Has there been any news from Singapore concerning our suspects or when the weapons might arrive?" He asked. "Just today I received word that they definitely are explosive devices disguised as ordinary travel stuff and be non-detectable by dogs. They also believe these gadgets are automatic and do not require outside input to detonate." Rory explained. "That means they can put them in luggage and check them onto the plane even without the passenger knowing what is going to happen. They could give the passenger some bogus message or something and

put it along with the other stuff in a normal suitcase for them to take on their trip. They wouldn't have to have suicidal fanatics to do that. They could give them to a family or anyone traveling to the US thinking they were just carrying information to some sleeper cell. Jesus, talk about diabolical. We've got to identify this stuff before they get it or we'll have the biggest disaster they have ever pulled off. Can you imagine what it would do to airline travel and the economy, let alone the loss of life?" Mick said, taking a deep breath. "I don't want to even think about it. We have to get this stuff away from them, one way or another. Even if news about their plan gets out it could interrupt airline travel and cause mass chaos." Rory countered.

CHAPTER EIGHTY

"It was loaded yesterday and the ship left just after midnight." The freight forwarder informed David Wong. He immediately phoned Chen Lee to inform him. "Get those Arabs on the phone. I want that money transferred now." He demanded. It would take eighteen days for the shipment to arrive at it's destination but he could keep the goods away from them if they did not pay as agreed. They would not know where to get their merchandize until he was paid and ready for them to know. He wanted to get another batch sold before they got theirs and created chaos. He called his pilot to see where Lin Yuang was in his quest for more materials. He planned to straighten the old man out when he returned. He did not like secrets unless it was he who held them. "I have not seen him since we got here. He told me it would take a couple of days to get all the things he needs. Do you want me to return to Singapore and come back for him later?" the pilot asked. "No, I want you to find him and get his miserable carcass back here as soon as possible. He'd better be working on the project and not screwing around. I didn't send you two on a vacation. I know he has many friends in Shanghai and likes to play around when he's there." Chen replied, more than a little frustrated. He wanted to get the new customer on the hook with a demonstration and get more money before anything happened to screw it up. He had raised the price to a level that made him lust for a quick sale. Wong called back and reported that the wire transfer had been completed and the money was paid in full. "At least that part of it went as planned." He thought to himself.

Maybe the rest would fall into place as well.

CHAPTER EIGHTY ONE

Ron and Ty were going over all the shipping orders that Dennis Wong had handled in the last few days, looking for any clue that might help them find out when the Arab's shipment would be leaving. The problem was; they didn't really know what they were looking for. They just kept poring over the bills of lading looking for something that would tip them off. Jake had called Mel to see if they had learned anything from the other Wong or Chen Lee that would help. Mel explained what they knew, which wasn't much, and said they were waiting for a demonstration of the device. They hoped that they could identify the disguised product in time to intercept the shipment. All they could do for now was wait for Wong to tell them when the demo would take place. Mel was considering kidnapping David Wong and dragging the information out of him. He knew it was a desperate, last resort, sort of plan but they were running out of options. It would not be easy in any case. Chen had people everywhere and Mel had no real options for hiding a captive. The whole area was Chen's back yard and Wong was very cautious. Still, it was a chance they might have to take. Time could be running out if they didn't get a break pretty soon. Nate decided to take a chance and call Wong and maybe apply a little subtle

pressure. He dialed the number Stan gave him for the Chinese embassy and was told that Mr. Wong would be away from his office for a few days. "Maybe we should try to get out to the gambling boat. If we run into Wong or Mr. Lee at least we'll know they're still here. I wonder why the delay, you'd think the greedy bastards would want to get on with it." Nate suggested. "Maybe they don't have enough of their magic potion to make another example. Or they're checking out your background. Something is up, I wish we knew what." Mel added. "Let's wait on the gambling boat idea for now. We don't want Wong to get nervous about us before we find out what the hell they are using to hide the explosives" He continued.

CHAPTER EIGHTY TWO

Lin Yuang had disappeared. Chen's pilot and the one bodyguard he had sent with them searched the old man's room and found that his belongings were gone and he had not bothered to check out. "Mr. Lee will kill us if we don't find him soon." The pilot screeched at the bigger man. "Stop whining, we'll find him. He's probably at a bordello in old town. He's as horny as a spring goat. I know where he goes when he comes to Shanghai." The man replied. They set off for the old section of town where Lin Yuang usually went for fun when he could get to Shanghai. They decided to search for him before alerting Chen Lee that he was really missing.

"What do you mean he's missing?" Wong demanded. "The buyer is ready and anxious.

I've had him checked out and can't see any reason to delay the demo." He continued. "He went to Shanghai to get supplies. I sent him in my own plane to speed things up. When I tried to reach him I couldn't. My pilot said he had gone to get the materials yesterday and has not returned. I told him to go find Lin and get his decrepit ass back here. He goes a

little nuts when he gets to his old haunts. He will regret this when he returns." Chen spat.

"What should I tell the buyer?" Wong asked. "Just tell him I had to leave town on a business emergency and will return shortly. We did not promise him an exact time for the demo, anyway." Chen replied. "Our other shipment is on its way; I hope we can get the next sale made before they start blowing up airplanes." Wong added.

CHAPTER EIGHTY THREE

Ty and Ron intercepted everything Dennis Wong had done since tapping his home computer as well as every deal he handled from his office at Joseph's company. "I can't see anything that looks suspicious in these freight bills; just a bunch of mundane Chinese stuff going to traders and department store chains." Ty complained. "Maybe they haven't shipped the explosives yet." Ron added. "We still don't know exactly what to look for and we know they will try to disguise the product to look like normal merchandize.

Besides, we don't know if they are getting one or a hundred of these devices." Ty said.

"Let's look at the smaller quantities going to England from Singapore. Chances are they are making the devices in Chen's home territory. If they are really new technology, he wouldn't trust anyone else to be involved at this stage." Jake offered. Ty divided the freight bills into three stacks and gave one to each of them to go over. "Here is a container that left yesterday from Singapore. It has several smaller quantities of merchandize going to various receivers, all in England. It's on a container ship of the Chinese Shipping Group's line. It's called the "Shanghai Star", one of the older, smaller container ships in their fleet. It looks like it has no other stops after Singapore and is headed for the Tilbury container port in the London area." Ty said. "Chen Lee has warehouse facilities in that district. Let's have a closer look at what's in that container."

Jake added. "There are several pallets of computer keyboards, several more of stuffed toys, two pallets of plastic luggage, two pallets of styrene pellets in bags, two more of kitchen appliances like electric can openers and coffee makers. Over half of the container is filled with silk men's shirts and women's silk skirts." Ty read off the list. "Who is getting the smaller units?" Jake asked. "ASDA, I believe that is England's version of Wal-Mart." Ron answered. "Let's get ahold of someone at ASDA and find out if they are really getting an order for such a small amount of luggage. Wouldn't you expect them to buy in much larger quantities than that?" Jake asked. "What about the styrene pellets?"

He asked. "They're going to a chemical supply broker, address in Leeds, London." Ty answered. "You call them and I'll check on the ASDA/Wal-Mart stuff." Jake told him.

They followed the same process on one other Singapore based container. The time zone difference meant they would have to wait until business hours in England before calling.

Since it was only four hours later in Singapore, Jake decided to call Mel for an update.

"I've got him. He's the one in the pullover and tan backpack." Mick told Rory over the radio. They had picked up the student coming out of the mosque the day before and tracked him to the University campus. Today they were following him back toward the mosque, watching from two cars so they could tag team him without his knowledge.

Mick could tell from the relaxed way the boy walked that he was unaware of their surveillance. He didn't appear to be more than twenty and had the disheveled look of a computer geek college student. When he entered the parking lot of the mosque they moved away to another street, out of sight. As far as they could tell this was only his second day at the mosque, unless they had failed to notice him earlier. Inside the mosque Rashid met the boy and led him to the office where the computer was glowing on an old

oak desk. "This would go a lot faster if you would allow me to do it at school. We have much better equipment there." The boy told Rashid. "We cannot allow anyone to know what we are doing.

You must do your work here." Rashid replied, trying not to alarm the boy with his tone. "OK, OK, just don't rush me, I'm doing the best I can with this old junk." "Allah will be proud of you, my son." Imam Rahman said, entering the room.

Rashid ignored the old man and went out. He was becoming more and more frustrated with the progress of the boy. Now that the suitcase bombs were on the way he was anxious to get his plan into action before anything went wrong. He still had to decide how to get the cases to the potential passengers once the flights were booked. He still felt they were being too ambitious. He believed that half as many flights would accomplish their objective and would cut the risk of premature discovery in half as well. His orders were clear and they left no room for independent decisions.

"Should we grab him when he comes out this time or wait and see how many times he returns?" Mick wondered aloud. "Let's just watch him a while longer. If he doesn't have any evidence on him to show what they're up to we'll tip them off and they may move the whole show somewhere else." Rory answered. "You're probably right. If he is programming a computer in the mosque they probably don't let him leave with anything that would connect him to their plans." Mick agreed. Rory moved his car around the block and set up where he could watch the mosque. Mick would come back and spell him in a couple of hours.

CHAPTER EIGHTY FOUR

"What do you think is going on? Wong should have set up the demo by now. I wonder if they're having trouble with the device or checking us out more thoroughly before

committing to show us their product." Stan asked. "I think it's time to put some pressure on our David Wong. No one would sit idly for this long after handing over that much cash. See if you can get him at the embassy and arrange a meeting somewhere else. Tell him Mr. Latiff is getting nervous and thinks he is getting screwed. Let on that you believe he is very dangerous and might do something rash if Chen doesn't get on with it." Mel replied.

Stan picked up his cell phone and called the Chinese embassy. The receptionist said Mr. Wong was out of town and asked if she could take a message. Stan asked when he was supposed to return and was told he was expected tomorrow. He repeated this to Mel and Nate and gave Mel a look that said "now what". "Let's wait until this evening and check out his usual haunts. If we don't see him around town we'll see if we can slip out to the gambling ship and look there." Mel decided.

CHAPTER EIGHTY FIVE

"We've looked everywhere, boss, Lin Yuang has disappeared. His room is empty but he didn't check out. All of his things are gone and no one saw him leave the hotel. We went to all his usual places in old town and checked out everything we could think of, but he has vanished." The pilot told Chen Lee. On the other end of the call Chen Lee was furious. He kicked over a waste basket, kicked it again and then screamed into the phone.

"You'd better find him fast! I won't stand for this! What the hell is he doing? What the hell did you let him out of your sight for?" He calmed down slightly, then continued "I'll send more men to help you search; spread some cash around to the police, somebody must know where he is." Now Chen had calmed down and began thinking about the old man. He wondered what reason there could be for him to disappear without a word. He paid the old fool more than he could ever make anywhere else. That should have

guaranteed his loyalty. Maybe he had been abducted or robbed and murdered; he was foolish about carrying large amounts of cash and going into unsafe places without protection. He would have to wait a few days and see if his men were able to locate him or worse he turned up dead in some alley. At least he had been paid for the first shipment of bombs and he had the deposit from the new customer already in his pocket. He could afford to wait, for now. He was still playing out various scenarios in his mind when David Wong phoned. "Mr. Lee, what is happening? Isn't Yuang back yet?" He asked.

"There is a problem; Yuang is missing in Shanghai. I have people searching for him. He seems to have disappeared." "What should I do about Latiff? Panidas is leaving messages at my office. He wants a meeting, no doubt to find out what is taking so long. If he believes we are cheating him he might try to kill me. I don't trust either of them." Wong worried. "Relax, just meet with them on the gambling ship where we can protect you. Do you really think they are more dangerous than we are, here in Singapore? You can tell them that some of our supplies have been delayed and it will only be a few more days. By then we should have found Yuang and gotten the demo ready. If not, I will deal with them." David Wong just stared at the phone; Chen had abruptly hung up, leaving Wong to ponder his next move. He decided he'd better call Panidas and set up a meeting at the gambling ship. Stan got the call in time to avoid searching the town and agreed to meet Wong at nine o'clock at the boat launch. Mel decided to go early and get on the ship ahead of the others.

Ron and Ty had gone over all the shipping orders from Wong's computer and from his records at work until they were convinced that the bombs had to be in one of two containers that were on the same ship. Both containers had various merchandize inside, a

combination of large and small orders. Jake had contacted ASDA in London and found that they indeed were expecting some luggage that had been on back order. Ty had similar results from the chemical supply house that ordered the styrene pellets. Several other small orders had also been checked by phone. Nothing seemed to be unusual. "I guess we'd better look at some other areas, just in case they are making them outside of Singapore." Jake reasoned. "Don't reject that Wal-Mart order just because they confirmed it. It's very common for portions of shipped goods to get damaged or lost, leaving the customer short and requiring a small back order to complete their stock. Chen could be hiding the devices within a legitimate order and planning to claim a portion was damaged. The customer would never know." Joseph explained. He had been listening in on the discussion and decided to offer his expertise. "Joseph's right. Chen could hide something in the luggage or use the normal stuff to surround the bombs on the pallet. It has to be a high percentage chance that the whole pallet would clear customs then he could get his devices out and ship the real order to the customer." Ron agreed. "If that's the case, we'll have British customs isolate both containers and go through them thoroughly. We might just get lucky. I'll get Sean to arrange that with the Brits." Jake advised. "We'd better keep looking at these bills and any new ones Wong handles, we might miss the real thing while we concentrate on these two containers." Ron added.

CHAPTER EIGHTY SIX

Mel picked up an "escort" with the help of the cab driver and made his way to the boat launch. Once on board he casually played at the tables with his new girl friend for a while and then they went into the dining room and ordered dinner. They had just finished dinner when he saw that Wong had arrived with Stan and Nate. They were shadowed by

two of Chen's bodyguards and went into a room off of the casino. Mel guided his date to a roulette table near the door to the side room and resumed playing. One of Chen's men stood near the door, watching the crowd. The other had gone inside with Wong and the others. "I have to apologize for the delay, gentlemen. It seems we have had some problem getting critical supplies. Mr. Lee has gone to the source to speed things up. He sends his apologies and has offered to extend you both unlimited gambling on this ship to make amends." Wong explained smoothly. "That is generous of Mr. Lee, but we did not come to you for entertainment. How much longer must we wait? My investors are not patient people. They are demanding to know why this has taken so long." Nate replied, his anger beginning to show. Stan moved uncomfortably in his chair and then tried to smooth things over. "Are we talking about two or three days or will it be longer?" He asked.

"You cannot get this product or anything like it anywhere else; surely it is worth a few extra days. Mr. Lee assures me that he will expedite the process as quickly as possible.

He could not give me an exact time frame but he is as anxious to conclude our business as you are." Wong replied, applying his well practiced charm. "What a snake oil salesman this asshole is" Stan thought to himself. "Let us all hope it takes no longer than a week." Nate said and stood up to leave. The stare he fixed on David Wong sent shivers up the man's spine. Chen's man began to reach inside his jacket for his pistol and then decided to let it go as Wong extended his hand to Nate. They shook hands and then Nate and Stan went out first followed by Wong and the bodyguard. Mel watched the procession from the roulette table. Satisfied that nothing was happening, he slipped the knife back into the sheath taped to his forearm. He told the girl it was time to cash in their chips and head for the launch. She collected their small pile of chips, tipped the croupier

and walked with Mel to the cashier's cage. Stan and Nate had gone down to catch the launch. David Wong and his two companions went back to the room where the meeting had been held. Mel waited while his lady friend used the restroom and then they joined the group in the launch for the ride back.

Back at the hotel the men gathered in Mel's room to discuss the evening's events.

"Something is definitely haywire. Why would Chen stall this deal unless they really couldn't get the device ready to demo?" Mel asked. "Wong tried to act like it was just an unfortunate delay in getting supplies, but I saw real fear in is eyes." Nate added. "That look you gave him even scared the big dude, Nate. I thought Hong Kong Fooey was gonna pull his gun and start blasting for a minute there." Stan explained. "It was more than that: he was spooked before I gave him the whammy. Something's fucked up on Chen's end. I wish we knew what it was." Nate added. "I'm afraid we're running out of time. Whatever Chen sold to the Arabs may have gotten to them by now. I'll call Jake and see if anything has turned up on that end. We may have to do something drastic if we don't get some answers pretty soon." Mel told them. He phoned Jake and brought him up to date. "I just talked to Sean Moore a little while ago. His man in Shanghai says that Chen Lee has people searching for a guy named Lin Yuang. It must be urgent because the whole city is looking for him. Chen has a reward out for him but no one knows what he wants him for. We checked him out and discovered he was a top chemist for the Chinese government's weapons program who went missing a couple of years ago. The Chinese believe he is dead. He may be working for Chen Lee on your project. Maybe he got scared and hauled ass. See if you can connect him to Lee." Jake said. Mel repeated the message to the others and said "Chen Lee is frantically looking for a scientist named Lin

Yuang. Maybe he's the problem. Jake says he was a chemist working on weapons in China. The Chinese say he disappeared and they believed him to be dead. If he got scared and took off, Chen might not know how to build whatever concoction it takes to make the bombs work. I'll call Jake back and have him see if Sean's people in Shanghai can help find him. If they can locate him he can tell us what we need to know to find these devices and disarm them." Mel called Jake and explained what he needed from Lin Yuang.

"When did Jake say the suspect ship is due in England?" Nate asked. "It's supposed to arrive at the end of this week. That doesn't give us much time to figure this thing out."

Mel replied. "Jake says they think they've narrowed down the possible containers that could have Chen's bombs on board. Let's hope he's right, maybe British customs can find them before they get out of the port." He added. "I think its time we put some real pressure on David Wong. I don't think we can afford to wait for Chen Lee to find his missing chemist." Nate offered. "I agree. We need to find out where he lives. If we can't catch him going to or from the embassy we'll have to grab him at one of the clubs or off the gambling boat." Mel answered. "I think it'll be too risky to try to get him at Chen's clubs or the boat. I'll contact Clay and see if he can come up with an address. He has to go home sometime." Stan explained. "We'll stake out the boat launch this evening, while you check with Clay. Find out where Chen lives while you're at it." Mel said. "I'll call his embassy office first and see if he is supposed to come in tomorrow. We can't just grab him in front of the embassy in broad daylight. The police would have us in no time." Stan replied. "You're right, we'll have to follow him when he leaves and try to ambush him somewhere away from there. If we try to take him at the boat launch he'll have Chen's bodyguards around him and we'd have a tough time getting away. We need to get him

when he's alone." Nate agreed. Stan had no luck at the Chinese embassy, David Wong was not scheduled to return for two more days. He left word at the blind drop asking Clay for the information on Chen and Wong. Later that day he went to the second drop and retrieved the answer. "David Wong lives within Chen Lee's compound. The whole thing is surrounded by a security fence with sophisticated detection devices and armed guards.

When he travels it's always in one of Chen's cars driven by one of his bodyguards." He told the others. "Then we'll have to try to get him when he's in the car or getting on the launch. We're running out of options." Mel replied. They decided to stake out the road near Chen's compound in the morning if they didn't find Wong by this evening.

Stan and Nate went out to the gambling ship to look for David Wong that night while Mel checked out the area around Chen Lee's compound. They stayed on the boat gambling and watching for Wong or Chen Lee until midnight and then gave it up and went back to town. Mel met them back at the hotel around two o'clock. "He didn't show up at the ship tonight." Stan said. "I found an area of dense trees and foliage about half a mile from the compound where we can watch for him without being seen from the road."

Mel reported.

Chen Lee's pilot had returned from Shanghai that afternoon to pick him up. Chen insisted that David Wong accompany him to Shanghai. He wanted Wong to use his government contacts to get help finding Lin Yuang. He was getting desperate to find the old man. He didn't want to lose the big payoff from Abdul Latiff. Lin Yuang would pay dearly for hiding from him, he told Wong.

Mel and Nate stayed at their stakeout until a little after ten the next morning. Several cars came and went but none of them had David Wong or Chen Lee aboard. When they got

back to the hotel, Stan was waiting in Mel's room. "I just got word from Clay that Chen Lee and David Wong have landed in Shanghai. They came in Chen's private jet last night. Wong has gone into a government office building and Chen Lee was seen in old town at a known gangster's club." "Great, no wonder we couldn't find them." Mel replied. "What do we do now?" Nate wondered. "We wait and hope they return right away or the CIA finds Lin Yuang before Chen Lee does." Mel answered.

CHAPTER EIGHTY SEVEN

"I have it! If no flights get cancelled or delayed you can have forty of them airborne before the first one lands!" the boy exclaimed. Imam Abdullah Al Rahman and Rashid stared at each other for a moment in shocked silence. Their intricate plan was finally going to be possible. "Allah be praised, this boy is a genius!" Al Rahman practically shouted to Rashid. "Indeed he is. Print that out for me now my young genius." Rashid replied, his eyes gleaming. Now all he needed was for the infidel Chinese to safely get the bombs to him, he knew he could get them to the passengers on time, one way or another. The boy could help him organize the distribution of the bombs now that the flights had been determined. It wouldn't be easy but it was going to happen. He could feel it. This would be a blow that the West would never recover from. Islam would eventually defeat all the infidels just as the prophet had predicted. Rashid would be revered as no other before him; he would be a hero for all of Islam, forever.

CHAPTER EIGHTY EIGHT

The search for Lin Yuang had intensified in Shanghai; unbeknownst to Chen Lee other forces were joining the hunt.

When David Wong contacted friends in the Chinese secret service for help, it unleashed a massive manhunt by the Chinese government to find the

old man. He possessed knowledge of military secrets that they did not want exposed. He had covered his tracks well when he ran off to work with Chen Lee; everyone believed he was dead. The CIA had agents searching as well. No one was having any success. Lin Yuang had once again disappeared. His escape route appeared to have been planned well in advance.

Two more days passed and there was still no sign of David Wong or Chen Lee. Mel decided it was time for a new strategy. "I'm going to meet with Jake in London. I want you to stay here with Stan and keep trying to get your hands on Wong or Chen Lee. The Shanghai Star has just docked in London. British customs agents will be looking into the suspect containers as soon as the ship is unloaded." He told Nate. "We may as well get Clay and Perry involved. Maybe with their help we can grab someone from Chen's yacht and squeeze some information from them about what the device looks like." Stan offered.

"Just don't get specific about who Nate works for. The less said, the better." Mel advised.

While Mel went down to check out and get a cab to the airport, Stan phoned Clay Strong and brought him up to date. "I'll send Perry to get you right away. We'll meet here at my office and make a plan for tonight." Clay told him. Stan introduced Nate and Perry on the way to the US Embassy and brought Perry up to speed on where the investigation had gone. "Clay has access to a speedboat, maybe we can get close enough to Chen's yacht to get on board or grab one of his crew. With Chen out of town they may be a little more relaxed than usual." Perry suggested. Clay couldn't come up with anything better when they suggested it to him so they made a plan to get someone on board Chen's yacht that night. They decided to take the speedboat out and reconnoiter Chen's ship for a way to get on board while it was still daylight. They discovered that the crew had left the loading ramp in position as though expecting a delivery or some other guests. "When the cat's away the mice get lazy. They must know that Chen is not coming back right away." Stan noted. "We'll wait until after midnight when most of the crew will be asleep. I'll make a pass a few hundred yards from the yacht and unload the two-man inflatable. You and Nate paddle it quietly up to the ramp and see if you can sneak on board. If you can grab one of the crew and get him into the raft we'll come back and tow you out of there. Perry and I will try to cover you from our position if you have to jump ship." Clay advised. He took the boat out about a half mile and shut the engine down. They spent a few minutes watching the activity on the yacht through high powered binoculars. Now and then a white uniformed deck hand would walk along the railing and then disappear around the forecastle. None appeared to be armed and no guards were visible anywhere on deck.

Satisfied, they took a circular route back to the docks. "We'll meet back here about eleven thirty. Perry and I will bring all the gear you will need. You guys get something to eat and get some rest. This might be a long night." Clay told them. When Stan and Nate returned to the boat, Perry was laying out two black wet suits, night vision goggles, knives, a blackjack, a piano wire garrote and various firearms. "Looks like you have all the bases covered." Nate said, staring at the arsenal. "Check this out if you think this stuff is good." Perry replied as he pulled the black cover off a silenced thirty caliber, belt fed machine gun that was set up to mount to the bow of the boat. "We're ready for world war three if you need it." He continued. Clay finished tying a small inflatable raft to the stern and then started the engines. As they pulled away from the marina Stan and Nate donned their wetsuits and readied their weapons. No one spoke during the ride out and Clay kept the engines running just above idle to keep the noise down. There were scattered lights on

boats moored in the marina but there was no moon and cloud cover masked the stars.

Clay cut the engines and glided silently to a stop about two hundred yards astern of the big yacht. Marker lights glowed on the ship's silhouette and a few cabin lights were visible below deck. Spot lights made the wheelhouse stand out above the dark water and the rotating beacon on top of the stack made yellow streaks through the evening mist.

Nate and Stan were practically invisible in the black raft as they paddled slowly toward the crew ladder. Nate tied the raft to the ladder with a large slip knot loop so he could release it quickly when they were ready to leave. The two dark figures crept up the crew ladder and slipped onto the deck. Stan took up a position near the exit from the wheelhouse while Nate made his way toward the stern. On the fantail he discovered a dark shape covered with a large tarp. He pulled the tarp up and switched on his penlight.

He was amazed to find an x-ray machine like the ones used by the TSA at airports. He turned off the light and pulled the tarp back down in place. He was just about back to Stan's position when a figure in a white uniform came out of the wheelhouse. The man looked toward Nate just as Stan whacked him with the leather covered blackjack. The man slumped to the deck without making a sound. Nate peeked inside the wheelhouse and then tried to help Stan get the big man on his feet. He was too heavy for them to carry down the ladder so Nate ran back toward the stern to look for a rope. He thought he might find one long enough to lower the big sailor down to the raft. Nothing was available so he went back to where Stan was holding the unconscious lump. "We'll have to heave him over the side and then try to drag him into the raft. It's the only way." He whispered. Stan nodded and grabbed the man under the arms while Nate went for his legs. They shuffled him over to the railing and folded him over it. He hit the water with a

loud splash just as they were sliding down the ladder. Nate went in first and got the man's head out of the water while Stan untied the raft and slid over to them. They struggled to get the limp sailor into the raft just as someone shouted from above and turned on a large searchlight. They began paddling furiously along the side of the ship where the light could not reach them. Someone was firing a pistol at them and shouting in Chinese. Soon others joined in the gunfire and tried to spot the dark raft with flashlights. Stan managed to get the raft under the overhang of the stern where the gunmen couldn't see them. More searchlights lit the area up like a carnival just as Clay drove the speedboat under the stern of the big ship. Perry helped them get into the speed boat and the three of them pulled the unconscious sailor on board. Above them on deck several crewmen were running back and forth firing wildly with pistols and one automatic rifle. Clay gunned the speedboat and shot out from under the stern but stayed close to the side of the ship until he gained some speed. The deck was in chaos and no one got a clear shot at them as they sped out of sight. In a few moments they were out of range of the gunfire and disappeared into the night. Stan was trying to revive their captive, but it was no use. "I think he broke his neck when he hit the water." Stan said. "Shit! We just stirred up a hornets nest and didn't learn anything." Clay spat. "Not quite. They have an x-ray machine on deck. They must have used it to see if they could get their device through airport security. Whatever it is, it must fit in a suitcase without raising suspicion." Stan replied. "We'd better dispose of our friend here before someone sees us." Perry said. Clay took the boat out to deep water, about an hour out and then they weighted the body down with chains and dropped it overboard. "We'll head over to Bin Tan and hide the boat. I don't want to take a chance we'll be seen at the marina." Clay said. On the way to Bin Tan Nate couldn't get the

suitcase bomb out of his mind. His bomb squad experience had shown him that bombers could be very clever at disguising their wares. "Do you remember the old joke about the guy who kept crossing the Mexican border with a wheelbarrow?" He asked the others.

"Every week he would come through the border station with a wheelbarrow full of straw or bricks, the border patrol guys were sure he was smuggling something but they never could find anything. Finally one day after he had gone through and was returning empty handed one of the border patrol guys asked him what he had been smuggling. He told them he was retired now so he would let them in on his secret if they left him alone afterward. They agreed. As he walked away all he said was *wheelbarrows*!

That has to be it. Somehow the suitcase is the bomb. Think about it, they can put clothes and normal stuff inside because the explosive is the suitcase itself. I don't know how they've done it but I'll bet I'm right. We have to get ahold of Mel before they put that luggage through customs.

CHAPTER EIGHTY NINE

Mick and Rory had watched the proceedings at the British Customs warehouse.

Everything in the two suspect containers had been opened, x-rayed, sniffed and inspected but nothing unusual was found. They were stumped. "Either they shipped the explosives by air or on a different ship or they have them hidden in something that hasn't been checked yet." Rory fumed. "If they're already here we'd better get back to Blackburn and see where our Arabs go to pick them up. I just hope they haven't gotten their hands on them while we've been here." Mick replied. Jake Powell had landed at Heathrow airport about an hour ahead of Mel's flight from Singapore. He called Mick Randall and asked how things were going at Customs. "We watched them check everything in the two

containers that you thought had the bombs in them and nothing was found. We plan to go back to Blackburn and keep an eye on the suspects. Do you want to come along?" Mick asked. "I'm waiting for Mel to arrive. I'll get a car at the airport and meet you in Blackburn in a short while." Jake replied. "There's a transport café just before the turnoff to Blackburn. One of us will meet you there." Mick instructed. He wanted to get up to the mosque as soon as possible. He had a bad feeling that he shouldn't have left the Arabs alone for this long. He sped out of London and flew toward Blackburn. Rory sat silently in the passenger seat, deep in thought. They arrived at the mosque before dark and found that the Imam's car was still parked in the lot. Mick walked down the street to where he had left his car and took up surveillance on the mosque. Rory circled the mosque, looking for unfamiliar cars or trucks and then drove out to the transport café to wait for Jake.

Mel was held up a while at customs while an unruly passenger argued with the agents about searching his bags. Once the melee had calmed down he went right through the

"nothing to declare" line and hurried to meet Jake at the car rental counter. "Have you heard from Nate?" He asked as they walked out to the rented Vauxhall sedan. "I tried to call him a couple of hours ago but got no answer." Jake replied. "I left in such a hurry I didn't have time to charge my phone and it's completely dead." Mel told him. "We can charge it up on the way to Blackburn. Mick Randall and his British counterpart, a guy named Rory Wells, are watching the suspects at a mosque up there." Jake added.

CHAPTER NINETY

Clay glided the boat into a covered boat house at the resort marina on Bin Tan Island and closed the doors behind them. Perry began unloading their gear and stowing it in a large locker. Stan and Nate had changed back into their street clothes on the way to Bin Tan,

Nate tried to reach Mel with no success so he tried Jake's number. He was unable to make a connection to Jake either. "You can call him on a secure line from my office when we get there if you can't reach him on the cell phone before hand." Clay told him.

They took a cab to the ferry and were back in Singapore in less than an hour.

Jake and Mel were nearly to Blackburn when Mel's phone rang. "Listen Mel, I found an x-ray machine on Chen's boat. I'm pretty sure that they have made bombs out of ordinary looking suitcases. I don't know how they've done it but it is the only thing that makes sense. I got to thinking about that old joke about the Mexican smuggling wheelbarrows and it just hit me. You've got to find that shipment of luggage that Ron was tracking from Singapore. Wong told us that they could easily get the explosives aboard any airline, as checked baggage, without even telling the passenger what he was carrying. Who would think to suspect the suitcase itself, instead of looking for a device hidden inside it?"

Nate was so excited he was nearly out of breath. Mel relayed
Nate's idea to Jake and they stared at each other for a brief
moment. Jake took the phone from Mel and spoke directly to Nate
"If you're right, we're in deep shit. That luggage cleared customs
already and we don't know where it is right now. Keep looking for
Wong and see if you can squeeze some answers out of somebody.
We'll go after that luggage." Jake pulled into the transport café
and found Rory Wells waiting by the phone booth just outside the
door.

"Jake?" He asked quietly. Jake nodded and they all went inside
and sat in a booth near the window. "Mick is in Blackburn
watching the mosque. We followed one of the suspects down to
London a while back. He appeared to be looking for a particular
warehouse but we couldn't tell whether or not he found what he
was after. Mick is convinced we need to wait for them to make a
move and then follow them. We've also

been watching a college kid come and go from the mosque. We
believe he is helping them write a program to organize the flights."
Rory explained. "That luggage was supposed to have been ordered
for ASDA. I'll call them and see if it has been delivered."

Jake said. It was too late to talk to anyone at ASDA so it would
have to wait until business hours tomorrow. "Do you know where
this college student lives?" Mel asked.

"He lives with his parents in a flat here in Blackburn. It's in the
center of the local Muslim population." Rory replied. Jake looked
at Mel and said "You want to pick him up and see what he
knows?" "I don't see that we have time to wait for them to make a
move.

Let's grab the kid now and shake some answers out of him." Mel
replied. "He might be at the mosque. He's been staying pretty late
there most nights. Let's go find Mick and see if he has seen him."
Rory suggested. They got into separate cars with Rory leading the
way for the short drive to the mosque. Rory went right on past
Mick's car and parked on the same side of the street. Jake parked a

little further down on the opposite side. Mick walked to Rory's car and got in the back seat. In a few minutes Mel joined him as Jake slid into the passenger seat next to Rory. "Have you seen the boy tonight?" Rory asked.

"Not so far, but if he's in there he'll be coming out soon. He usually goes home right about now." Mick answered. They waited half an hour but the boy did not show. Mick gave them the address where the kid's parents live. "I'll stay here and watch for Rashid.

Rory can take you to the neighborhood and keep the car ready. You'll have to sneak through some back yards to get to their apartment. Getting in will be the easy part, getting away might be a different story. You'd better take these." he said as he removed two handguns from under the seat and handed them to Jake. Rory drove them to a park across from the apartment complex and gave them general directions to the kid's apartment.

"They live in a two story on the far end of the row. The kid lives in the basement. There is a separate entrance on the alley side of the building. If you get him, don't come back this way, it's too slow. Just go up the alley and I'll pick you up at the next street. Good luck." They walked off into the trees and made their way to the alley beside the apartments. The lights were off in the building and only a few were visible on the entire street. Mel slipped into the doorway while Jake peeked around the front of the building.

Mel tried the door, it was unlocked. He could make out the shape of someone sitting in front of a desk with a laptop computer glowing. No other lights were on in the tiny room.

Mel covered the boy's mouth with his free hand and shoved the barrel of his pistol tight against his temple. "Make no sound or I'll blow your head off." He whispered hoarsely into the boy's ear. He kept the gun pressed against the boy's temple while Jake applied a strip of duct tape over his mouth. He made no attempt to resist, his eyes bulging with fear as they led him up the stairs and out into the alley. They each put a hand under his armpits and literally carried him up the alley at a brisk walk. Rory was waiting with the lights off and the motor running when they reached the street. Mel shoved him into the back seat and climbed in beside him as Rory drove off. They drove to a wooded area several miles from Blackburn. At the end of a dirt track they came to an ancient cottage that Rory used occasionally as a safe house. They pulled the boy out of the car and pushed him into the cottage. Mel sat him down in a straight backed chair and taped his hands behind the chair. "Do you have a saw or a big knife handy?" he asked Rory, still leaving the tape across the boy's mouth. Rory nodded and then went into the kitchen and returned with large butcher knife. Mel showed the knife to the boy and then said "We are going to ask you some questions. If you answer them truthfully you'll be home safe in no

time. If you lie or refuse to answer I will stick this knife into your knee joint and slowly remove your lower leg. If that doesn't work I'll repeat it with the other leg. Do you understand me?"

The boy nearly fainted and nodded his head up and down, his eyes staring at the knife.

Jake ripped the tape from his mouth and began the questioning. "What exactly are you doing for the Imam at the mosque?" the boy hesitated a moment and Mel put the tip of the knife against his knee. "I'm helping them organize some airline flights, they don't know much about computers." "Why do they need a program for a few flights?" "A few flights? I had to get forty flights into the air before the first flight landed. Do you have any idea how difficult that was?" What was the first flight?" "London to San Francisco, over the pole." He was freely cooperating now. Maybe it was fear, maybe ego. He was more of a computer geek than he was a radical Muslim. "Do you have a copy of the program?" "It's on my laptop at my house. They wouldn't let me work anywhere but the mosque, but I couldn't complete the program with their old junk. I did the real program at home and then copied it to their computer. They couldn't even tell what I was doing."

"We can't go back for his computer now in broad daylight." Rory offered. "You don't have to. If you get me to a good computer I

can go online and retrieve anything I need from my laptop." The
boy volunteered. "That's the spirit. I'm going to untie your hands
and take you to a computer. If you keep cooperating we will let
you go home as soon as we are finished." Jake said. "If you try to
escape or warn anyone my friend here will make you suffer
beyond belief." He continued, nodding at Mel. "I have my laptop
at the room back at the transport café. Let's take him there right
now." Rory suggested.

Morning mist was rising gently from the fields as the sun came up;
it was going to be a

nice day. No one in the car noticed. The boy, Parviz el Azziz, sat
between Mel and Jake in the back seat, more relaxed now but just
staring at the back of the front seat. Rory parked behind the café
and unlocked the room. Mel and Jake ushered Parviz quickly
inside. Rory booted up the computer and entered his password
then waved the boy into his chair. Mel stood off to one side of the
writing desk, the knife still visible in his hand.

The boy's eyes lit up when he saw Rory's computer. He had never
had the chance to operate anything this advanced. He quickly got
online, his fingers flying over the keyboard. "I have it. It will only
take a few moments to download. This is an amazing unit." His
hands caressed the sides of the keyboard in admiration while they
waited for the download. He punched the print key and the printer
quickly produced three pages of airline schedules. "Unbelievable!
I wouldn't have thought this possible if I wasn't holding it in my
hands." Rory exclaimed. "They plan to have forty flights explode
while landing. Once they are all in the air there is no escape. No
matter where they try to land they will explode, turning back won't
make any difference." He continued. "We've got to find that
luggage. They're not going to ASDA, we need to find out who
picked them up from Customs. Maybe they're in one of Chen's
warehouses." Jake said. "Why don't we just stake out the mosque
and nail them when they get here?" Rory asked. "They might not
be coming to this mosque. They would be smarter if they
distributed them from somewhere else. These guys aren't stupid."
Mel replied. "How does Rashid plan to get the bags to each of the

passengers?" He asked Parviz. "I don't know. He wanted me to help organize that, but I just got the flight program finished and haven't worked on that part of it yet." His eyes told Mel he wasn't lying. "He will be expecting me to be there today. I have been going to the mosque everyday after my last class." He added. "Call

Mick and see if any new cars or trucks have come to the mosque since yesterday." Jake instructed Rory. The cell phone startled Mick; he had dozed off for a few minutes. He answered the phone and glanced at his watch. He had only been asleep for thirty minutes or so. He listened to Rory's report and decided to take a walk to check the parking lot and surrounding streets. "There doesn't seem to be anything new or unusual in the lot or around the area. Do you want to try to get a warrant to search the mosque? Maybe we can just grab the suspects and hold them until we find the luggage." He said when he returned the call. "We don't have anything on any of them that we can use to get a criminal warrant. The politicians would never let us just go into a mosque and arrest them on suspicion." Rory replied. "They're going to know something is wrong when our friend here doesn't show up. They expect him by 4:30 this afternoon. Maybe they'll get nervous and go out looking for him and we can catch someone outside. Is that tracker still active on the Imam's car? If it is why don't you meet us out here at the café. I doubt they will be going anywhere this morning. We can track them if they do." He added. His next call to the Customs agency confirmed that the luggage pallets had been picked up by a Crown Cartage truck yesterday afternoon. He placed another call to Crown Cartage to find out where the shipment had been delivered. They gave him an address near where he and Mick had followed Rashid before. "Our luggage was delivered to this address yesterday.

Let's get down there and see if it's still there." He suggested. They decided to go in three cars with Rory leading the way. Mel tied Parviz up and put the tape back on his mouth.

He told him he would leave him in the room where he would be safe until they returned and then he would let him go. The boy curled up on the bed and closed his eyes. Mick was just leaving the café when he noticed the Imam's car was moving. He called the

others and alerted them. They decided to meet at the first service plaza on the M-4 and let the Arabs get ahead of them. Rory was parked near the exit and watched them go by.

"There are four of them in the car. It looks like Rashid is driving, Al Rahman is in front and the other two are in the back seat." He told the others. Mick decided to follow their car at a safe distance, while the others would speed up and get to the warehouse ahead of them. He followed them to an exit near Heathrow and into a residential neighborhood.

Rashid stopped behind an old Thames van. Mahmoud and Ahmed got into the rusty old van and took off. Mick called the others and reported the change. He followed them back to the M-4 and on toward the East end where the warehouse was located. Rory located the building first and then drove around to another street to park. Jake followed and parked behind him. Mick called again and said that the old van and Al Rahman's car had entered the warehouse and closed the doors as he passed by. When Mick arrived to park by the others he opened the trunk of his car and displayed four AR-15 assault rifles and extra ammunition as well as a small bag with concussion and fragmentation grenades.

There wasn't any traffic on the street right then so they picked up the weapons and walked quickly to the alley that led to the next street. From the end of the alley they could see the warehouse entrance. There was more traffic, mostly delivery trucks, going in both directions in front of the warehouse. Mel waited for a break in the traffic and then darted across into the alley on the other side, next to the warehouse. He carried the weapon vertically alongside his leg to make it less noticeable. Jake followed after the next break.

Mick and Rory covered the entrance from their position in the alley. There was only a row of ventilation windows about twelve feet up from the street that ran the length of the building. Some were tilted open, a few were broken, most were closed. Mel went to the

other end of the alley and found another set of doors facing the street. They were corrugated metal like the rest of the building. He pried them apart enough to see inside.

Two pallets of boxes sat on the floor. One of the men, he assumed it was Rashid, had opened a box and removed a black plastic suitcase. He was gesturing to the others about it and pointing to the handle. He slowly opened the case and let the others look inside.

They were all smiling and nodding at each other. From where Mel was, it looked like any other hard sided suitcase. The men began removing all the suitcases from the cardboard containers. When they were all lined up out of the boxes the Imam brought out a black light from the car and began scanning the tops of the cases. Some he moved back a foot or so from the others. The remainder he left sitting as they were and motioned for the others to load them in the van. Mel went back to the alley and told Jake what he had seen.

They slipped back across the street and rejoined Mick and Rory. "They separated the suitcases and loaded some in the old van and just left the others on the floor. I couldn't tell them apart from where I was, but they must have marked the bombs somehow. The Imam used a black light to find the real ones." Mel told them. "I think we should let them come out and see where they go. If we go in shooting we might blow up the whole block and us with it." Jake said. "If they go back toward Blackburn we can have the police setup a road block just after they get off the M-4. There is nothing but cow pasture for a few miles right along there. If the police can stop the traffic both ways we can catch them in the open without risking anyone else." Mick suggested. "I've got to call the Major. We can't just go at this alone. Let's let him set up the capture and take the credit for it. Why expose ourselves now?" Rory insisted. "Do it then, but we're not backing off until those bags are safely out of action." Jake replied. Mel stayed in the alley and watched the building while the others went for the cars. A short while later the doors opened and the Imam's car came out followed by the van. One man jumped out of the van and closed the warehouse doors. Mick's GPS tracker was still working so following the Imam's car would be simple. Rory got on the phone to his superiors and filled them in. Major Castleberry listened carefully and then ordered two helicopter teams to fly ahead to a point along the two lane road suggested by Rory Wells. He also sent two armored personnel carriers with commando teams to speed ahead to the area and set up a road block. Al Rahman's car led the van at a leisurely pace to avoid any chance of being stopped by the police for speeding. This gave the Major's men plenty of time to get in position and clear the southbound traffic on the two-lane. One of the armored squads parked out of site near the M-4 and waited for the suspect vehicles to pass and then followed them a short distance behind. Rory kept them apprised of the suspect's position by cell phone. After the car and van left the M-4 Jake, Mel, Rory and Mick followed them at a distance while the second armored unit blocked the north bound traffic. The plan to trap the suspects alone on the narrow road was in place. The road was fenced on both sides and there was nothing in this stretch but cow pastures. The rolling terrain allowed the Major's forward unit to block the road with the armored vehicle and the stone fences provided cover for the commandos. The helicopters had dropped off their two squads and then flew out of sight. When Rahman's car topped the blind hill he was shocked to see the military vehicle sitting crossways in the road at the bottom. He slammed on the brakes and slid to a stop a hundred yard from the roadblock.

Unfortunately the old van did not have decent brakes and Ahmed had to swerve into the ditch to avoid hitting the Imam's car. The van remained upright but was hopelessly high

centered in the deep ditch. Mick's car was in the lead and stopped in the opposing lane, leaving room for Jake's car alongside. The terrorists were trapped. Ahmed and Mahmoud jumped out of the van and climbed over the fence, heading for the pasture on the dead run. Rashid and Al Rahman fired up the car and drove straight at the military vehicle at high speed. Rashid was driving and made a desperate attempt to pass by on the right hand side where the ditch was shallower. He nearly made it but dug into the soft ditch and careened into the fence. The car rolled over and back onto the road, passenger side down.

It was instantly surrounded by armed commandos. Both men were killed in the crash.

Across the field, Ahmed and Mahmoud saw the commandos and ran up the hill in the opposite direction. Mel cut them off and yelled for them to stop. Mahmoud pulled a pistol out of his belt and fired several shots in Mel's direction. Jake had run down the road toward the van and now was coming up behind the two men. Mel had dropped to a prone position facing the two Arabs. Jake fired two shots from behind them, they stopped and whirled around just as Mel rose up and put two rounds through Mahmoud's head. Ahmed dropped his weapon and put his hands on his head as Jake came up behind him. Jake yelled at him to get face down on the ground. He fell to the ground and put his hands behind his head. By then Mick and Rory had caught up and picked up the dropped weapons. Several commandos who had run up the hill were now able to place plastic ties on Ahmed's hands and get him on his feet. Fortunately, no one had gone near the van because at that moment Lin Yuang's fears about the stability of the detonators was realized. The van exploded into a huge fireball and was blown into the air. The concussion from the blast knocked some of the soldiers near the Imam's car off their feet.

The doors from the van landed in the fields on either side of the road; there wasn't much left. The heat from the blast had melted the old van into a smoking pile of twisted metal.

Jake and Mel slipped off to their rental car and made a u-turn and headed off toward the M-4. They stopped when they met the armored unit and explained what had happened and advised them not to let any cars through until the mess could be cleaned up. Jake called Mick and reminded him that they had left young Mr. El Azziz tied up at the old cottage. "I'm on the way to get him now. Rory is busy with the commandos and will have his hands full for a couple of days. Will you stick around long enough to have a few drinks and dinner on us later?" "We need to be on our way, our presence might complicate things for you. Just let us thank you and Rory for all the help. We'll see you for that drink another time."

CHAPTER NINETY ONE

They were nearly back to the airport when Nate called. "Chen Lee just returned from Shanghai. Apparently he has not found the old man; word on the street is he has a big reward out for him and every creep in Singapore and Shanghai is looking for him."

Jake gave him the short version of what happened to the bombs and then told him they were heading back to Singapore on the next flight. When they arrived in Singapore they went back to their hotel to meet with the others. Luckily they hadn't checked out before leaving for England so they still had the original room situation in place.

"Should we pressure Wong a little more and see what shakes out?" Stan asked. "With Chen back in town, they are running out of excuses for delaying the demo." He added.

"Has word gotten here about the blast in England?" Mel asked. "There was news about an explosion, but nothing definitely tying it to a terrorist plot. The limey press always

suggests terror connections when anything happens, but your friends must have done a good job of misdirecting them for now. The TV news did not mention any survivors of the blast, so the one guy you said they captured must have been moved out of the area without being seen. No survivors, no public trial. Gotta give the Brits credit for the way they handled the whole mess." Nate answered. "We've got to get our hands on Lin Yuang before anyone else does. I think he must be the only one who knows how to make that undetectable explosive. Otherwise, Chen Lee wouldn't be so interested in finding him." Jake said. "If he is hiding somewhere in China, we have no chance of finding him, but I don't think he could be because the Chinese government was looking for him before all of this started. He must be somewhere around Shanghai or maybe he got out on a tramp ship. Chen would know if he tried to leave by any commercial means" Stan suggested. "By now even the pirates are probably looking for him; he must have had an escape plan in place before he went to Shanghai. He couldn't have disappeared on the spur of the moment without some prior planning. He would have known that Chen would never let him get away if he suspected him of wanting to leave. I have to wonder why he wanted to get away. Chen had to be paying him very well and he was keeping him safe from the Chinese government." Jake said. "Maybe his device wasn't as foolproof as he told Chen it was. He may have decided to get away before anyone found out. We still don't know what kind of triggering mechanism he had or what caused them to go off in the truck. Maybe the impact of the crash caused it, but maybe it was some flaw in his design. Something made him scared enough to run out on a pretty decent setup with Chen Lee. He either already knew or strongly suspected that something might go wrong before the terrorists were able to complete their plan. Either way he would not want to incur the

wrath of Chen Lee; particularly if he had not received full payment for the bombs." Nate suggested. "The question is, what do we do now?" He added.

CHAPTER NINETY TWO

When Rory and Mick got back to the cottage they found young Mr. El Azziz asleep on the cot where they had left him. He hadn't tried to escape or even loosen his bonds. Mick woke him gently with a tap on the shoulder and removed the tape from his mouth. "The Imam and his two mates have met with an unfortunate accident and will not be coming back to the mosque. We are going to give you a chance to go on with your life as though you were never involved in this terror business. Here's the deal; you never mention any of this to anyone and you never get involved again with any of these radical bastards and we will get you home safely. You will always be watched and we will know if you ever breathe a word to anyone. If you break the rules you and your entire family will disappear forever and you may meet up with the fellow who promised to remove your knee joints with a knife. We believe you are not really a terrorist and we want you to go back to your family unharmed. Do we have a deal?" Rory asked. The boy just nodded and was silent for a moment then finally choked out his reply. "I was just intrigued by the challenge to write their program and I feared they would harm me or my family if I refused to help them. I will never do anything like that again, I swear by Allah." Mick undid his hands and feet and then slipped the black hood over his head and said "We want to believe you but you must realize we cannot just trust you. Never forget our deal and you will be safe." It was dark when they arrived a few blocks from the boy's home and let him out.

He walked away quickly and never looked back. "I'll give him a couple of days and then

make a surprise visit just to remind him to keep silent. I think he is too scared to do anything to screw up his deal." Rory said as they watched him go.

CHAPTER NINETY THREE

Lin Yuang's disguise had allowed him to take the Z5 train from Shanghai to Beijing as soon as he had left Chen Lee's pilot at the airport. He counted on them not looking for him right away and never expecting him to come here. He had purchased the ticket under an assumed name on the last trip to Shanghai just in case anything went wrong in Singapore. He had carefully stashed the ticket, his disguise, forged Canadian passport and extra cash in a locker at the train depot. He knew how to lose himself in the capital city and planned to hide here until he could arrange a way out of China. He had money stashed in several Swiss banks and was carrying enough cash to get anything he needed in Beijing. He knew Chen Lee would be searching for him in Shanghai and would have people looking for him everywhere but he would not suspect that he would risk being found in Beijing by government agents. He had not heard the news about the explosion in England

and hoped that nothing had gone wrong with the suitcase bombs.
He was certain that Chen Lee would kill him as soon as he could
get the formula for his explosive from him. The Canadian passport
he was using allowed him to check into one of the newer tourist
hotels downtown. He would have to stay away from places where
Chen might have people watching for him. He assumed correctly
that Chen would put a large enough bounty on him that no one
would pass it up to protect him. He wanted to contact an old
girlfriend but was afraid to let her know he was in the area. Chen
would certainly send someone to interrogate her. He had to lay low
while he worked on the next part of his

escape plan. He decided that North Korea was his best option and
began plotting a way to get there safely. He knew there were
trainloads of grain and coal going to Shenyang and on to
Pyongyang. He had to find a way to bribe his way onto one of the
trains headed there. He found a government freight broker in
Bejing who accepted cash for getting him included as part of the
train crew on a train leaving in two days. He just had to hide out
until it left. He was certain that North Korea would accept him in
exchange for his services as a weapons expert.

CHAPTER NINETY FOUR

Although Chen Lee had received all the money from the first
suitcase bomb venture he was still furious that Lin Yuang had
disappeared before he could make the next deal with Abdul Latiff.
No one knew for certain that the explosion reported in Britain had
anything to do with the suitcase bombs. At least no airliners had
exploded anywhere yet. He thought there would still be enough
time to make at least one more deal before anyone knew about the
airline plan. He desperately needed to find Lin Yuang and get him
back to work or at least get the formula so it could be sold. He
feared that the old man had made a deal on his own. So far, efforts
to find him had turned up nothing. How had the old man managed
to disappear? Surely the reward would get someone to turn him
over.

David Wong was doing his best to keep Abdul Latiff interested while the search continued, but it probably would not work for much longer. Chen was still fuming over these thoughts when Wong called to tell him the customer was demanding to know when they could get on with their business. "Take them out to the Emerald Queen tonight, I will meet with them there around ten o'clock" Chen ordered.

"That was Wong. He said Chen wants to meet us at the boat tonight around ten." Nate told the others when he snapped the mobile phone closed. "I wonder if he located the old man or is just going to stall for more time." He added. "I think I'll go down town and snoop around some of Chen's guy's hangouts and see if there is any chatter about someone collecting the bounty before we head out there." Stan suggested. "Good idea.

Mel will shadow you in case anyone gets jumpy. Then we'll split up and make our way out to the boat before ten." Jake replied.

Stan made a list of the places he planned to visit and went over it with Mel. They couldn't risk being seen together anywhere so they decided to alternate arriving first at each place. Mel put one pistol in its customary place at the small of his back and another in his jacket pocket. What the 32 caliber PPK lacks in firepower, it makes up for in easy concealment and reliability. He placed extra magazines in various pockets within easy reach. If they encountered trouble he wanted to be able to either get one gun to Stan or at least have enough rounds to cover them long enough to get away. He knew that they would have little chance of escaping in Chen's part of town if things got hairy but hoped to increase their odds any way he could. He waited thirty minutes after Stan left before making his way to the first dive on Stan's list. It was one of the underground gambling joints he had been to before and he had no problem spotting Stan at one of the card tables. He made his way to an empty seat at another table where he could keep an eye on things while playing some Pai Gow. He noted that Stan had chosen a table near the exit with a seat that allowed him to have his back to the wall. Inwardly, he reminded himself that Stan had learned his craft very well which gave him some comfort. They stayed about an hour and then Mel cashed in and headed for their next rendezvous. Stan had

been very careful not to ask any questions but listened to the conversations around him.

So far there had been no mention of anything happening concerning the hunt for Lin Yuang. He noticed one or two goons that he figured were part of Chen's army of local enforcers. Hemet Mel at the next dive and headed for the boat launch to meet the others.

As soon as they boarded Chen Lee's ship, they were greeted by one of Lee's bodyguards who told them that Chen Lee had not returned and said they would be contacted as soon as the demo could be arranged. They decided to get back on the launch and go to the hotel where they met in Jake's room. "I guess this means that they haven't found the old scientist and won't be making any suitcase bombs in the near future" Jake told them. Lets split up and go to New York and Dubai until something pops up". Ron and Joseph can keep an eye on Mr. Wong and the rest of us can go home and wait for news from Doug.

end

Document Outline

•